Other titles by D.A.Broughton

America, Amerike, Amerigo
sequel to *The All Seeing Eyes*
(due for release 2011)

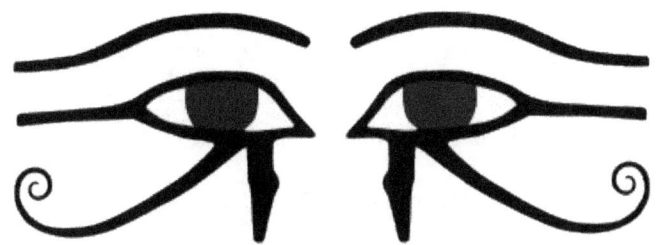

THE
ALL SEEING
EYES

D.A.BROUGHTON

Imox Publishing

Published by Imox Publishing in 2010

First published in the United States of America 2010 by Imox Publishing

Imox Publishing House
Enfield, NH
USA

ISBN: 978-0-615-37294-5, 0615372945
Printed and bound in the United States of America

Library of Congress Control Number: 2010906739

For Laura, my wife
For making me the person I am today.

Disclaimer:

I am not, not will I ever be a person intolerant of other people's views on religion. This book is not intended to be viewed as a work based upon hatred, blasphemy, or any way used as a tool to influence the flames of mistrust between religious groups. I take no responsible for other people's actions upon reading this literary work and furthermore will distance myself from all actions that have a negative impact on society. My quest in writing this book was plain and simple, the unraveling of the truth which has remained hidden for centuries. Should you choose to believe it or not it is entirely up to you, all I ask is that you open your eyes and your mind to other possibilities. I just chose to follow the path laid in front of me, now your choice is the same.

D.A.Broughton

PREFACE

"This war would never have been possible without the sinister influence of the Jesuits. We owe it to the popery that we now see our land reddened with the blood of her noblest sons. Though there were great differences of opinion between the South and the North on the question of slavery, neither Jeff Davis nor anyone of the leading men of the Confederacy would have dared to attack the North, had they not relied on the promises of the Jesuits, that, under the mask of Democracy, the money and the arms of the Roman Catholic, even the arms of France were at their disposal, if they would attack us.

I pity the priests, the bishops and monks of Rome in the United States, when the people realize that they are, in great part, responsible for the tears and the bloodshed in this war. I conceal what I know, on that subject, from the knowledge of the nation; for if the people knew the whole truth, this war would turn into a religious war, and it would at once, take a tenfold more savage and bloody character.

It would become merciless as all religious wars are. It would become a war of extermination on both sides. The Protestants of both the North and the South would surely unite to exterminate the priests and the Jesuits, if they could hear what Professor Morse has said to me of the plots made in the very city of Rome to destroy this Republic, and if they could learn how the priests, the nuns, and the monks, which daily land on our shores, under the pretext of preaching their religion, instructing the people in their schools, taking care of the sick in the hospitals, are nothing else but the emissaries of the Pope, of Napoleon, and the other despots of Europe, to undermine our institutions, alienate the hearts of our people from our constitution, and our laws, destroy our schools, and prepare a reign of anarchy here as they have done in Ireland, in Mexico, in Spain, and wherever there are any people who want to be free."

"Is it not an absurdity to give to a man a thing which he is sworn to hate, curse, and destroy? And does not the Church of Rome hate, curse and destroy liberty of conscience whenever she can do it safely? I am for liberty of conscience in its noblest, broadest, highest sense. But I cannot give liberty of conscience to the Pope and to his followers, the Papists, so long as they tell me, through all their councils, theologians, and canon laws that their conscience orders them to burn my wife, strangle my children, and cut my throat when they find their opportunity! This does not seem to be understood by the people today. But sooner or later, the light of common sense will make it clear to everyone that no liberty of conscience can be granted to men who are sworn to obey a Pope, who pretends to have the right to put to death those who differ from him in religion."

ABRAHAM LINCOLN TO PRIEST CHARLES CHINIQUY, 1864

"It has served us well, this myth of Christ"

Pope Leo X

"The most heinous and the must cruel crimes of which history has record have been committed under the cover of religion or equally noble motives."

<u>GHANDI</u>

"The word god is for me nothing more than the expression and product of human weaknesses, the Bible a collection of honorable, but still primitive legends which are nevertheless pretty childish. No interpretation no matter how subtle can (for me) change this."

<u>ALBERT EINSTEIN</u>

"The truth is incontrovertible.
Panic may resent it,
Ignorance may deride it,
Malice may distort it,
But there it is".

<u>WINSTON CHURCHILL</u>

CHAPTER I

The golden globe permeated the sky with a halo of gilded brilliance against the lazuline sky, minuscule particles of silica danced in the wind to a silent tune, whilst heat haze trickled like water into a fast flowing river.

From the horizon a lonely figure appeared like a ghost in the night, riding a white steed. The ghost decked in the silver armor of a knight, carried in his right hand a shield made from bronze, upon which a vermillion cross was emblazoned on it, his left hand, empty except for the reigns of his steed, hung loosely in front of him.

Days had passed since The Knight left the Temple behind, yet his faith remained strong, with the horse his only companion he wandered the land searching for the truth. The Master of the Temple had sent him out on a quest to find about the word coming from Jerusalem: "Was the son of God truly dead?"

There had been stories about this man passed on by pilgrims to the Temple's Master, the last one troubling him greatly. "Betrayed by a friend, Jesus, the son of God, had been taken to a place of execution, and put to death. The pagan King Herod, afraid of losing his kingdom to the lowly offspring of a carpenter, took his life away for there would be no other King sake himself."

The sun began to sink slowly into the horizon, turning the brightness of day into the darkness of night. Creatures appeared from the shadows; snakes, serpents and unholy beasts appeared before The Knight, determined to tear the flesh from his bones.

Thirty Three score and six beasts readied themselves for the battle, with legion upon legion of the damned marching together as one. The Lord Sabaoth, suited in black armor, in command at the head of the brigade, sent forth 7 serpents, followed by 7 more, their eyes filled with fire and their hearts filled with hatred.

The Knight unafraid (for he was full of courage), dismounted his noble beast with the silver locks that crowned his head blowing gently in the cool desert breeze and drew his sword from its sheath, planting it firmly in the barren wasteland.

"Forgive me Father for what I am about to do and May the courage of my brother's give me strength to kill these unholy creatures." he prayed as he rested his hands on the hilt.

With one graceful movement, The Knight took the sword from the deserts vice like grip and took the life of the nearest serpent, its head surgically removed from its body,   causing a volcanic eruption of blood to spurt from the torso and christening the desert carpet with a crimson baptism. The Knight seeing his foe perish raised himself upwards and readied his blade for the next attack.

Two unholy creatures launched themselves at their assassin, with ferociousness and evil intent, striking his armor with venom filled fangs. The Knight laughed saying thusly "You think a mere wicked serpent's bite can dent my armor, think again my little friends. I dispatch thee back to thy maker" and with that the head of the first serpent fell graciously to the floor.

As The Knight's sword ploughed its way into the creature's neck, the second creature took a great displeasure at the sight that its eyes feasted upon and attacked The Knight with an unholy cry. Cries of pain, soon resonated through the desert's never ending wastelands, as the life of the aggressor was terminated with a swift blow to the head by the sharpened blade of The Knight.
Creature after creature attacked The Holy Warrior until all were slain and their corpses left rotting on the desert floor. "My Dear Lord Sabaoth", The Knight said wearily gasping for air "it appears that your evil plan has failed"

"It appears so" replied the Evil Lord "however you must not underestimate the powers of my master"

"Your Master?" queried The Knight "And who might that be?"

"His name is The Unholy One, the one you shall kneel before, for he is the ruler of hell and all its dominions, the one true Master of all of mankind, the taker of life, and the drinker of souls and in his name I ask him to raise the dead from beyond the grave. Lord Satan hear my prayer and raise those, whose life belongs to you so that they may serve for your glory".

Darkness instantly came to pass, as the rains from the tears of damned fell from the broken sky onto the corpses of the fallen army, breathing life into broken skin and flesh."Your God has forsaken you now" Lord Sabaoth riposted "See how he is left his only son to die on the cross, and for what? To redeem man of his sins? Man has always sinned; man will always sin. Join me now and serve the one true master".

"Never" shouted The Knight back to his adversary "Never, as long as I live I will never join you".

"Then so be it. Kill Him!"

From the darkened sands (overcast by the shadows of evil) rotting cadavers slowly started rising from the grasp of death into the service of a malevolent master, fingers of skeletal remains coiling themselves around the legs of The Knight, dragging him down to the ground. The Knight tried reaching for his blade but alas it was to no avail, for his hands were engulfed by the bones of the undead.

The Knight lay helplessly on the floor, clinging to the hope that good would prevail. Alas the prayer he committed to his Lord fell on the desert plans as the evil Lord Sabaoth commanded the creatures thusly, "Wait. Before he dies let me see if he wants to beg for his life". He leant forward in recognition of The Knight's foolish but brave actions, "So my friend are you ready for beg for your mortal life?"

The Knight replied "I'd rather die as a free man then live as a slave".

Lord Sabaoth angrily retorted, "Then so be it".

As the clouds darkened overhead The Knights' own sword found itself in the hands of a new master, bowing to the greatest which he yielded, before embedding itself into the neck of The Knight.

CHAPTER II

Reality turned the nightmare world into the dawn of a new day, as Tom awoke to the sounds of the morning trying to wake his comatosed body into life, the birds conducting an operatic aria in rehearsal for the days performance, while the radio burrowed itself into his sub consciousness probing for signs of life, "Good morning and here is the 7 o'clock news for July the 7th 2007".

"God damn it", grumbled a half awake Tom wiping the sleep from his eyes "what the hell is good about 7 o' damn clock in the friggin morning?"

Tom had every reason to grumble, for a bottle of fine whiskey with two vodka chasers, had given him the hangover of all hangovers, and a citation from a more than zealous cop, who had the audacity to prevent him from showing his butt to a group of revelers coming out of a local bar at 1am in the morning.

His sweat ladened body arose from the man made sarcophagus that had been his prison. Furrows of an ageing man ploughed their ways across an anguished face, as pain planted seeds of desperation into the gouges left behind by father time; eyes of a life etched with misery struggled to open. Sleep deprivation driven by constant nightmares began to take its toll; his half dilated pupils began darting around the room, as the shadows on his walls danced a ballet of monotonal rainbows.

"Jeez Louise" he swore cursing the world as it came into focus "Why do the goddam frigging radio presenters have to be so twatting nice in the morning? Here take this you overly pleasant annoying bastard".

From the darkness of his barely opened eyes, a pillow shaped missile was launched airborne hurtling towards its target, the radio. Unfortunately (or fortunately depending on your perception of things) Tom's aim was surprising good, as his target took the brunt of the attack. Several cans of beer, one being half full, became collateral damage, along with a several containers of sleeping pills and numerous pictures of his children.

"Fuck...Fuck...Fuck" he cussed under his breath "It's going to be one of those fucking days, I guess", and he was right in his assumption, it was going to one of *those* days, even for someone as menial as him, for unbeknown to Tom wheels had been set in motion that would ultimately change his life forever.

The six o clock shadow that caressed his face, sat in stone silently reminding him of the previous night's pathetic attempt to dull the pain of a broken marriage in a bottle of fine Scottish whiskey. Several months had passed, yet the pain was still fresh in his mind, his first attempt at being married started out well, years passed by without any sign of trouble, but all that changed with the birth of a second child, a son, named Tom also.

The person he was married to suddenly began to change in her respect for Tom, no longer was she a loving and caring mother and wife, but now she was hell bent on trying to break him of the last thing he owned, his dignity. It wasn't until one day last fall, when he came home early, hoping to surprise her by taking her flowers to celebrate their anniversary, when he stumbled upon a scene that would change his life forever.

In the sanctity of their own bedroom, a place where their children had been conceived, the woman he thought he knew was in the arms of another man, making passionate love to each other. Heartbreak, distress, anger, each one subjecting his body to wave upon wave of negative emotions. Police were eventually called when the angry Tom landed a pristine upper cut to his wife's lover, causing a small torrent of blood to flow freely from his broken nose.

Months passed by, as his home, his money and his family was divided by a judge sitting behind an oak paneled desk in a small court room, in the town where he resided. Access was granted to him to allow him every two weeks to spend time alone with his two bewildered children. He felt betrayed; not only by his wife, but the court system too, for he had been the innocent party in this, he was made to feel like a leper, outcast from society for doing nothing more than trying to earn a decent wage to maintain his wife's extravagant lifestyle. The uttered words of a man frustrated with life turned into abject despair as the telephone rang, "I knew it......I twatting knew it" he thought to himself, struggling to make sense of the sound that pounded like a jackhammer in his head, "If it's that fucking ex-wife begging for more money, she can fuck off, I've already made my payment this month."

Several rings passed before Tom managed to stagger haphazardly towards the telephone, "Look Rachel" he stormed, irate at being called so early in morning , especially when he was trying to shake off the after effects of over indulgence, "You've had your fucking money this month and if you think...."

The color from his face drained when he realized it was not his ex-wife who phoned him up so early in the day, but his boss calling him to instruct him on his new assignment. "I.......I......I'm so sorry Mr. Edwards....I.....I....I thought it was my ex-wife" he stammered, "Yes...yes....I understand that you're not.....but..."

His heart pounded, as the words poured from his mouth, the moisture on them evaporating with every new syllable he spoke, "Ah hah..... yep.....yep...I understand" he clamored as his pulse slowly began to return to normal "So the plane ticket will be waiting for me at the airport? Ok....Ok.....sure, I can do that, thank you, and I'm sorry about shouting at you like that...Ok...Bye"

The instructions he was just given entered his head, but it took a little time for him to fully understand them, "Israel?" he uttered to himself, "I'm off to fucking Israel. Jesus H. Christ, it is going to be one of those fucking days".

For the first time in his professional career, Tom was being sent off on an assignment he knew little about, to a place he knew little about, a place he had only seen in the news on his cheap little Japanese imported television set, which occasionally took the brunt of his anger at the world outside. His once caring soul turned into that of a raging alcoholic by the misdemeanor of others, intent on his own self destruction, the opportunity to prove himself once more, had landed squarely at his feet, whether he would swim or drown, only time and his battle to quell his own personal demons would tell.

CHAPTER III

The airport was a metropolis constantly on the move, never ending, never still, like the seas, the ebb and flow of an ever changing population in a minuscule world came and went with a regular occurrence. A cacophony of noise sang from the cathedral's pulpit, as modern day pilgrims began their travels to global destinations, sounds of people in union, inaudible, scrambled, garbled, never making any sense, as words of pleasure, words of misery, were spoken with such unclarity that it made a noise like no other.

Tom hated the airport, he hated the hustle and bustle of it, people coming and going, never standing still, constantly moving. He never truly understood the mass appeal of air travel, although he often theorized that people's love affair with flight was a need to feel free, untapped by the bonds of an earth bound existence, an existence enhanced by a desire to explore, just like their forefathers before them and their fathers before them. Yet something felt missing, something missing from their lives that urged them to the corners of the earth in search of peace and tranquility.

Tom laughed inwardly when he heard that saying 'The Corners of the Earth', the earth was spherical. How did it have corners?

He remembered times as a child when his mother would say "I can see you out of the corner of my eye doing that Tom, stop it please"

It used to confuse him; did his mother really have square eyes? Could she really see out of the corner of her eye? Not now, now it bewildered him; the funny things we say and take for granted made him question the use of strange sayings in every day events. Tom was nervous, his mind always wandered when he was nervous, nervous about what though?

It couldn't be the flying, he had flown many times before, and he knew he wasn't afraid of travelling alone, so what was it? Whatever it was it had preoccupied the place in his mind that was reserved for thinking, and now it was empty, empty enough to remind him it was time to check in.

"Hi" said Tom as the approached desk of El Al airlines "I'm Tom Raust I believe you're holding a ticket for me?"

"Can I see your passport Mr., er" asked the reservations clerk, her recently capped teeth outlined by her ruby red lipstick. Tom couldn't help but wonder, as he stood staring at the mole on her left cheek, if she would take offence if he gave a quarter to have it removed (a la John Candy in Uncle Buck), but he neither had a quarter nor the personal fortitude to do so.

"Raust, Tom Raust" he reminded the clerk, slightly taken a back by the fact that he had to give his name yet again, "Sure, here it is"

From the inside of his jacket pocket he produced the official document and gave it to the person behind the desk, "You're a newspaper reporter Mr. Raust?" she queried with an inquisitive look on her face.

"I am" he confirmed placing the returned passport into its original hiding place, "I'm flying out to Israel to cover a story for my paper"

"Mr. Raust, Mr. Raust" the clerk muttered under her breath as she browsed through the prepaid flight tickets, "Ah here we are Mr. Raust, your flight departs at 18:13. Mr. Raust, your seat number is G7, a window seat. You only have the one suitcase Mr. Raust?"

"Yes just the one" he stated as he placed his beaten, red leather suitcase on the conveyor belt.

"Just a few questions Mr. Raust then you can be on your way. Did you pack this yourself? "

"Yes" Tom replied (although he had an urge to say no).

"Has this been in your possession all the time?"

Tom paused and thought about the time he lent it to his brother, but he was sure this didn't count, "Yes" he said.

Tom's younger brother Jack, had been missing from his life since the divorce was made absolute, he had been the only one to stand by him in his hours of need, the times when he wanted to cry and breakdown, Jack was there. When he wanted someone to stagger home with him in a drunken self pitying stupor, Jack was there. When his thoughts turned suicidal, Jack was there. Jack had been a constant pillar of strength always lending him support when he needed it the most, then late one night whilst Tom was working on a story about a house fire in the center of town for the newspaper, he got a phone call from his brother that he was disappearing off on one of his self seeking journey's to somewhere remote "To cleanse the soul of all impurities", as he put it. Jack would occasionally, when things became a little dramatic in his life, seek solace from civilization by taking himself off to remote places where no one on earth would find him, but now it was his own turn to go to places new.

"Has anyone else asked you to take anything on board?" prompted the reservations clerk.

"No", Tom abruptly answered eager to get this voyage into the unknown off and running.

"Thank you Mr. Raust and have a pleasant flight" the clerk said passing Tom his ticket.

"Thank you" replied Tom watching his suitcase disappear from sight "I'm sure I will".

As he walked away from the desk he was bumped into by a bearded Middle Eastern man, a newspaper in one hand and a mobile phone in the other, seemingly attached to his ear,

"Excuse me" he apologized "I am so sorry, I did not mean to bump into you on purpose, please forgive me"

"It's okay" Tom answered back, picking up the stranger's belongings that had dropped to the floor when the two men bumped into one another, "no harm done".

"Medad is a clumsy, clumsy man, sorry let me introduce myself. I am Medad, Medad Amiti"

"I am Tom, Tom Raust" said a surprised Tom who was being shook firmly by the hand.

"Please Mr. Raust let me offer you some refreshment as an apology", Medad said continuing to apologize to the slightly perturbed traveler.

"It is not necessary", Tom replied taken aback at the generosity of someone he had just *'bumped'* into.

"In my country it is" stated Medad.

"Oh and what country is that?" asked Tom, his eyebrows rising with bewilderment.

"Israel, Mr. Raust, Israel"

"I'm flying out to Israel on business too Mr., er?"

"Medad, Medad Amiti"

"I'm sorry, I'm very bad with names" apologized Tom as his forgetfulness made him illiterate of the stranger's name, "and please no more Mr. Raust, it's too formal, call me Tom".

"No apologies necessary Mr." Medad paused for a moment before continuing, "Tom, so how about you and I get a nice glass of Coca-Cola?"

"If you can get someone to put vodka in it Medad, I'm your man."

"You are my man?" Medad inquisitively replied unsure of Tom's sexual preference for men or women.

"It's just a saying, my friend", Tom laughed alleviating Medad's fear of his new found friend's social standing, "It's just a saying".

Tom and his new found friend went off to the lounge to wait for the departure of their aircraft to Israel, talking to each other on the way about their line of profession, and the need to fly to a foreign country for what seemed a futile exercise in nothing more than spending someone else's money.

"So my friend", Medad said as they sat at the bar drinking alcohol free beverages, "your newspaper is sending you off to Israel and you know not the reason why?"

"Not a clue", Tom answered sipping his drink through a straw like a small child, "but I figured it's not for me to reason why. So what about you, why are you here?"

"I'm an importer and exporter of fine antiquities", replied Medad grabbing a handful of complimentary pistachio nuts from the bar.

"Interesting line of work", commented Tom declining Medad's offer of the free food in front of them.

"Not always", came the reply between mouthfuls of crunched nuts in the mouth of Medad, "Sometimes it's like a wild goose chase, like it was this time. I had a lead on an old Templar Sword, but it turned out to be nothing but a late 19th century copy"

"Waste of time then?".

"Completely. Nevertheless it is what it is".

"And what's that?"

"An opportunity to get away from the mother-in-law", Medad laughed amused by his own joke.

Tom was starting to warm to this new friend, he was funny, he was confident, but most of all he was truthful in the words he said, and that was what he most admired in this bearded stranger, the fact that he told the truth, unlike several people in his past, this was the first person he had ever met who was honest in his approach to everything he undertook, he wished that whatever lay ahead, their paths would cross again.

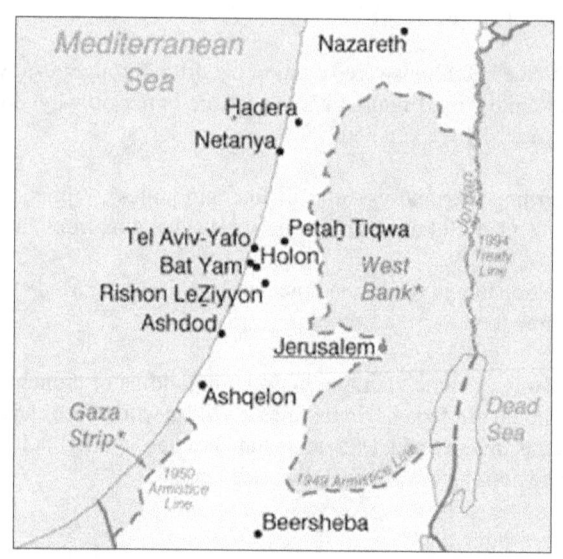

JERUSALEM
ISRAEL

CHAPTER IV

Israel was a sensory overload for Tom, new sounds, new sights, even new smells, each one bombarding his conscious awareness with an intenseness never experienced before. To his new companion it was home, to him it was a journey into the unknown, an experience to be savored like a good wine, it was an intoxicating vision and he planned to get drunk on it.

"Wow", he exclaimed with his new friend Medad at his side, "It's beautiful".

"Medad told you correct did he not?" replied the Israeli journeyman as he took pride in showing off his home country to Tom.

"That you did my friend, that you did", Tom confirmed with a pleasure in his voice that echoed the sentiments he was feeling.

"Will you excuse me for a brief moment Tom; I need to organize some transport for us?" Medad said excusing himself. Medad walked around the corner of the airport terminal and disappeared out of Tom's sight, the mobile telephone, which Medad had been carrying in his inside jacket pocket, was produced and a mysterious number dialed.

"Hello", Medad said, "It's me, we've arrived safely".

The voice on the other end acknowledged the message and queried Medad on the traveler with him."No, no" Medad answered "he suspects nothing; we will drop him off at the hotel as arranged".

The faceless, mysterious person gave further instructions to Medad "Yes. Yes. I understand. I will contact you later as soon as I have further news. I take it transportation is on route?"

The answer was in the affirmative making Medad respond, "Ok, Ok, and Bye". From the safety of his hiding place, Medad walked back

to Tom who was unaware of the conversation that took place.
Tom queried, "Everything ok?".

"Yes Tom, everything is fine, transport is on its way", Medad
answered hiding his secret from Tom like a master spy trying to
elude the enemy.

"I'm going to be too pleased to lie down; I've got the worst jet lag
ever"

"Are you sure its jet lag Tom and not the three bottles of
complementary wine you drank?" laughed Medad remembering the
10 hour flight they sat together drinking their way through several
bottles of cheap Italian wine.

"It could be", Tom agreed, remembering the sweet musty flavor as it
rolled over his taste buds, "It was very agreeable".

"More like it was very drinkable, my friend".

"Are you saying I'm an alcoholic Medad?" retorted Tom with a
slight snarl, who for the first time since their meeting, was angered
by Medad's remark.

"Not at all Tom, but you were kind of knocking back the wine".

"Medad, if you've lead the life I've had, you would understand".

"I don't wish to pry", Medad said concerned for his friend, "but for
you to drink like that, it must be a painful experience".

"It is", Tom confessed with anguish in his eyes before correcting
himself, "it was"

"You wish to tell me Tom?".

"I'm not sure I can my friend, a lot of pain, a lot of emotional
scars".

"That is not good Tom, let me guess women trouble?"

Tom half-heartedly laughed "Yes, how did you guess?"

"Women Tom", Medad declared with a voice that spoke from experience, "they're our greatest joy and at times our greatest pain; she was in the bed with another man I am guessing?"

Tom nodded solemnly, not saying a word, the pain in his heart and in his eyes was burdening him with an ache in his empty life, he remembered about all the good times he had with Rachel, the first date, the first kiss, the first child born, so many good memories they once shared, but now they were gone, erased in Tom's mind by the infidelity of the love of his life. The trust on which they based their relationship cast into the winds of shattered promises made to each other in a place of worship, hatred now replacing love as the thought of another taking his place as the father to his children filled his mind with anger, an anger that still burnt deep in his soul.

"Children?" queried Medad breaking Tom's train of thought that journeyed to his past.

"Two, a boy and a girl", Tom answered, slowly producing a photograph of two children, before showing it to his companion, "She's called Emma and he's called Tom. It's a family tradition; the eldest son of the first born male is called Tom. My father was called Tom and his father before him"

"Very pretty children you have Tom".

"Had Medad, had. They live with their mother now".

"That is not good for the soul Tom", Medad replied sympathizing. He was about to console his friend when he noticed a car pull up to the sidewalk, "Ah. Tom our ride is here".

"Nice car", said Tom noticing the shiny automobile, "What is it?"

"I believe it is a Mercedes Tom, you approve?" Medad asked.

"Totally, Medad, totally, I've been dreaming about buying one of these for some time, but my ex-wife keeps taking all my money away from me"

"Here", said Medad, "let me get your luggage for you, while you get comfortable."

"Are you sure?" queried Tom

"I am sure", answered Medad, "you are in our country now, and you are a guest, so please be making yourself comfortable, while I am putting the luggage in the trunk".

"Thank you", said Tom, as he made his way to the car door.

The driver of the car, seeing Tom approach got out and went around to open the door for him, puzzled, Tom, looked at the driver, then looked at the interior of the car , before making himself comfortable on the upholstered leather seat, a silent thud followed, as the driver shut the door.

Tom gazed out of the tinted windows at Medad, as he talked to the driver, he tried to lip read the conversation, however as he soon discovered, Arabic is a tricky language to understand without lip reading, let alone with. Whatever they were saying Tom could tell from their body language that they both were unhappy with something, but what it was he could not tell, maybe it was something he had or hadn't done. The other car door opened and Medad popped his head inside, "Where are you staying Tom?" he asked.

"Let me look at my reservation slip Medad", said Tom fishing around inside his jacket pocket, before finding a tattered and crumpled piece of paper, "I'm at the David Intercontinental".

Medad muttered something in broken English, before issuing instructions to driver, who also muttered something, both shaking their heads in disbelief at the location of the temporary residence at which Tom was a guest. As soon as Medad got in the car he asked, "Are you sure, you are just a newspaper reporter Tom?"

"Yes", he replied, "why?"

"The David Intercontinental is a 5 star hotel and is one the most prestigious ones around".

"5....5 star?" stammered Tom with excitement, "Me? 5 star, get out of town".

"No not out of town, Tom. In town. In town" Medad said with a puzzled look on his face.

"But" replied Tom trying to explain his bad choice of words.

"Let me guess", interrupted Medad, "it's just saying?"

"Yes" replied Tom laughing "it's just a saying".

As Tom and Medad set off in hot pursuit of the glamorous lifestyle that someone decided Tom needed, they both couldn't help but wonder what Tom had done to deserve this treatment, maybe someone decided Tom needed a break from the mundane, maybe they decided he paid his dues to society, whatever the reason it was clear that Tom was upgrading his lifestyle from that of a mere underling to someone who deserved better treatment.

CHAPTER V

Like a palm tree growing in the desert, The David Inter- continental Hotel stood lonely, on its own, it lay beside a man- made oasis in the concrete wasteland, fauna and flora interspersing the lush green grass that swayed in the breeze, as a menagerie of colored fabrics fluttered back and forth like butterflies on the wing, their bright colors echoing many of the world's populated countries, each one hung from a perpendicular perch like a sturdy oak tree.

A macadamized, meandering path lead to the front door, columns of granite stood like giants who had gazed upon Medusa's stare, strength, stature, and importance, each one graced the facade with a delicate finger of decadence, a poised gracefulness for all to see, and those who saw the imposing piece of architecture were treated to lavish life style (albeit temporary), full of tempting sinful experiences, it was a joy to behold.

As the horseless carriage carrying Tom and his friend Medad entered the grounds of the hotel, Tom gasped in wonderment, "This is where I'm staying at?"

"Apparently so my friend", replied Medad shocked at the extravagance in front of his eyes; "Somebody must love you".

"I doubt that very much", Tom murmured quietly, whose breath had been stolen from him, "I doubt that".

Like an ice skater performing at the Olympics, the car gracefully drew up to the front door of the architectural masterpiece, as it stopped with a gentle deceleration Medad turned to Tom and gave him his business card.

Medad Amiti
Importer and Exporter
Tel: 285-863-46787

"This is where you can reach me, should you need anything, and I mean anything, ok?" Medad told Tom, forcing the small card into the pocket of Tom's jacket.

"But", Tom interrupted, not comfortable with having so much generosity placed as his beck and call.

"No buts Tom, we are friends", Medad explained to the astonished Tom, who was taken aback at the kindness of someone he barely knew.

"Ok", said Tom shaking Medad firmly by the hand, "Thank you very much".

"Now go Tom. You must have much to do".

Tom left the comfort of the conveyance and walked with admiration into the main lobby of his temporary dwelling, as his walk to the front desk was some distance, he had time to notice how the interior was even more grandeur then exterior.

From the ceiling hung giant chandeliers, whose brilliance cast a mirage of incandescent luminosity onto the floor below, here a lucullan carpet traversed from wall to wall with a soft velvetiness, as it gently caressed the walls with a textured sea of colors, towards the rear, a cliff of intricately decorated royal oak desks protruded upwards housing a plethora of mercantile machinery.

A smartly presented woman, working behind the desk, observed Tom motioning forwards to her and placed her pen down on the work station in which she resided.

"Good day sir", came the friendly greeting Tom as reached the reservations desk, "How may I help you?".

"My name is Raust, Tom Raust. I've got a reservation" he explained.

"Just one moment Mr. Raust, let me check for you on the computer", she replied entering his name into the computers records, "Can I see your passport Mr. Raust?"

Tom produced his passport from the interior of his jacket and handed it to the clerk.

"We've also got a message for you from your office Mr. Raust", stated the woman handing back his passport, along with a nicely folded piece of hotel stationary, "and here is your key Mr. Raust, you are in Room 412, we hope you enjoy your stay with us"

A credit card shape entry key was forced into his hand, which he accepted with bewilderment, he was more used to low end, low class living with heavy keys that looked like they belong to a gaoler, "So much for modern technology", he thought to himself as he looked at the entry device.

"Thank you, I will", he answered flipping the key over, and over, each time examining it with raised eye brow. After his brief lapse back into his childhood, he remembered about the note from his office:

Tom,
You have a meeting with the PRIEST at the
Temple Of St.George in Lydda (LOD), at 11am.
Mr.Edwards

"A priest?" he thought to himself, "Why the hell a priest? I'm not the religious correspondent; I suppose Mr. Edwards knows what he's doing".

As he read the message from his superior, a friendly, familiar face strode through the entry way, "Tom...Tom", Medad said as he was transecting the foyer towards the elevator which stood on the far wall, where Tom was waiting for a car to descend to the ground floor.

"Medad?" asked Tom as his eyes turned to the voice calling his name, "I didn't expect do see you soon. What can I do for you?"

"You forgot this Tom", Medad answered slightly out of breath before depositing Tom's beaten, red, suitcase on the floor.

"Ah, hell", Tom swore under his breath.

"You ok Tom?"

"Yeah I'm fine Medad", Tom replied, "Medad what do you know about the Tomb of St.George?"

"Not much Tom", answered Medad, "only what I learnt at school and that was St. George, an important figure in the history of Israel, has a Tomb and this, er, Tomb is a place where both Christians and Muslims both pray. Why? Why you ask?"

Tom, showing him the message from Mr. Edwards his boss, replied "It's my next assignment".

"I'll be happy to take you there tomorrow", offered Medad who was genuinely at loose end the next day.

"Are you sure?" Tom wondered with astonishment, uneasy at the generosity of his new friend.

"Yeah I'm sure Tom; I got nothing planned for tomorrow".

"Thanks Medad, I got to go and er", Tom murmured sheepishly looking at the crimson colored luggage at his feet.

"Ok Tom", Medad said placing a guiding hand on his friend's shoulder, "I'll pick you up at 10am, we should be early. It's always good to be a little early when meeting a priest for this first time".

"Thank you".

"Not at all Tom, Not at all", Medad stated turning to face the door from whence he came.

As the bewildered Tom headed inward towards the elevators, his mind began to turn over, thoughts, hypotheses, ideas, questions, each one formulating in his brain.

"Why am I here? Why am I meeting the priest? Why is Medad being so generous? And why do I get the feeling I'm being watched? If so then by whom?"

So many questions, and not enough answers, questions with no answers, answers to the wrong questions. If he was to navigate the moral maze presented before him, the only answer Tom had was that time would provide all the necessary information, his only worry was would there be enough time before he lost his sanity, his life or both ?

CHAPTER VI

A prisoner of his own mind, Tom, for all tense and purposes, was a man on the edge leaning on the precipice of oblivion, fueled by a cocktail of sleep deprivation, alcoholism and prescription drugs, his life had become a recipe for disaster. It was just a case of waiting for someone to light the blue touch paper.

When he managed to get any sleep at all, he was frequently plagued by nightmares, a spiritual manifestation of emotional scars left by a life lead hard, visions of an abusive father, would tear into his sub consciousness with regular occurrence, as he fought for control of his inner demons, demons which later on in life which would cause him to hurt those people around him he cared about.

He lost his mind, his house, his marriage, but his greatest pain was caused by the loss of his children, his greatest joy became his deepest sorrow. The loss to Tom was etched in his eyes for the entire world to see, a pain so great, so terminal at times he felt suicidal, but he figured death was the easy way out, so he carried on with his painful existence, drinking heavily to fill the void in his life.

A full day travelling had caught up with him, so he thought, as he was tired, tired of the dealing with the shit in his life, tired of dealing with other people's shit, tired of being a second class citizen in world where he deserved better, tired of being treated like a lackey by his ex-wife who would only show up when the money ran out, tired of having no self-respect, no self-control, no morals, he was tired of being tired.

As he lay on a bed he didn't own, in, a room he didn't own, surrounded by things he didn't own, he began to wonder when he was going to get a break, just a onetime measly little break, just a onetime measly little break so he could begin to live a normal life again.

"It's not too much to ask it God ?", he asked to anyone who was listening, but then he realized the futility of his request, for he was not a God faring man, not since the days when his prayers to be delivered from his evil father went unanswered, now he was a practicing atheist and proud of it too. He told those who told him God really existed and he should believe in Him, that once definitive proof was available to him that an omnipotent being existed then he would only be too pleased to join the massing throngs, until then he was happy to be a non believer.

As Tom lay there on his bed, he slowly drifted in and out of unconsciousness, praying for the shadowy ghosts in his mind to stay hidden in the recesses of his guilt driven mind, so at least for once he could sleep, soon Tom was leaving behind the conscious world as colors of a physical existence turned into the monotonal apparitions of a nightmare dominion. In this state of awareness, blurred visions projected on to Tom's mind's eye, images he thought he knew but quite couldn't recognize. He lay there, paralyzed with fear at the sight of the apparition, watching, waiting for a sign.

A voice he knew, and despised rang true, as the visions in his head faded into the darkness, "Tom, get off your ass you lazy bastard, stop feeling sorry for yourself".

"D...D...Dad?" shivered Tom nervously, the prospect of meeting up with the Father who relentlessly whipped him when ever he felt the urge, sending shivers of discomfort up his spine.

"Yes it's me, you poor excuse of a man", his Dad replied snarling like a pit-bull terrier.

"W.W.What do you want?" stammered Tom.

"I want you to stop freaking wasting your life."

"B...B...But".

"Don't but me young man", interrupted his dad, "Its time you grew a set of balls and started acting like a man, instead of being the chicken you are"

The voice left his audio perceptive part of his brain and another one took its place.

"Tom when are you going to stop drinking?".

"Rachel?" Tom asked as the voice of his ex-wife entered his sub conscious thoughts.

"Forget about seeing the children until you sober up you drunk", Rachel snapped angry with her ex-husband's lack of effort at kicking the habit which put their marriage into an early grave.

"That's not fair Rachel I am trying to get sober", protested Tom, the anxiety in his voice causing his pulse to race a little faster.

"Well you're going to have to try harder, because until you do the children will not be visiting"

"Tom, Tom don't listen to her", another voice said drowning out the angry Rachel.

"Medad?"

"Yes Tom, it is I", Medad answered.

"What the hell is going on?" Tom asked inquisitively.

"Trust me Tom, trust me when I say to you, have the courage of your convictions, the courage to do what is right, when it is called for, for you have a greater importance then realize."

"But how will I know Medad?"

Medad did not answer, so Tom shouted nervously, "Medad? Medad? Are you there Medad?"

Medad never replied as the conscious part of Tom's mind awoke stirring his body into life."What the freaking hell was that all about ?", Tom said removing the sleep from his eyes, his retinas dilating letting in more light, bringing color back (albeit hazy) to his current surroundings. As he became more accustomed to the light, the focus of his attention was drawn to the alarm clock that rest on the bedside cabinet, it did not present a sight that was welcoming, in fact it was a little hostile.

"Jesus Christ", he swore observing the numbers on the time piece, "Time for me to get a move on".

Tom dove headlong into a time warp paradox as he prepped himself for his meeting with the priest at the Tomb of St. George's, "I hope he appreciates it", thought Tom to himself as finished off dressing, by placing a knotted neck tie around his uncomfortably new shirt.

Tom left the comfort of his hotel room, confidently closing the door behind with a sharp thud and proceeded to walk to elevators at the end of hall way, his descent to the hotel lobby in the vertically motioned coffin, was much more full of promise then the one ascending had been the previous night, hope replaced doubt, confidence replaced low self-esteem, he was now ready to take on the world, and to hell with it, he was fighting back, naming names, taking prisoners, the world had better be ready, for he was on the march to victory.

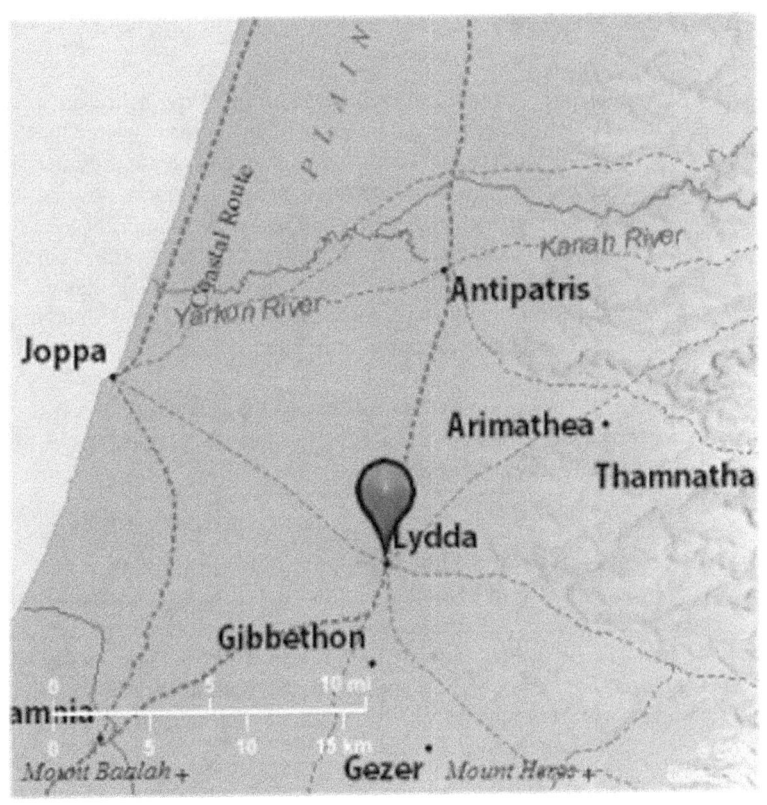

LOD (LYDDA) ISRAEL

CHAPTER VII

Lod a small city about 15km southeast of Tel Aviv, held Tom's awe in the palm of its historical hand, as it guided him towards the Church Of St. George (home to the Tomb Of St. George) with gentle caress of an ancient people proud of its heritage, pilgrims by the score made the journey daily to see this historical monument to a saint, whose beliefs and ideals cost him his mortal life on earth. Tom approached the Church with interpretation; his nerves on the edge of fragility, made him shudder with a nervous twitch, his friend Medad sensing a little apprehension asked "Are you ok Tom?"

"Question of having to be Medad, everything is so beautiful it takes the breath away", he replied as the city and it's famous church overwhelmed his sense of being.

The entrance way to the church caught Tom's attention as they walked inside, for above the door, carved eloquently from stone, was what appeared to be a man on a horse killing a mythological beast, as he studied the carving his attention was drawn to man on the horse for he seemed familiar, he seemed familiar to the point that Tom was sure he knew the imposing figure, his memory however couldn't quite recall where, or how, so for the time being he emptied the thoughts from his mind.

A small flight of stairs lead to an area of the church, where a small group of pilgrims were looking at the architecture of the church, enthralled by the detailed carvings that decorated the columns which took the vertical load of the ceiling, Tom's attention however was draw to the Crusader basilica which dominated the holy place of worship.

Tom and Medad (who had joined his friend) were both studying it with great enthusiasm, each one noticing how delicate the artistry was, the brilliance at which the artwork was conceived blinded them to their surroundings and the people in close proximity.

"Impressive is it not? A voice from behind them softly asked.

Tom turned slowly around, slightly afraid to see who was behind them, was it friend or was it foe? As he turned to see who it was, a long bearded man, in a black cassock stood before him, "Father Makom?" he queried, uncertain of the man that was tapping his sandaled foot with impatience.

"Yes my child, how may I help you", replied the holy man, his mouth starting to broaden with an all knowing smile that spread joy to those around him.

"I am Tom Raust, the newspaper reporter", Tom said relieved to find this person standing in front of him was the correct interviewee, "I believe I'm expected".

"Ah yes", Father Makom said with unease in his voice, "I am aware of your newspaper's request"

"I take it", exclaimed Tom wondering why the priest was not entirely happy, "you don't approve?"

"Not entirely Mr. Raust, however I have been told to fully co-operate and that I will", Father Makom said. Father Makom paused for a brief moment before continuing, "Tell me Mr. Raust, are you religious man?"

"To be honest Father Makom I am not", confessed Tom, reaffirming his belief that religion was not for him.

"Honesty in a man that is good Mr. Raust. I like a man who is honest", said the priest clasping his hands in a prayer like stance, " I am asking you as to many lies have been concealed in the doctrines of religious ideals, much blood has been spilt in the name of God, people evicted from their homes because their beliefs in another God conflict with those who worship another deity, it is a bad thing people do to each other in the name of God Mr. Raust".

"I'm astonished you say such a thing", confessed Tom who was puzzled by the priest's attitude to religion. He had expected him to be forthright in his opinion, and try to make him '*convert*' to his way of thinking but this was unexpected and caught him slightly off guard.

"Why Mr. Raust? Does killing your fellow man because it doesn't conform to your ideals sound logical sense? I hope not because surely that's against the moral fiber of most decent men?"

"I'm in total agreement with you", Tom said defending his position on faith, "Throughout history people have used and still use God as a reason to explain the unexplainable. More wars have been started throughout man's time on earth because of religious ideals, instead of questioning the obvious"

"Good, you have an inquisitive mind, I like that, it shows you are not afraid" smiled the priest putting an arm around the astonished newspaper reporter, "Mr. Raust, we have much to discuss, your friend can wait here while we talk, come".

Tom, still in shock, looked over his shoulder for reassurance, however it was not forthcoming, for his friend Medad had his hand over his own mouth trying not to laugh.

"Look around you Mr. Raust", prompted the religious cleric, "People of all faiths, all dominations come here to visit and pay homage to the anointed saint. Why do you think that is?"

"I'm not sure", replied Tom as his eyes feasted upon the glory that held within the Temple, "and please call me Tom".

"It is because of one man's vision for religious tolerance".

"So who was St. George?" Tom asked who was almost certain that this was the man that haunted his nightmares.

"Ah. That my friend is a good question. You know of the legend of St. George?" the priest replied as they walked side by side in discussion through the holy shrine.

"What little I know, is that St. George was a man who slayed a mythological beast".

"Ah the legend of the dragon story. That my friend is what most people know", said the priest showing Tom a spiral stairwell made from rock carved into the floor of the church, "The real man behind the fabled tale of a dragon slayer, was one of religious tolerance, a total understanding of others people's faith and the personal fortitude to do what is right when it was called off him, something even you, the most skeptical man Tom Raust, can appreciate. Come let me show you something I am sure will interest you".

The pair of intellectual equals descended slowly into the crypt, the walls cold with the passing of time, decorated the journey downward with an eerie feeling of déjà vu, light from an artificial man made source illuminated the sepulcher with a humble glow as it caressed the room with a loving touch.

"Here my friend", demonstrated the priest outstretching his frail but spiritually strong arm, "Here is the final resting place of St. George".

Tom apprehensively walked to the sarcophagus of the anointed knight, that took pride of place in the tomb of a meek little church, his eyes fixating on the golden relief that shone brightly in his vision, not daring to look away, "I...I...I know this man", he stuttered with disbelief.

"How do you know him my child?" Father Makom gently asked, his voice try to comfort Tom.

"I...I...I've seen him, this man, St George in my dreams", he sighed enunciating the words with a finger point at the gold and colored carving in front of him. Tom was reluctant to tell the priest of the repetitive nature of his nightmares, for he sensed Father Makom was not a believer of messages from past life existences (if indeed that's what they were), and to tell him that the visions he had were evil might undermine the nature of his visit to this holy shrine to a man he knew little about.

"In your dreams?" queried the holy man.

"Yes in my dreams, my subconscious, whatever you want to call it", he replied with a bewildered look in his eyes, disbelieving the vision presented before him. "Tell me", Tom asked continuing, "Was he beheaded by any chance?"

"After being tortured several times yes he was", Father Makom replied.

"This man in my dreams, he too is beheaded".

"Are you plagued by these dreams Tom?" the priest asked concerned for the man's soul in front of him.

"All too frequently", admitted Tom shaking his head, reluctant to let his visions on anyone else but himself.

"These dreams you are experiencing, will eat your soul alive if you let them", stated the priest with an all too knowing tone in his voice.

"How...how...how do I stop them?" asked Tom as a little tear formed in the corner of his eyes, ready to do anything to get an undisturbed nights' sleep.

"You must find out what really happened to this man in your dreams. You must do the right thing by him and for him. You must do the right thing for your own sanity Tom Raust. If you don't, then heed my warning, the devil will have you soul".

Tom brushed the tears from his eyes and softly spoke, "He's half way there already".

"Then my friend", the priest said putting a comforting arm around his fallen comrade, "We shall begin your quest now Tom Raust for this heavy burden on your soul is eating you up, if you do what needs to be done then, in time, these visions will transform themselves from darkness into light."

"Now?" queried Tom," but...but...but".

"No buts ", demanded the priest, "For the devils work is at play in your mind, the sooner we start, the sooner your demonic visions will disappear". Tom sighed for he knew the priest was right, it was time to unburden himself of these troublesome nightmares, but he was a little afraid, afraid that it might take him on a journey to places of persona that would cause him more pain then he could cope with, then what?

"Tell me Mr. Raust have you sampled Israeli Wine before?" asked Father Makom interrupting Tom's train of thought.

"No, never, why?" he said questioning the Father's methodology.

"Then it's about time you did my friend", said the Father with a smile on his face, "It's about time you did".

Tom sensed the goodness within the man standing beside him was pure, he sensed too that he was trying to help Tom in ridding himself of these troublesome nightmarish visions that kept him awake at night, whether or not he was doing the right thing by allowing his guard to finally come down, only time would tell, but for now the trust between the two men was a strong bond that only comes when both seek a simple answer, to a simple question.

Will you let me help you in your time of need?

If the answer was yes, then both men could proceed in their prospective goals, if not then all hope would be lost and ultimately his soul would be claimed by a darker presence then anyone would dare dream of.

CHAPTER VIII

A river of red, clear, alcoholic beverage flowed slowly into the crystal clear goblets like lava from a volcano, the intoxicating scent of fermented grapes drifted into the nasal cavity, while the clarity of its color presented the eyes with a pleasing scarlet glow of a wondrous liquid heaven. A taste of extreme pleasure rolled off the tongue like ambrosia from the gods as it slid over the palette, igniting the taste buds with a roaring fire, sending the brain neurons into rapture, whilst delighting the body with a warm feeling of impending happiness.

A trinity of free thinking individuals sat savoring the decadent nectar, while discussing intensely the rights and wrongs of spiritual enlightenment.

"So what you are saying", asked Medad, "Is the church should not ask for or receive donations of any kind?"

"No", explained Tom gesturing wildly with his hands, "What I am saying is, the people in the church, use the church as a means to line their own pocket instead of giving the money to those who truly need it".

"Explain please Tom Raust", chimed in the priest who was intrigued but open to Tom's persuasive argument.

"Ok", replied Tom ready to take the fight head on with the religious zealot in front of him, "Take the Catholic church for instance. They offer forgiveness of any wrong doing, in return for either a couple of prayers or a charitable donation, now tell me that is not wrong".

"I totally agree", responded the priest his hands gesturing praise with Tom's perception of the modern church, "However not all churches or faiths are like that, here people give donations to their church, not because it is expected of them, but they do so freely because the church uses the money to help those less fortunate. However Tom is correct in his thinking about people lining their own pockets at the expense of those weak in the mind. Do you know for instance, that the Roman Catholic Church was founded in the same year as a financial crisis threatened the very existence of Rome itself? No? I thought not, perhaps Mr. Tom Raust that could be something you must think about? Yes?"

"I certainly will give it some thought", answered Tom unsure of the Father's remarks, however it did make him think, think about the possibility that perhaps the foundation of the Roman Catholic church was nothing more than a money making scheme to help Rome in its conquest of Europe.

"I propose a toast", said Medad lifting his glass upwards "Helping those less fortunate than you, is not a requisite of getting into heaven, however is it a deed that should be done freely and without hesitation. Cheers".

The other two men clinked their glasses with Medad, all in total agreement with the sentiment echoing in the Father's private quarters, "Cheers" they all said in unison.

"Oh Tom before I forget", said Father Makom, "This is for you" presenting him with a yellow bound book.

"The Dummy's Guide to Feng-Shui?" queried Tom slightly taken aback by the unusual gift bestowed upon him, he was not a big believer of divine retribution, all that *'what goes around comes around'* stuff; he was of the adage that life was what you made it.

"Oh, I'm sorry", apologized the priest noticing he had given Tom an inappropriate present, "That's what you get for not wearing glasses".

"More like the wine", Medad muttered to Tom under his breath so the priest could not hear. Tom looked, at Medad with a raised eye brow, before shaking his head with a sly grin on his face, both knew what the other was thinking, it was crystal clear and both were secretly laughing on the inside.

"Here we go", said Father Makom correctly presenting Tom with a small leather bound book.

"What's this?" asked Tom starring at the artifact placed in his hand.

"It's a book containing information about St. George", replied the priest, "We've got similar copies of this in pamphlet form for the tourists. However this one is for you".

"Why...why...thank you", answered Tom taken aback by the priest's surprising generosity.

"Go ahead and read it", the priest told Tom with a slightly glazed look on his face.

"What now?"

"Why not?" interrupted Medad placing his crystal goblet back on the desk in front of him.

"Why don't your friend and I leave you to read it in peace?" the priest asked rising slowly from his seat, "I need some fresh air anyway".

"I agree", said Medad who too was in the process of elevating himself from the seat which had made his backside numb.

"We'll check in on you in a little while", promised the priest who was ushering Medad out of the priest's office with a comforting arm.

"Have fun", laughed Medad as he closed the office door behind him.

Tom poured himself another glass of wine, settled himself in the priest's chair, which was slightly more comfortable than the one he sat on and began to read.

'Their was much confusion about St. George, Was he a real man? Was he a fable? What ever the answer, people have believed the anointed Saint was a true man amongst men, his life of servitude and undying sacrifice a lesson for all of mankind.

George's life as infant started out in Lydda, Palestine, to parents of a noble family between 275AD and 285AD. His father, Geronzio was a Roman army official from Cappadocia, his mother Policronia from Palestine were both Christians, both had strong spiritual values which they imparted on the young George.

At 14 tragedy struck young George when he lost his father, at the age of 16 tragedy struck George again when his mother too died, this left him fatherless, motherless at an age when he was in most need of guidance. The need of this orphaned man for someone to give him direction in his life, lead the young George to the imperial city Nicomededeia , where he presented himself to the Roman Emperor Diocletian *(244AD - 311AD)* to apply for a career as a soldier.

Diocletian, having known and served with his father Geronzio welcomed George like a long lost son.

George's career under the guidance of Diocletian flourished, promoting George, who was then in his late 20's to the rank of Tribunus (serving as an Imperial Guard to the Emperor at Nicomedia).

During his time in the Roman Army, George served under Emperor Galerius Valerius Maximianus *(260AD - 311AD)* in the Egyptian and Persian campaigns *(approximately 298AD)*, where he met and became friends with a young Constantine *(272AD - 337AD)*.

In the year 302AD, Diocletian (who was then under the influence of Galerius) issued an edict that every Christian solder serving in the Roman Army either convert to paganism or be arrested.

George objected to this when he was approached by the Emperor, as the Emperor tried to convert George to paganism. Enraged by the man who he treated like a son, Diocletian offered land, money, and slaves the son of Geronzio if would make a sacrifice to the pagan gods, George denounced the pagan gods as false gods and refused to be bribed.

Diocletian, recognizing that George would not be tempted to pray to any other God, had no choice but to execute him., as Roman officials prepared for George's execution, George sensing his time on earth was near an end, gave away all his wealth, to the poor, the needy and the destitute.

Whilst in the captivity of the Roman persecutors, George was subjected to several bouts of torture, including three lacerations on a wheel of swords, each time being revived and brought back to life, however on April 23, 303AD George was executed by decapitation before the city walls of Nicomedia, after his death the body of St George was returned to Lydda (the place of his birth) for burial.

A church in Lydda built during the reign of his great friend Constantine (who later became Constantine the Great) was consecrated to "a man of highest distinction", the name of patron was not disclosed however, because of Constantine's love for his friend, and it was assumed to be George.

The original church was destroyed in 1010AD, but was rebuilt and dedicated to Saint George by the Crusaders, however during the Third Crusade *(1189AD -1192AD)*, this too was destroyed by the forces of Saladin, Sultan of the Aryyubid dynasty), a new church to replace this one was not built until 1872 where it stands to this day.'

"I need to find out more about this man Constantine", thought Tom to himself as he closed the book with a gentle thud. The sound of the book echoing in the priest's chamber stopped and the door to the office gently opened, with two of his closest allies walking through to see the progress he made.

"You ok Tom?' asked Medad.

"Medad what do you know about Constantine the Great?" asked Tom inquisitively

"Very little Tom", answered his friend truthfully, "The only thing I know is what they taught Medad at school. This man Constantine built a city called Constantinople which is now called".

"Istanbul", Tom interrupted with excitement.

"Yes Istanbul my friend. How you know?"

"It's a question in Trivial Pursuits", laughed Tom with a smile on his face that belittled the fountain of his knowledge.

"What is Trivial Pursuits?" asked Father Makom who was puzzled by the fountain of Tom's knowledge.

"I'll tell you about it later Father", promised Tom, "Tell me Medad", said Tom continuing, "Do you know anyone in Istanbul?"

"I have a long lost uncle there", stated Medad, "Why?"

"I've never been to Turkey", said Tom getting out of the Fathers chair, "All of a sudden I've got this sudden urge to go and visit".

"Ah", said Medad with a smile on his face, "I understand. I will go and make contact with my long lost uncle".

Tom was going to say an appreciative remark to Medad; however the Israeli businessman had already left, leaving Tom alone with the Father.

"I take it", asked the priest, "the book was useful?"

"It was Father", replied Tom, "would you mind if kept hold of it?"

"Not all my child", acknowledged the priest, pleased that his gift had been useful, "Not at all. Now Tom Raust tell me about this thing called Trivial Pursuits".

"Ok Father", said Tom laughing," I tell you all about Trivial Pursuits while you pour us some more of that delicious wine".

"That my friend", replied the priest pouring the wine into the crystal goblets, "is the least I can do. Cheers".

"Cheers", Tom responded, clinking the priest's glass. It wasn't long before the night fell as the two men talked themselves into an alcoholic state, blissfully unaware of the events that were to unfold before them.

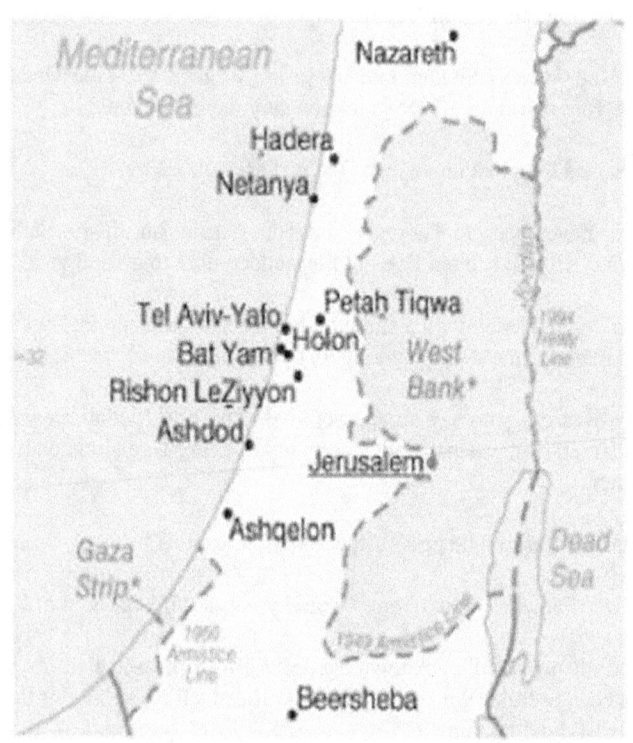

JERUSALEM
ISRAEL

CHAPTER IX

The morning slowly crept out of the shadows with a weary sigh, a sky of clouded nocturnal ambience drifted away on the breeze of light, as creatures of the night returned to their homes like vampires to their coffins, a world once held captive in a prison of darkness slowly broke out from its cell into a freedom of gilded radiance.

Gentle beams of haziness prodded their way into a dormant encephalon that belonged to man, who as a result of being tempted into drinking fermented grape juice, was suffering the effects of over self indulgence, his mind, his body, his soul crying out for relief from the self inflicted pain he was suffering.

"Never again", promised Tom as his eyes tried breaking free from his sleep ladened body, "Will I drink with a priest", the desert that ran over his tongue ran for miles in all directions, only interspersed occasionally by an oasis of acid laden breath that forced its way from the bottom of his pit less stomach.

He tried lifting his head off the sweat ladened pillow, but the forces of gravity and an annoying thud in his frontal lobe forced him back down, "Oh my head", Tom ached as he cupped his throbbing head in his hands.

Tom felt like he had been asleep at the fun fair, his stomach was somewhere doing inverted loops on a rollercoaster, his vision left spinning on a never ending merry-go-round, his sense of taste dry from eating those giant pretzels you get from those vendors whose personal hygiene left a lot to be desired, even his hearing was dancing to a melodic beat deafened by the giant boom boxes they seemed to play with that "dance" music he hated, Tom was in his own self indulged purgatory and he was paying a heavy price.

As he lay festering in a pit of self pity and self loathing he got a feeling in the bottom of his stomach that something was not quite right, and he was correct, for a gurgling sound started forming in the lower part of his abdomen. A small silent gurgle at first, bubbled away like a cauldron in a witches coven, before manifesting itself into that of a semi active volcano about to explode for the first time in centuries, "Oh Jesus H.Christ", he swore jumping out of his bed and running to the bathroom faster than an Olympic sprinter, as he reached the porcelain obelisk an eruption poured violently from his mouth.

"Frigging priest", he blurted, sending the offending sea of acid down a tunnel of fresh clean water, "That's it I'm totally done with the booze, I got to get sober before that man kills me". For Tom, it was not the first time he had promised to get clean, his wife, Rachel had tried to convince him that their marriage was suffering as a result of his over self indulgence. She had tried to convince him to seek professional help in his addiction, but in the end she gave up and sought solace in the arms of their neighbor, a man Tom thought he knew and could trust. Tom's years of self abuse had taken its toll on his health, his happiness but much more than that, his family, now he drank to forget, forget about the pain that he endured through his own self pitying destructive path to hell.

He had only just stumbled back to bed, when a knock on the door made him re-open his pain driven eyes, "Ah hell" , Tom groaned under his breath, "I wonder who that could be ?"

A slow zombie like walk was all that Tom could muster, his limbs struggling to keep pace with the rest of his body, his eyes barely wide enough for him to see where he was going and his stomach threatening to launch another vomit missile into space, as he slowly opened the door a friendly face breached the sanctity of Tom's undead state.

"Good Morning", smiled the visitor.

"What's so frigging good about it Medad?" queried Tom, his mouth just about managing to form the word of a semi decent greeting.

"Aren't we Mr. Cheerful this morning Tom?" asked Medad laughing at his friend's disposition, the beard he was growing hiding most of the delight he sensed at seeing his friend's own over indulgence, his brown eyes sparkling with mischievousness at the prospect of making Tom more ill than he already was, darted around the room looking for signs of a night spent under the coat of an intoxicating grogginess.

"What do you want?" Tom slurred struggling to make any sense out of the words he thought he was speaking.

"Well I brought coffee and aspirin", replied Medad still laughing at Tom.

"You better come in then", yawned Tom who was silently pleased with the liquid breakfast, just so long as it wasn't one of those nasty tasting protein shakes his brother used to give him when they were suffering the after effects of a heavy nights drinking, he didn't care what it was.

"So how's the hangover?" Medad inquired shutting the door loudly behind him, trying to goad Tom into issuing a profanity. Tom however didn't bite; he was far more concerned about getting rid of the nasty taste in his mouth.

"I've had worse", confessed Tom, remembering the time at his bachelor party he got so drunk , he didn't remember being pushed by his friends while naked in a wheelchair from the hospital, until his picture appeared on the local TV news show the very next day.

"Here drink this", Medad said handing a plastic cup of steaming black coffee to Tom.

"Thanks", replied Tom uncertain of the coffee brand that his friend had deemed fit to bring him.

"I'd wait till you drink that before you thank me".

"Why?"

"It's not Western coffee my friend", explained Medad hoping Tom would welcome a break from his more European flavored coffee, "it's Turkish".

"Turkish? I've never had Turkish coffee before", Tom said looking at the infused liquid before him.

"Well drink up then Tom", urged Medad eager to find out what his friend thought of the *'local brew'*. Tom smelt the gift Medad had brought him before taking a small sip of steaming hot liquid.

A smile of bewilderment spread across Tom's face as the coffee slid effortlessly down his throat."Wow. That's like drinking liquid caffeine", he said excitedly, "Thanks Medad, it's just what I needed. So". Tom paused for a moment before taking another sip of the delicious brew, "What do I owe the pleasure of your company?"

"I managed to get in contact with my uncle", Medad told Tom smiling at his friend's enjoyment of the coffee he had brought for him.

"Uncle. Uncle. Oh god yes your uncle Medad and?"

"He said it would be his honor and his privilege for him to pick you up at the airport in Istanbul, but he would only do it on one condition".

"Which is?" asked Tom nervously, remembering all the conditions his ex-wife used to demand in return for seeing his children.

"That you stop with him in his house in Turkey".

"Will you tell him thanks but, no thanks I don't want to impose"?

"But Tom", Medad explained, "he was most insistent, he will take it as an insult to his family name if you do not accept his generous offer".

"I wouldn't want to that now would I Medad?" Tom said taken aback by the generosity of someone he not even met yet, "Would you please tell him then, I graciously accept".

"Good", replied Medad, "He will be most pleased".

Tom was in a state of euphoria when he suddenly remembered about the man who paid his meagerly salary, "Ah hell"; Tom swore handing the coffee cup back to Medad.

"What is wrong?" asked Medad slightly perturbed.

"I've just remembered I've not been in contact with Edwards for a couple of days now, he's going to be steaming mad", said Tom looking for the telephone.

"Edwards. What is Edwards?" Medad inquired.

"Not what Medad, who. Edwards is the man who pays my salary", answered Tom sadly remembering that most of the money he earned went to his already over paid ex-wife, thanks to an overzealous female attorney hell bent on seeing Tom squirm with every ounce of his body as he was a classic "drunken husband who was not only a threat to his wife, but to the children also".

"He is your superior?"

"In name only Medad", Tom answered quickly pressing several buttons on the telephone, which he allocated on his bedside cabinet, "in name only".

"Shall I go then?" Medad offered pointing to the hotel door which lead to the corridor outside.

"No. It's okay you can stay", said Tom answering his friend while shaking a hand, affirming his desire for Medad to say, "Hello Mr. Edwards, its' Tom, Tom Raust".

A voice on the other answered and asked Tom in a surprisingly calm manner how the interview with the priest went."It went surprising well Mr. Edwards, there is one small snag though", said Tom explaining the details of the interview between the priest and himself, "The story doesn't quite end there."

As Mr. Edwards talked to Tom in length, further details began to emerge about Tom's need to go to Istanbul to complete the story, "So that means it's okay for me to fly to Istanbul then ?", asked Tom hesitantly, "No. No. Accommodation has been taken care of, my contact over here has arranged for me to stay with his family. Yes.

Yes I understand. Ok Mr. Edwards. Bye".

Tom place the phone back on the receiver, as a look of astonishment engulfed his persona with the touch of angel. "I don't believe it", Tom said retaking the coffee from his friend.

"What don't you believe?" queried Medad.

"He was fine with whole thing", Tom replied.

"Why does that surprise you?"

"He's never that nice", Tom stated as he had flashbacks to the time when he and Mr. Edwards argued over the content of his latest piece of literary work, on the closing down of the drug rehabilitation unit two towns over.

"Maybe he's pleased with the progress you are making?" asked Medad searching for an answer to his friend's predicament.

"I'm not sure", confided Tom, "but whatever it is, he's approved the flight to Istanbul".

"So that is good is it not, my friend".

"Not really ".

"Why is that?"

"The flight leaves in 3 hours time and I've not packed or washed or anything like that".

"Good Lord", exclaimed Medad in astonishment, "We'd better get a move on".

"We'd better had", agreed Tom who was already on his way to clean himself from the previous night's endeavors.

"Would you mind if I used your phone while you are getting changed?" Medad asked pointing to the telephone.

"Sure thing", answered Tom, who by then had turned on the faucet in the shower.

Medad looked in the bathroom to make sure Tom was in the shower, and began to dial slowly, "Hello. This is Medad", whispered the Israeli businessman making sure Tom didn't hear what he was saying, "Our friend is off to Istanbul". As soon as the words left his mouth and silently as he could, and without malice, an exchange of information began between Medad and the mysterious person on the other end of the phone. The end of the conversion was reached when Medad asked, "You want me to give him the usual gift?"

He paused listening with intent to the instructions he was given before replying "Ok, ok, my friend. Bye".

Medad shouted to his friend still in the shower, "Hurry up Tom will you, time is very short".

"Time is very short", he said whispering quietly under his breath, for Medad knew that with every second that passed danger grew ever closer, and as danger grew ever closer, Medad knew that people would be sent to hinder the progress of his friend Tom.

<u>ISTANBUL</u>
<u>TURKEY</u>

CHAPTER X

One by one they slowly appeared, a menagerie of personal effects, all shapes, all colors, slowly forcing their way into the light from the darkness, like a new foal being born, they staggered and swayed around until gravity took effect and they fell with a resounding thud onto the man made carousel. Modern day pilgrims gleefully reclaimed their prize possessions, as piece by piece floated by on a cushion of impending disaster, each one performed a waltz of mystery and intrigue waiting for their audience to acknowledge its contribution to the theater in which they stood.

A lonely, little red and battered suitcase slid slowly onto the merry-go-round. In the company of others it looked insignificant and feeble; however it was loved and respected by one person for it had travelled the world with him, no questions asked, no unselfish demands and no chance of it ever deserting him.

"Ah my faithful friend", thought the weary traveler as his fingers clasped the handle of the red suitcase, "Another city, another country, another what the hell am I doing here?" He let out a brief, but silent sigh of tiredness, the bags under his eyes burdened his face with fatigue. The plane trip had not been a pleasant one, cramped conditions, poor on board service and several bouts of turbulence had worn his patience thin, however he was here safely, in Istanbul, the jewel of the Middle East.

Tom's worn out carcass moved slowly through the airport terminal, as he searched for some sign of relief. A man on a mission, devoid of sleep and hungry through malnourishment, his eyes scanning for signs of a person who he had never met, a male individual who he had hoped would give him refuge and some insight into what was going on, for at this moment in time everything was a blur, nothing made any sense and it was making his head explode. Slipping into a parallel universe that was his mind, the lonely wanderer paid no attention to his surroundings, faces became a blur as voices dull with monotony drifted into the ozone of the concrete jungle.

From out of the blue like a lightning bolt, a voice came with true crystal clarity, "Mr. Raust, Mr. Tom Raust?"

"Yes I'm Tom Raust", replied the astonished Tom wondering how this man knew him, "and you are?"

"Don't be alarmed Mr. Raust", the stranger replied sensing fear in Tom's voice; "I'm Emre, Emre Osman, Medad's uncle. Nice to finally meet you. How was your trip?"

"It was kind of interesting", Tom answered as his heart beat slowly returned to a more normal rhythm. "How did you know it was me?"

"Medad gave me a very good description", stated Emre with a smile on his freshly shaved face, the hair on his head gelled and teased into complete submission, as his eye's observed the world through the glass of a metal ringed pair of designer spectacles.

"Ah I see", said Tom his eyes beginning to feel the after effects of another two hours spent in flying from country to country.

"Plus your name is on your suitcase", stated Emre pointing to the small luggage label attached to Tom's luggage, "Come my friend", he continued, "You look tired and hungry".

"That I am Mr. Osman, I'm afraid airline food leaves a lot to be desired", Tom replied remembering the less than appetizing meal served as a mid flight snack. He would hardly call rubber chicken, stringy green beans and what appeared to be carrots served in a gelatinous sauce a meal, it was more like a suicide note from the chef that dreamt it up.

"I'm not surprised and please call me Emre" replied the Turkish patriot as the two men walked to the exit deep in conversation, "What brings you to my part of the world?"

"I'm looking into the Legend of St George", Tom answered, "It appears he had connections with the former city Constantine".

"Ah the Legend of El-Khader", corrected Emre understanding

Tom's lack of local knowledge.

"El-Khader?" inquired Tom with a look that denied any previous knowledge of the man in question.

"Yes El-Khader" Emre answered "In my religion Tom, we see St. George as one of the human manifestations of the spirit known as El-Khader"

"I'm a little confused Emre", responded Tom as the furrows in his head got larger and deeper with slight anxiety at the prospect of maybe having already found a misplaced lead in his search for more information about St. George.

"There is a tale my slightly confused friend, that may or may not help you in your understanding of the legend which you seek", Emre said offering a way out of Tom's dilemma, "'The Feast of Mar Elias (Al-Khadr, El-Kidr, El-Khader) came and the young men stood together making their vows. One said: "I will give a goat," another "I will give a sheep." Then Jiryis, the son of a widow desired to offer something. They had but one cow."Then," he said, "I will sacrifice a cow," and he went and killed the cow.

At evening time his mother called and said, "Where is the cow?" He said, "I gave it to Al-Khadr." His mother said, "You have cut our lives. Let me not see your face again". That night the young man had a vision. A white haired man appeared to him and said, "Fear not, I am Al-Khadr; thou shalt go to Constantinople and to the king's palace. Only each day thou shalt call a blessing upon me".

So the young man went far away to Constantinople and he went to the king's palace. But he was dressed as a fellah (a peasant, farmer or agricultural laborer) and they sent him away from the door of the palace. Again the vision appeared, saying as before, "Fear not; I am with you. Only do not forget to ask a blessing on me every day," and this he continued to do. After many nights Al-Khadr came and showed him where seven storehouses of gold were hidden. Then the young man went again to the palace, offering to reveal his knowledge, and this time he was allowed to enter in and was made welcome there and he gave all the gold to Queen Helena. Then the saying came true, "He who gives gold, May marry the

Sultan's daughter", for Jiryis was dressed as a prince and married to the king's daughter.

That night, his wedding night, he forgot to ask a blessing on Al-Khadr. In the morning he woke to find himself back in Jerusalem, standing at the Bab Al-Khalil, dressed as a fellah and only the ring on his finger to remind him of his bride, the king's daughter. Months passed and he lived miserably in Jerusalem, ever imploring forgiveness of Al-Khadr.

After a while Queen Helena decided to travel and build churches. At every place where she stopped she built a pillar and a sign was placed on the pillar - some say a light, some say a bell - so that news could be sent back to Constantinople. At last the queen arrived in Jerusalem and with her came the king's daughter and her baby.

Now the baby was not content, but cried all the time for his father, day and night, and there was his father, a poor fellah out of work, hanging around the Bab Al-Khalil.

One day those who stood near the young man said to him, "Why do you not go and work for the queen who is trying to find the Cross? She needs workmen to dig for her". So he went and was accepted and worked with the workmen, and that same night Al-Khadr appeared to him and showed him where the True Cross lay. Next morning he first revealed the secret to the queen and then showed the ring to the king's daughter, and as soon as ever he came near her, the baby, his son, stopped crying.

After the Cross was found, Queen Helena sent the news to Constantinople by means of her pillars. So by the wisdom of Al-Khadr the True Cross was found and through the gold of Al-Khadr all the churches of Queen Helena were built.'"

As Tom listened intently to Emre's fable, something strange was beginning to dawn on him, something he had not noticed before and that was the reoccurrence time and time again of the number seven. His alarm clock went off at 7am, Mr. Edwards called him up on the 7th July 2007 (07/07/07), his plane number was G7, hell even his hotel room number back in Israel added up to the number 7 (Room 412 - 4+1+2 = 7), and now this story of St. George contained seven storehouses of gold. There must be a reason why the number seven kept cropping up? But Why? What was the significance behind the number 7? He decided for now to keep quiet about this revelation until their came an opportunity to find the meaning of the number seven, and then, only then, would he find the answer his was seeking, "So what you're basically telling me is that St. George (or El-Khader) helped Queen Helena find the whereabouts of the True Cross? And If I understand it correct, that this means that due to Jiryis living in Jerusalem, then that means that's where the True Cross is? ".

"Correct on both accounts Mr. Raust", affirmed Emre pleased at this stranger's grasp of an old fable handed down generation to generation,

"I'm pleased my story telling was better then I remembered being told as a small child by my father".

"Does the name El-Khader mean anything then Emre?" Tom said inquisitively.

"It is derived from the Quran", Emre said offering insight into the other incarnation of St.George, "and it means 'The Green'. The Quran is a book of divine guidance and direction for mankind, for those of us in the Muslim faith".

"Does that mean St. George is *The Green Man*?"

"Well sort of Tom", Emre answered, "The spirit attached to St. George is the *'The Green One'*".

"And?".

"*'The Green One'* is an immortal being who wanders the world invisible to humans, only appearing once in a while in human form to rescue the righteous from danger or preach to the ungodly".

"How did this all begin, this myth of *'The Green One'*?"

"According to legends", stated Emre trying to remember the lesson he was taught in school, "This myth, this legend, whatever you want to call it has roots in Syrian and Babylonian fertility gods, Adonis and Tammuz, Islam adopted it very early on, the connection to St George with El-Khader, however is a mystery it maybe simply an adaptation of the famous 12th century myth of St. George killing the dragon to save a Libyan princess".

"That sounds like Perseus killing a sea monster", Tom commented as a look of bewilderment etched its way into his already burned face. For once Tom surprised himself at having remembered something at school he took little interest in, Perseus the founder of Mycenae and first mythic hero of Greek mythology did indeed kill a sea monster by the name of The Cetus in his rescue of the princess Andromeda (but what he did not know was that The Cetus was the large whale that swallowed Jonah as depicted in the bible).

"Ah", replied Emre pleased that his *apprentice* had grasped what little knowledge he was imparting, "You know your Greek mythology".

"Only the little what I remember from school", Tom replied not entirely confident of the name of the monster killed by Perseus, "I think it's called The Cetus or something like that".

"You know more than I do", Emre said laughing at his new found friend's sudden expertise in Greek mythology, "Let us talk some more about this thing called The Cetus as we journey to my home. Come our taxi cab has arrived".

As Tom turned to face the bustling city a yellow taxi pulled into close where the two men stood, it reminded him of home and the yellow taxis where he lived. For a brief moment in time he stood motionless, his staring eyes transfixed on the car before him, journeying back in his own mind to his beaten down one bedroom apartment in the middle of Manhattan's bustling metropolis.

"Tom, Tom we go now please?" Emre asked a little mystified at Tom's reluctance to get into the yellow cab.

"I'm sorry Emre. Yes we go now", apologized Tom as he was brought to reality by the voice of the Turkish man penetrating his journey back to another time.

As Tom and his new friend set of to Emre's home, he couldn't help but wonder if this was a wild goose chase or whether he was on the precipice of something bigger then he could possible imagine, "There was only one thing he could to", he thought to himself, "and that was to wait and see what paths were to unfold before him, hoping that whichever one he chose would be the right one to follow".

CHAPTER XI

The morning broke with a fresh sweetness about it; clouds of pure white fleece drifted their way through the seas of aura as the rays of the sun bathed the earth in a tender glow. Swarms of people (brought out by the birth of the new day) began busying themselves; slaves to the system they rat raced themselves to the trappings of modern life desperate to earn the pot of gold at the end of the suburban rainbow.

A pair of likeminded suburban warriors viewed this way of life with distaste, neither caring for the misery it brought or the greed which it nurtured, an explainable curse to an unexplainable desire for wealth and the status that society placed upon it, "I hate city life", Emre professed to Tom as they both observed the city through a window in Emre's home.

"Me too", sighed Tom with a sadness in his heart, "society has placed too much emphasis on the accumulation of much wealth as possible".

The profoundness of Tom's reply came from years of a poverty stricken life on a small farm in Ohio, where he lived with his Mother and Father and his brother Jack on a small holding, farming cattle (and the occasionally Bison when the money was good). The run down shanty like farm eventually went the way of most small holdings in the Mid West during the 1970's, the price of crude oil and cheap foreign imported meat placed the homestead in the hands of the banks, forcing Tom and his family to the city of New York. His Father took work as a Taxi Cab driver learning the streets from a small pocket map he kept with him at all times before retiring in his later years due to ill health, the money was mediocre but at least they had a roof over their heads and food in their stomachs.

When she wasn't taking care of the family or her husband, Tom's mother, occasionally took sewing in from people who knew of her from an advert in the taxi cab which Tom's father drove, charging a nominal fee for a variety of services offered.

As Tom got older and started working, his mother warned him about girls who would only hang around him for his money, he took the advice with a pinch of salt, going the way of most young men with money in their pocket, the bar, to pick up girls and drink, it was at one bar in particular, in the lower end of Manhattan, where he first met Rachel, they laughed, and giggled, having fun together, with one another, as long as Tom had money they had fun.

The first time his parent's met Rachel, Tom's mother took him aside and warned him that this girl was a gold digger only after his money; Tom brushed the remark off with all the nonchalance of a man who thought he knew better than anyone else, how wrong he was.

Rachel was driven by greed, money and trying to out better the Joneses, it wasn't long before she had run up thousands and thousands of dollars on her credit card, forcing Tom to work longer and longer hours at the newspaper where he worked.

"Greed only brings problems", Emre said agreeing with his new friend.

"Sometimes it creates more problems than it actually solves", commented Tom admitting what he learnt through bitter experience.

"Too many people have been killed because of this modern curse", Emre remarked admiring his friend's position on society's infatuation with wealth and money.

"People have died because of the lack of it; people have killed others because their lust for money has turned them from the straight and narrow".

"Ultimately it will be man's undoing".

"That it will my friend", Emre agreed, "That it will".

"So", Tom said turning his head away from the view which pained him," I could really use some help finding out more about this man who befriended St. George. Do you know anyone who could help?"

"I don't personally", replied Emre, "however I'm certain someone at the museum will be pleased to help you with your questions".

"That sounds fine to me", Tom said as he made his way to the front door of Emre's house.

"Good. Good", Emre said as a smile light up his face, "I thought I would you show the Column of Constantine on the way there, we pass it so we might as well have a look at it".

"Column of Constantine?" asked Tom as the two men ventured into the back streets of the city and proceeded to make their way through the rich tapestry of Istanbul's streets and alleyways in search of the museum.

"It's quite an impressive piece of architecture Tom", answered Emre.

"Really?" Tom proclaimed raising an inquisitive eye brow, "Tell me more".

"It was built in approximately 330AD under the orders of Constantine the Great to commemorate the declaration of Byzantium as the new capital city of the Roman Empire".

"I bet that went down well with the Romans", Tom said to Emre as they turned into what Tom thought was a major thoroughfare running through the city. Tom noticed on the sidewalk, two distinctly elderly gentlemen smoking through what he thought was a hookah. Tom had not seen one since he was at college, when his friend Eric had brought one to smoke some marijuana through. Eric van Outen, a child of Dutch immigrants, was a rebel, a man who did not care for society's rules; it was kind of ironic, how he eventually turned out to be a court room judge presiding over some of history's most bizarre trials revolving around children allegedly being sexually abused by people of power and trust in the Mormon religion, but that was typical of the man, unpredictable to the last.

"Yeah like a lead balloon" confessed Emre whose vocabulary had been slightly westernized from his time listening to the BBC world service news on his ancient radio he had as a small boy given to him by his father.

"Did it cause a lot of resentment between the Romans and the Byzantium people?"

"There are no records of any dispute between the Romans and the Byzantium people, but you can guarantee there was. Wouldn't you be just a little aggravated?"

"I would be more than a little annoyed", stated Tom, "I would be furious".

"So would I", responded Emre agreeing with Tom, "Strange how there's no records of how the Roman people felt."

"Maybe there is but they've not been found yet".

"Or they've been hidden".

"What, on purpose you mean?" asked Tom a little perturbed by the fact that some of histories records had been concealed for a specific reason.

"Stranger things have happened my friend. Ah here we are the Column of Constantine", Emre said as the two men entered a part of the city known to local people as Yeniceriler Caddessi.

"In the days", Emre explained, "When Constantine was ruler, the column was at the center of the *'Forum of Constantine'*. It was dedicated to Emperor in 330AD in a bizarre mix of pagan and Christian ceremonies".

"Pagan and Christian?" asked Tom, "Why was that?".

"That I'm not sure about", replied Emre, "maybe it was something to do with the fact he was a pagan then converted to Christianity".

"That's strange", said Tom as an inquisitive look ran over his face that relayed the thoughts he had were spinning around in his head like a washing machine on full spin.

"There are many myths about Constantine's conversion to Christianity. Maybe you should ask someone who knows more about it then me".

"I will Emre and I also", but Tom didn't finish his sentence for the pair of journey men had reach their goal, The Column of Constantine, the sight that entered Tom's retina took his breath away for the Column grand in many different ways, the size, the architecture, the ornateness of the carvings all weighed heavy on his perception, each one adding to the complete picture of a most exquisite modern day marvel.

"How?" asked Tom quietly under his breath.

Emre shrugged his shoulders saying "No one knows Tom for sure, but it surely takes the breath away".

All Tom could do was nod in agreement for his heart and his mind were taken over by the spectacle of nine cylindrical porphyry blocks pointing their way towards the heavens, each one perfect in size and shape, never moving, the monument stood as sturdy as the day it was created. "Legend has it", interrupted Emre, "that the statue of Constantine as the Greek God Apollo, which used to adorn the top of Column held a fragment of the True Cross".

"For real?" queried Tom knowing that the True Cross was the name for the actual remnants of the cross on which Jesus was alleged to have been crucified.

"Well it is only a legend Tom", Emre reminded his friend, "and legends also say that at the foot of the Column, a sanctuary hid other important biblical artifacts".

"Such as?" Tom inquired.

"The Crosses of the two thieves crucified alongside Jesus, the baskets from the loaves and fishes miracle, an ointment jar belonging to Mary Magdalene, the palladium of ancient Rome and a wooden statue of Athena from Troy".

"Mary Magdalene the alleged wife of Jesus?" questioned Tom as his thoughts turned to the distinct possibility that this fable of Jesus marrying the woman Mary Magdalene was more than just a made up story.

"The one and only".

"How did they get over here to Istanbul then?"

"The story is that Constantine's mother Helena went on a pilgrimage with St. George to Palestine to recover artifacts relating to the True Cross, however there is no documented proof that this really happened", answered Emre explaining Tom's question as fully as he possibly could. For a brief moment Tom and his friend Emre stood silently side by side, each man in his own right stood isolated from the world lost in his own inner thoughts.

"We should be pressing on Emre", Tom said after returning from his subconscious mind, "There's still the museum to go and see ".

"Yes, I agree", Emre replied reluctant to leave the awe inspiring monument behind, "There's still much to do and yet we've barely scratched the surface".

"Why have I got the feeling we could be about to open Pandora's Box", said Tom to Emre as the two men set off to find the Museum.

"I don't know", answered Emre as they sat off in transit for the knowledge contained with the museum, "but if you're right then we could be in for an enlightening journey".

"That", Tom acknowledged "could be the understatement of the year".

"Let us go and find out then my friend", Emre said with anticipation, "what the box of Pandora has in store for us".

Tom and his new friend Emre, went forth into the unknown, not knowing, not caring to know, what the future would bring, whether it was riches beyond their wildest dreams, or whether it was nothing more than satisfaction in a job well done, they only had the eyes fixed on one thing, the museum and all the glories it held within.

CHAPTER XII

The crossword alleys bordered the tapestry of the houses, the fabrics patterned into a maze of brick and mortar that sometimes bewildered visitors in a labyrinth of bizarre ritualistic routinely strange sarcophagus of noise and vision, between that and the different languages spoken, a person could find themselves lost in a mirage of time and space, each one more precious than gold and both equally in short supply.

Patterns of fine particles suspended in a gas released themselves into the sky creating fine whispery snakes, as upwards they drifted on the gentle breeze that caressed the city with a lover's kiss, while slowly they danced a waltz of grace and beauty before disappearing into the blueness of the earth's curtain. From the depths within a small band of wandering troubadours walked the streets in search of a fountain of knowledge from which they wanted to quench their thirst, a thirst so great, so intense, that the wanderers took little heed of the danger that was apparent, for to fail in their quest now would bring intolerable misery to the people who had placed great faith in them and failure was not an option they felt entirely comfortable with.

Their journey had started from humble beginnings to a place, which now had firmly held them within its grasp, a prophetic journey so life changing, that neither man nor beast would be the same individual again. As further along this chosen path they walked, secrets once hidden would become visible, faiths once strong would be weakened, even the morality of the flesh would be wounded with a weapon much deadlier than the gun, but neither man cared, nor did he dream to care for this was the path he had chosen to walk upon.

Carefully they walked, placing each foot on the ground, moving forward, forward into the unknown as an entity that binded itself to each man, an entity that both men sought as a friend, a guide, a savior, in times of sorrow, in times of desperation, in times of poverty, in times of riches, an entity each man would seek from within, an entity known simply as the truth.

"Surely each man must seek the truth?" Emre said to Tom as they circumnavigated the bustling streets of the city unsure of his friends reply.

"Or his own version of what he deems to be the truth", stated Tom sensing the uncertainty in his friends voice.

"I'm not entirely sure what you mean", said Emre still a little puzzled by Tom's remark.

"The truth is dependent on your own perception of what the truth is", commented Tom, "It can vary from person to person as each person's moral values color their perception of what the truth really is".

"But isn't the truth the truth?" argued Emre.

"To a certain extent yes, but the truth can be tainted to become a different variant of what the truth once was, take for instance this St. George myth".

"Or El-Khader", Emre reminded his friend.

"Or El-Khader", continued Tom, "The real St. George actually existed, the real truth about him is he was tortured for his belief in the Christian faith, but the truth was tainted into becoming this myth about St. George slaying the dragon but it is generally accepted as the truth".

"I see Tom", said Emre who had just began to see what the point of Tom's argument was, "So the truth as it originally once was can be changed, altered, to what we generally accept the truth to be".

"Precisely", replied Tom who was relieved that Emre was starting to appreciate the subtlety in his argument, "We as a race have become quite adept at changing the truth to what we want the truth to be".

"Hence the legend, the myths", continued Emre.

"The stories, the fables, fairytales", Tom said interrupting Emre stressing each point with a finger wag.

"The truth as it was, no longer exists".

"Well it does to a certain point, but then it gets twisted to how we want it to be. Take the myths surrounding Jesus for example, no one really knows what happened to him, no one can be 100% certain of the life he lead, hell for all we know he could be living it up in the South of France somewhere laughing his ass off at the stories made up about him."

"Well my friend", stated Emre who now totally understood what Tom was trying to make him understand, "We better ask the right questions then".

"That my friend", said Tom, "is something we can both agree on".

"I agree", said Emre smiling as he realized where they were, "I'm sure these people might have some of the answers to our questions".

Tom laughed as he noticed the impressive building that stood isolated in the middle of the city, "I take it this is the museum ?", he asked as the two men walked on a tile road way that lead directly to a quadruplet of marble columns supporting a pyramid like structure.

"It certainly is", said Emre.

"Did you know about this?" Tom asked Emre as a wooden advertising board standing on a tripod came into focus.

"You mean Da Vinci's Vitruvian Man?"

"Is that what it is?"

"Yes", answered Emre studying the billboard, "It's Da Vinci's Vitruvian Man and according to the advertisement it say's it's on loan from Gallerie dell'Accademia Venice".

"The what?" said a slightly annoyed Tom who was far from happy at what appeared to be a plan of deception on Emre's part.

"The Gallerie dell'Accademia in Venice, it's a museum of pre-19th century art which is the permanent home for Da Vinci's Vitruvian Man", Emre answered translating the writing on the advertising board from Turkish into English.

"Overrated crackpot", Tom snarled to Emre who had his fill of Da Vinci related news items. Time and time again it was he, who Mr.Edwards, his boss, had sent to cover stories through the Americas to certain individuals who claimed they had solved a true *'Da Vinci Code'* only to find out they were spotty teenage boys in their first semester of college, barely out of diapers wanting their 15 minutes of fame.

"What do you mean?" asked Emre surprised by Tom's reaction was more venom filled than he originally anticipated.

"Da Vinci is overrated, there's no definitive proof he was that great inventor, he was probably just the illustrator of other people's idea's, the paintings are substandard and as for the alleged DaVinci code".

"You're not a big fan then?"

"No I'm not".

"I'll make you a deal then?" said Emre sensing a challenge.

"Oh and what's that then"

"I'll take you to a coffee bar in town which serves the best coffee you'll ever taste in your life".

"In return for?" asked Tom sensing what was coming next, yet still managing to wonder how Emre knew of his love of coffee.

"You'll accompany me to look at this work of art".

"I accept", said Tom putting his hand out to shake Emre's hand.

"Deal?" queried Emre clasping Tom's outstretched hand.

"Deal", said Tom as a cheesy grin spread over his face.

"Let's go then", said Emre as he walked down the path to the front of the museum.

"What now?" asked Tom.

"Yes now, something wrong with that?"

"Nothing, just I wasn't quite expecting to go now considering we've got to find someone who has expertise on Constantine".

"Don't worry my friend", said Emre who had placed a guiding hand on his bewildered friends shoulder, "there will be plenty of time to find someone who can answer your questions. Come let us go now".

"Ok", replied Tom hesitantly, "but you're buying the coffee".

"That my friend is the truth", said Emre to his friend, as the two men continued their journey forward into the unknown.

CHAPTER XIII

The translucent bolder sentry closed firmly as the two vagabond thieves entered the Aladdin's cave of treasures, riches beyond their wildest dreams draped themselves on the columns that supported the cathedral ceiling, as glass coffins of knowledge lay motionless on the manmade grass each one holding the corpse of an historic event within its confined walls. Stories desperate to be passed on lay in wait, eager to be told to a captive audience, yearning for a chance to be free, free from the shackles of time, a time when the knowledge they possessed bore ideas of a much simpler yet idyllic life.

Further into the annals of time stealthily the two men went, as each step they trod moved them further from their existence in the modern world and closer to a man whose genius gave birth to an abundance of much sought after knowledge. These men on the pathways of uncertainty and desperate to pray on the alter of enlightenment, they wandered deeper and deeper into the citadel in search of their holy grail, occasionally seeking magi who would be found wandering the empty plains looking for those lost or in need of assistance.

From the distance a white light shone, penetrating the darkness with a small beacon of hope, enticing those who had wandered from distant kingdoms into a belief that their quest was almost completed, for some it had, for others it had just begun.

"This my friend", Emre confirmed showing Tom the artwork by Leonardo Da Vinci, "is the Vitruvian man".

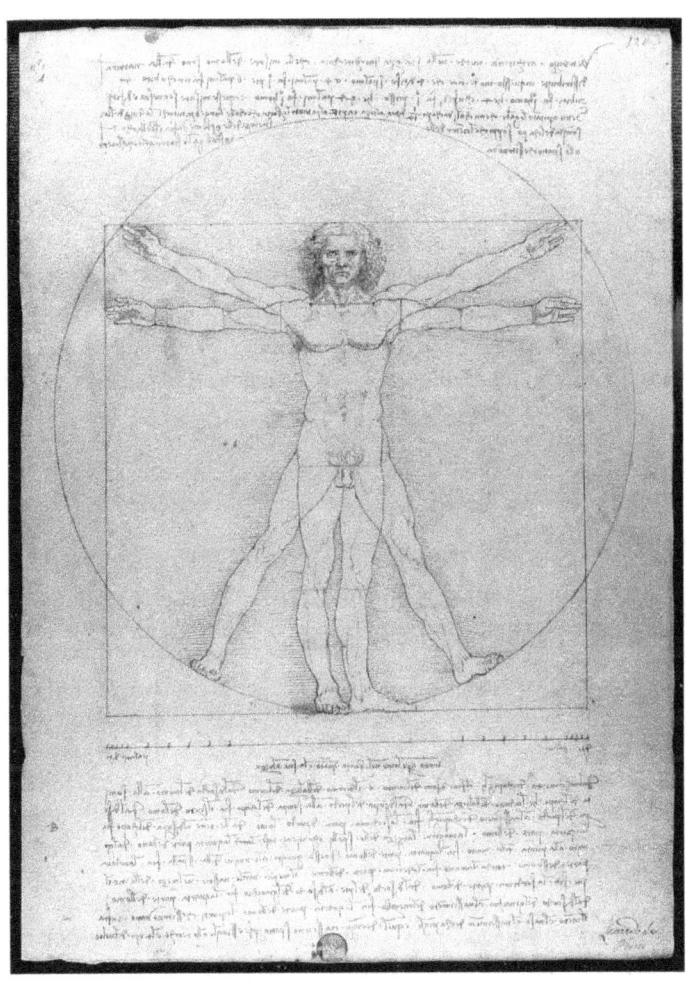

Fig. I - The Vitruvian Man by Leonardo Da Vinci

"Why is it called the Vitruvian man and not the self portrait of a man who was drunk at the time?" sneered Tom who was unenthusiastic with what was presented to him.

"Still not impressed are we?" Emre said to Tom who was not happy with his friend's negative thinking.

"No I'm not", Tom replied his eyes confirming what his mouth was saying.

"Why?" asked his friend who was determined to make Tom's life difficult.

"It's just the picture of a naked man done by someone who was a 2nd rate artist", explained Tom, his voice strong and firm as he gestured the symbol of clarity with his right hand conducting the orchestra of his mind.

"2nd Rate? DaVinci?" Emre questioned Tom's remark and his distaste for what he classed as someone who was truly the master of his craft.

"Yes Da Vinci, come on Emre look at it, what is it really supposed to be about, this Vitruvian man?"

"This Vitruvian man is one of Da Vinci's most important works; it defines the proportions of man".

"I bet it wasn't one of his own ideas then", sniped Tom certain in his belief that Da Vinci copied the theme from someone else's work.

"You're right it wasn't".

"I knew it", shrugged Tom shaking his head in a way that told his friend *'I told you so'*.

"The original concept was drawn up by a man called Vitruvius who was an architect. He was the one who defined the proportions of man in his book De Architectura.", explained Emre pausing in his thoughts before continuing, "Vitruvius had been a Roman soldier serving under Julius Caesar as an army engineer, where he specialized in the construction of ballista and Scorpio artillery war machines used in the sieges of towns during the rise of Rome's military expansion of its Empire, places like North Africa, Hispania, Gaul and Pontus".

"So what was Da Vinci's interest in it then? " asked Tom a little put off by his friend's surprising knowledge of a man he himself, knew little about.

"Da Vinci was fascinated by the anatomy of the human body." stated Emre as he stood admiring the work in front of him, "In fact Da Vinci wrote a book on the Anatomy of Man after he illegally obtained dead bodies through which he studied the workings of the human body".

"Ok then Emre", retorted Tom sensing an opening in the argument, "If he was so interested in human anatomy then why are all the hands on the drawing in different positions?"

"What do you mean?" Emre said astonished by his friend's attention to detail.

"Look at the hands", exclaimed Tom pointing to the hands on the picture, "They're all different, if it was supposed to be anatomically correct, surely they would all be the same?"

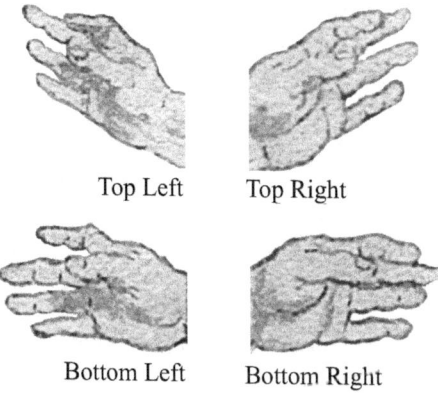

Top Left   Top Right

Bottom Left   Bottom Right

Emre took Tom's remark very seriously, looking closely at each finely detailed hand in question. The position of the fingers were different, every single one of the hands did indeed have a distinct pattern to its brethren."Tom", Emre quietly whispered his friend's name.

"Yes Emre", answered Tom who couldn't quite understand the need to suddenly whisper.

"I think you could be on to something there".

"What do you mean like a *'secret code'* or something", Tom said who still wasn't taking his friend's need for whispering seriously.

"I do", Emre murmured barely able to believe what his eyes were telling him.

"You're serious aren't you?" Tom replied as he stood back a little further to get an overall view of the picture.

"Yes I am", said Emre whose demeanor had suddenly turned from that of a heated discussion to one of a more serious nature.

"What's the code then?" asked Tom who suddenly had stopped joking and was now more serious than he previously was.

"I've no idea Tom", Emre confessed scratching his head, "You got any ideas?".

"Hmmm let me think", Tom mumbled rubbing his hand over his chin in hope that a spark of ingenuity would light a fire in his head, "It can't be the number of fingers as they're all showing but........" he hesitated for a moment as his brain began to show him something else, something he hadn't expected.

"What is it Tom?"

"The fingers are all in certain positions almost like they're", he paused for a moment as he restudied each finger individually with a greater intensity.

"Like what", asked Emre impatiently.

"Like they're making the pattern of a letter but something doesn't quite add up. When Da Vinci wrote did he have a special, unique way of writing?"

"From what I understand he used to write mirror imaged", stated Emre puzzled but delighted what Tom was discovering.

"I've got a feeling that this code, if a code truly exists in this picture, is mirrored. Is there any way we could get a copy of this and take it home?"

"I've got a computer at home we could get a digital copy".

"Good", said Tom, "then let's go and dissect this code".

"You've changed your tune", Emre remarked who was now delighted by his friend's attitude.

"I love a good mystery", replied Tom, "However I still reserve the right to be skeptical".

"That my friend is the best way to be", Emre assured Tom putting a hand on his friend's shoulder.

As each man left the vicinity of the master's work both asked the same question, "What does the code say?" both equally determined to see if a code existed and if it existed then what was the message. Time they decided would provide the answer they were looking for, if only to confirm or dismiss the plausibility of a *'true Da Vinci code'*.

CHAPTER XIV

The fields of cognitive content lay barren, windswept by the ravages of time and infertile by droughts of inactivity, nothing grew, not even one tiny seedling, devoid of ideology and lacking in the creativity of forethought, nothing short of a miracle would bring lushness back to this desert and return nutrients to the soil beneath. Year upon year the farmers of this god forbidden place would cultivate the earth in a hope that one time their labors would be rewarded, but alas it was all in vain for the gods deemed that this place was to remain forlorn and barren until a certain time when their efforts would give them a glean, so rich, so overflowing that they would be hungry no more.

Time came and went with regularity like the tides of the seas, never stopping, constantly flowing; as did the hope that this land would, one day, be a lush paradise upon which the knights of truth would triumphantly announce their return. As the passing of the seasons moved closer to the spring equinox, a miracle was being born, for on these barren fields, a small insignificant seed was being brought to life.

"I suppose the first logical step, considering Da Vinci used to write in mirror image, would be to reverse the hands", a hesitant Tom remarked not entirely sure of the direction they were going.

"Considering the way Da Vinci used to write that would be a good starting point", replied Emre confirming Tom's opening remark.

"Let me see", Tom thought to himself as he studied the options on the computer screen, "Flip Horizontal 180 degrees, where are you?"

For a small moment Tom's eyes transfixed themselves on the computer screen that decorated the small office in Emre's home. The office itself was a unique room in a mundane house, books by the score, antiquities by the dozen, and enough dust to fill a vacuum cleaner twice over. It didn't bother Tom and why should it? He was used to dealing with other people's filth bearing habits as part of his job, that was what he was paid to do, dig through the filth and the grime that others used to protect their secrets, secrets worth dying for.

"Ah there you are", Tom remarked clicking the mouse button on the required function directly under the pointer on the screen.

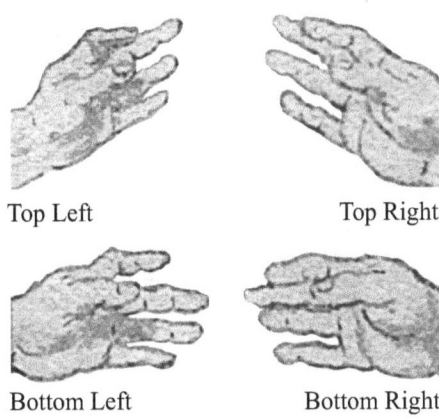

Top Left   Top Right

Bottom Left   Bottom Right

Fig. III - Hands on the Vitruvian Man (Reversed)

"I see what you mean about the hands now Tom", stated Emre studying the images with great interest, "They're all in different positions aren't they?"

"See", confirmed Tom with an all knowing smile that encompassed his slightly beaten cortex, "I told you so".

"What does it mean though?" queried Emre.

"I'm not entirely sure", Tom admitted leaning back in his chair trying to figure out the hidden meaning. The chair disapproved of Tom's action with a small squeak of pain prompting the occupier to return to a more natural stance, "It kind of looks like the hands are in the shape of letters though".

"Really?" asked Emre, "How so?"

"Let me show you Emre", explained Tom moving the mouse pointer on the screen, creating an image so his friend could comprehend what he thought he had seen.

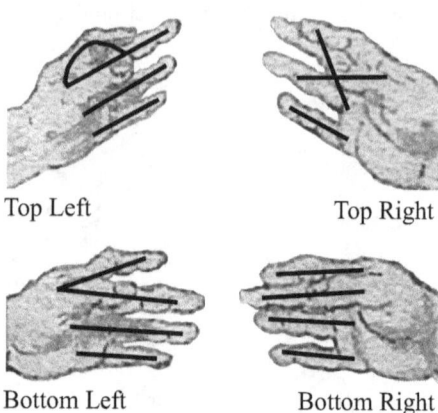

Top Left   Top Right

Bottom Left   Bottom Right

Fig. IV - Hands on the Vitruvian Man (Reversed and Lines Drawn)

"I can understand how you get DII, VII and IIII", Emre told Tom as they both sat looking at the screen in front of them, "How do you get the IX though ?".

"I think its IX because the last two fingers are crossed, like this", Tom explained answering Emre's question by showing his own finger's in the pattern produced on the screen," Thing is I'm not sure what the hell is DII IX VII IIII", Tom continued uncertain of the significance pertaining to the letters he had drawn.

As Tom and Emre sat motionless in time and space, a telephone that lay somewhere else in the house began to reverberate, "Excuse me Tom", said Emre as he pushed himself to a vertical base.

"Sure thing", Tom replied acknowledging his friend's departure.

With his friend gone, Tom turned his attention to bizarre combination of letters that ran across the computer screen, "Maybe" he thought to himself, "I'm taking it too literally. What else could it be?"

The wheels of reasoning began to turn slowly in his brain, trying to decipher what these letters meant. Time after time an idea came to him, but he dismissed it for one reason or another, however one came to him that could *NOT* be dismissed, "I know they're not alphabetical symbols, perhaps they're symbols of a different kind, maybe just maybe, they could be Roman Numerals", he thought to himself quietly, "What would that give me now ?", he paused trying to recollect his knowledge of the ancient number system, "Well DII I think is 502, VII is 7, IX is 9 and IIII possible could 4 even though 4 is usually IV, so that gives me 502,7,9 and 4. What the frigging hell does that mean?"

The thoughts in his head ran head long into a brick wall, a wall which he could not penetrate through, however his thoughts were to soon turn into another darker emotion.

"Tom", sighed Emre re-entering the room with a solemn look on his face that beguiled the emotional state he was in, "I've got some bad news".

"W.W.What is it?" stammered Tom afraid to ask what the sadness in Emre's voice meant.

"Medad has been killed", sobbed Emre as a solemn face of sorrow drew its lines of anguish across his face.

"Medad killed. How?" asked Tom struggling to contain his grief for his newly deceased friend.

"His house was set on fire", Emre said putting a comforting hand on Tom's shoulder trying to find solace in his own grief.

"But...But...Why?"

"That my friend I don't know. I've got to go back to Israel and help with funeral arrangements".

"I want to come too".

"That my friend is not advisable".

"Why?" Tom asked confused why a return to Israel was not on the cards.

"It is too dangerous for you".

"What do you mean it is too dangerous for me?" Tom said alarmed now by the thought that a threat on his very person could exist.

"If someone killed Medad on purpose, they will probably want to kill those people connected with him too".

"What do you mean *'If someone killed Medad on purpose'*? What aren't you telling me Emre?" Tom prodding and probing what Emre knew and wasn't telling.

"All I can tell you my friend, is that his death is being treated as suspicious", confirmed his friend as best he could.

"And that means?"

"It means you were seen with him. It means people are aware of your existence. It means they expected you to be with him when he was killed. It means your life is in peril too, should you return to Israel".

"I understand", relented Tom slowly shaking his head in disappointment, "but I don't agree with it".

"I know you don't", said Emre, "but in time you will understand why".

"I hope so", replied Tom.

"I know so", Emre stated placing faith his friend's ability to do what was required of him, "I've got to go, there's a taxi waiting outside for me. Continue your work here. Break this code. Do this not only for yourself but for Medad too, for he had faith in you, the faith to do what is right, at the right time, for the right reasons".

"I appreciate what you're telling me Emre", said Tom to his brother in grief, "and I will continue this work we have both started".

"That my friend", Emre replied trying to hide his own sorrow, "is all I can ask of you, sometimes you have to remember you are more important then you realize".

As Emre left Tom to attend to his nephew's funeral, Tom began to think that something was amiss with Medad's death. Emre obviously knew more than he was letting on, that he was certain about, but what he was unsure of was Emre's reluctance to let him go. Then there was the quickness of the arrival of the taxi for Emre to take him to what he thought was the airport (although he could not prove that). It all seemed a little preordained, a little too neatly organized and that set off alarm bells ringing in his head that something was amiss. Whatever Emre was up to, Tom decided to keep his suspicions to himself, for now.

CHAPTER XV

As darkness fell the windows of the soul lay open, restless, only moving when the gentle evening breeze moved slowly over them. Inside they lay heavy burdened with the tears of sadness, while the outside they lay heavy burdened with weight of the world. Fatigue and a wandering mind left an indelible mark, as one by one the sorrows of a departed friend fell softly.

Tom went to the window in his room and looked out towards the city, the stars painting a mirage of diamond clusters in the sky reminding him of his own insignificant place in the world, each one a reminder of tears shed for people he had loved and lost, his wife, his children and now his friend.

Tom briefly let out a sigh of disappointment with the world and returned to his bed. He suddenly felt very alone and very afraid, the years of never achieving anything really worthwhile burdened his sense of fulfillment with a darkness that encapsulated his mood. Reaching for the truth, he decided, was sometimes a weight that lay heavy on his heart, for uncovering the truth might make the world a worse place to live in, his reasoning however soon convinced him that the truth must be told, for too many secrets were held, by individuals, wanting to hold the world for ransom.

From the darkness of his soul, and from the darkness of his mind, he rose to seek the answers that made him at times question his own sanity. He had made a promise to a friend, and to a friend that no longer existed that he would continue this journey and seek out the truth, whatever the truth was.

Tom went down into the office that Emre had furnished with paintings, sculptures and books from every corner of the globe, anything and everything, from bizarre carvings to prints of renaissance painters, to books on and by Da Vinci. "Books on Da Vinci?", Tom thought to himself turning on the Tiffany lamp that guarded secrets held captive by the darkness, "I wonder what books he's got?".

Tom stooped down to get a better look at the cornucopia of written words that bound themselves to the shelf on which they stood, "*Da Vinci's Books on Anatomy, Da Vinci's Notebooks' Part 1, Da Vinci's Notebooks Part 2, The Complete Works Of Da Vinci*. Jesus Christ this guy's a freak on old Da Vinci". He paused for a moment, thinking about the code he had *'discovered' in* the Vitruvian man, "Maybe there's something in the notebooks I could use. Maybe Da Vinci annotated his works", he thought as he reached and pulled the two books on Da Vinci's notebooks from the shelf on which they stood.

The two books, one red, one green, felt heavy in his hands, as did the expectation that perhaps an answer lay contained within. Although they were not the original (Bill Gates had those), they were ideal, for not only were the original Italian versions present (along with several annotated drawings), the English translation stood side by side on the same page with its more illustrious counterpart.

Tom pulled up a chair for himself and sat down, preparing himself to read what he was sure was a complete waste of time, but nevertheless he opened the book and began to read. As he read however, he noticed something a little strange about the way it was laid out. Each page contained several paragraphs detailing Da Vinci's work, but the unusual thing was each individual paragraph was numbered. Surely that couldn't be the numbers he and Emre found in the Vitruvian man? Could it?

His heart began to pound as he quickly, turned the pages, 371,372, almost there 481, 482 and then he found what he was looking for, paragraph 502.

Paragraph 502 was entitled '*HOW, IN IMPORTANT WORKS, A MAN SHOULD NOT TRUST ENTIRELY TO HIS MEMORY WITHOUT CONDESCENDING TO DRAW FROM NATURE*'.

He had found 502 but what were the other numbers for? Maybe it was the letters? He began counting the number of letters in the heading, 7th letter equals M, 9th letter equals O, and 4th letter equals I.

"*MOI, MOI?*" Tom asked of himself, "what the hell is *MOI?* Apart from the French word for *ME*"

Tom studied the paragraph even more, his mind beginning to question whether it wasn't the letters but the actual words themselves. He began to count and as he did, his jaw dropped with astonishment as the pieces of the puzzle slid together to form a picture that he finally understood, "No it can't be" he thought to himself as the words joined together to make sense to him, so he recounted the words, again and again, each time he got the same answer, with his heart in his mouth he reached for a pen and paper that lay on the desk and began to write.

<u>502ND PARAGRAPH</u>

7th Word is SHOULD

9th Word is WORKS

4th Word is TRUST

If I rearrange these words I get the phrase *'should trust works'*.

Fig V - Secret Message Contained in Vitruvian Man

"Oh my fucking hell", Tom swore, "There is a god damn fucking code and the key is these stupid freaking ass notebooks?" He picked up the notebooks and kissed each one with divine pleasure, for he, this mortal man had found a code, a clue in the picture that no-one else on earth discovered. His yearning to tell the whole world was overpowering yet he knew in his heart it would have to remain a secret for now. If he was certain about this *'true code'* by telling the whole world, people would call him a heretic, a crackpot, someone who had failed society and was not worth taking notice of. He needed more proof, more evidence that this code really existed, but would doing so open people's eyes to the truth or would it close people's eyes to what was being told in these pictures?

The message contained within in this one picture, was a message asking for trust, a trust in the works of this master who previously he had a complete antipathy for. Should he trust the message completely or should he just wait for more evidence to justify his excitement?

Whatever his decision would be, there could be no undeniable proof that this picture contained a secret message and he was the one that had broken the first clue in a true *'Da Vinci Code'*.

CHAPTER XVI

The distance between the present and the past is short, a kiss, a heartbeat, a spoken word, a breath on the wind. We spend too much time worrying about the future, for without the past there is no future, and without the future there would be no past. Our ancestors created the world in which we live now, our forefathers died and bled for our existence, yet we take their sacrifice sometimes a little too much for granted, for the blood on their hands taints the air we breathe, the pain which they endured runs deep in the seas and oceans while their undying devotion to protect our existence pollutes the lands with the cries of mothers whose children have died in the service of their country.

Tom sat alone, pondering, contemplating, wondering, worrying, worrying about his place in the world, worrying whether people would understand or care about the death of another Palestinian child, why should they ? It didn't affect their life so why should it bother them? When people really sat and thought about it, the death of one lonely Palestinian should disturb them, disturb them to a point that nightmares ensued, for the taking of a life at the hands of another is wrong, so morally wrong that to give justification to such an act is just the same as physically holding the weapon in your hand, "Life is hard", he decided, "Death is easy".

As time drifted along on the breeze of ideology, he began to wish his friend would soon return, for being alone made Tom lock the cells doors of his own mind, a place where he would go and seek solace at times of dark emotional turmoil, sometimes torturing his persona with negative thinking, occasionally they manifested into dreams seeded with evil, sometimes they were projected into his very soul as negative emotional life draining tears of abject misery.

For the first time since his divorce from Rachel, sorrow had taken Tom's heart captive. It vexed him like it did before. Why was it always him that had to suffer the loss of those close to him? What had he done to deserve this pain? It was not fair; he had more than his fill of picking up the pieces of his shattered life.

Minutes turned into hours, hours into days, grief turned into anger, anger into hatred. Such a wasted emotion hatred Tom decided, yet he had spent years hating people who had done him wrong, people who he felt he had trusted, returned to make that trust tarnished with the folly of greed and infidelity, yet in his heart he knew that perhaps maybe he was the one at fault. How can so many people he felt he knew despise him and all be wrong? He couldn't entirely be certain of his actions, for they were all in a theater of an alcohol induced coma, as years of self abuse contained within the glass confinements of a whiskey concoction gave birth to the Dr. Jekyll and Mr. Hyde characters that he had become. The pain that he had suffered as a child at the hands of an abusive father only enhancing the monster deep within.

The skies above the city that had become Tom's refuge began to weep as did he. From his observation point in Emre's house he continued to watch the minuscule particles of water fall softly to the ground. He began to wonder that maybe this loneliness, these anguish driven thoughts were his penance for his years of neglect, neglect of those he had loved, neglect of his family, neglect of his peers, but most of all, the neglect of the true Tom that lay dormant within the shell of this hollow man.

When alone he would often question his sanity, diving into the dark recesses of his own mind to find nothing that would answer this question one way or the other. Maybe he was a little mad, a little dangerous, a little reckless, but he was comfortable with it, for it was like a friend to him that stood by him in times of need as difficulties arose and went.

Tom considered the sanctity of this union between himself and this 'friend'; maybe, just maybe it was time to ask for a divorce. He had grown tired of constantly battling demons that this friend brought. The tiredness tattooed his face with pain ladened ink as the ravages of time ran across his grey tarnished cutis only to be met by the blemished natural protective covering that lay over his internal parts.

The rains slowly subsided as the sun began to bring warmth once more, enhancing the earth with a rainbow crown, adorning the people below with a golden reverence, as once again life was given to the city and those that dwelled within its walls.

Tom smiled as he watched the rainbow arc over as he began to think about life changing circumstances, for he was on this journey, not only for this quest for truth and knowledge, but he also felt like he was on a journey of self discovery. A journey to discover who he really was, a journey to exorcise the demons that lay within, the prison door that held him within opened, as his comrade in arms returned from lands afar.

"Emre your back", enthused Tom who was genuinely pleased to see his long lost friend.

"It's good to see you", acknowledged Emre who stood embracing Tom.

"How was everything?" queried Tom.

"A funerals a funeral", murmured Emre solemnly, "How did you get on?"

"Well", said Tom as he ushered Emre into the office, "I think I've discovered something".

"You did?"

"Yes I did".

"So?"

"So what?" smirked Tom who was prepared to keep his friend on tenterhooks a little longer.

"What did you find my friend?" begged Emre, eager to find out what Tom discovered hidden in *The Vitruvian Man*.

"This", demonstrated Tom, as he showed the piece of paper on which he had written his discovery.

Emre took the paper with anticipation and slowly read what Tom had written.

502ND PARAGRAPH

7th Word is SHOULD

9th Word is WORKS

4th Word is TRUST

If I rearrange these words I get the phrase *'should trust works'*.

Fig.V - Secret Message Contained in Vitruvian Man

"502nd Paragraph? 502nd Paragraph from what?" Emre asked inquisitively.

"These", claimed Tom handing Emre his own Da Vinci's notebooks.

"For real?"

"Yes for real".

"Wow", exclaimed Emre as he slowly positioned himself on a chair, "Do you mind if I?"

"Not at all", replied Tom, "I'd feel a lot happier if someone else would confirm it too."

Emre sat in his chair and began to count the words just as Tom had done, "Ah you mean the 502nd section".

"Section, Paragraph, Note. It's all the same".

"Yes it is", chortled Emre, pleased that Tom could take a joke as much as he could dish it out.

"And?" asked Tom.

"I get the same as you my friend", stated Emre answering Tom's question.

"What do you think?"

"I think you could be onto something. What do you want to do next?"

"There's nothing else we can do yet", said Tom, "we better continue with our original quest".

"To find out more about Constantine?" queried Emre.

"Yes. Unfortunately", remarked Tom a little disappointed, "Although we've broken part of the code it doesn't point to anything else, so there's nothing else to go on".

"So we go back to the original source of your investigation?"

"I think so".

"That sounds quite logical".

"That's what I thought", confirmed Tom.

"Oh", exclaimed Emre as he reached inside his coat pocket, "I almost forget, I'm supposed to give you this".

"What is it?"

"It was Medad's, he wanted you to have it", said Emre handing Tom, a beautifully decorated silver watch. Tom looked at the time piece in his hand, wondering what he'd done to deserve this honor, he was certain (in his mind at least), that this was an item of Medad's he did not deserve to have.

"Me? Why Me?" asked Tom gazing at the watch in his hand.

"Why not?" said Emre, "You were his friend".

"Thank you", said Tom as he slid the watch on his wrist, "now wherever I go a little piece of Medad will go with me".

"Now come my friend let us eat, I'm hungry".

"Was the airline food that bad?"

"Yes it was", confessed Emre laughing at his experience with the bad food he'd been served on board the aircraft, "How did you put up with it?"

"I didn't, I threw up in the bathroom immediately".

"Between you and I", admitted Emre," I did the same thing too".

"Then my friend", said Tom smiling "welcome to the club".

As the two friends shook hands, Tom felt, although he lost one friend, he had gained another. It was like one door had closed and another one opened, "Maybe", he thought, "just maybe that this was meant to be, whatever it's meaning though, I will never forget you Medad. Never".

CHAPTER XVII

The chance to venture into the streets and alleys of a fresh, vibrant city was a delight and Tom was delighted to have his friend back, for not only had he missed him physically, he had also missed the chance to interact with someone who inspired him to greater heights of mental awareness. He had never thought of himself as a great thinker, a philosopher who could articulate with the most brilliant minded individuals, yet here he was thinking, formulating ideas and plans that he never would have dreamt possible.

"So if there is a hidden code then why is it still hidden?", asked Tom.

"Because people don't look", answered Emre.

"Why do you think that is?"

"Sometimes to know something is wrong is better than to correct years of a hidden truth".

"Interesting", said Tom.

"Also convenient", replied Emre, "if people are happy with a false truth then what's the point of revealing the real truth".

"So why do you think it was hidden then?"

"That is a good question", said Emre "maybe the truth was hidden to protect those who knew what the truth was".

"Do you think that by revealing the truth they would be persecuted?"

"What is the usual reason for hiding something?"

"To protect whatever is being hidden from those individuals seeking to destroy it?" guessed Tom.

"Correct. And why do you suppose they would wish to destroy it?" asked Emre.

"To prevent anyone else from knowing the truth?" queried Tom.

"Yes", answered Emre," and also because those people have the greatest to lose".

"Such as power, money, influence?"

"Power especially Tom, sometimes people under estimate the lure of power. Take something like a cult which controls a mass of people by fear or through mind control, their power to control the weak minded is their greatest power, yet is also their greatest weakness, for they dread losing it".

"Hence the number of reasons why when a cult is cornered, positioned into a place from which they will ultimately lose their power, mass suicide occurs".

"Exactly Tom", replied Emre, "never under estimate the power or the lure of a cult, do so at your own peril".

"I take it you have had personal experience of a cult then Emre?"

"Yes, I have" confessed Emre remembering the time he had found out his nephew was in a cult that he did not approve of, "Medad was part of a cult before we managed to rescue him".

"He never said he was", stated Tom trying to recollect Medad mentioning such an ordeal.

"He didn't like to talk about it Tom", sighed Emre reflecting on his nephews past, "and I never asked, so we just left things like that".

"Do you think that was influential in his death?"

"Possibly, Tom, I did find out while I was in Israel his house was deliberately set on fire".

Tom stood still for a moment, pausing in his tracks and in his thoughts before turning to his friend, "So you mean to tell me you suspect Medad was what? Murdered?"

"My friend I suspect nothing, I only know what I know".

"What exactly do you know?" asked Tom who was beginning to suspect that Emre was holding back on certain things.

"I know that Medad was killed in his house which was deliberately set on fire".

"You know by whom, don't you and that's why you told me to stop here, here in Istanbul?"

"I have my suspicions", confirmed Emre, "but it is too risky, much too risky to get you involved".

"Why?" asked Tom.

"These people are fanatics, undying in their devotion to their beliefs, and these people will stop at nothing and I mean nothing to kill those people who stand in their way".

"And?"

"And I'm frightened of getting someone killed because I've said too much".

"But don't you think I've got a right to know?" questioned Tom.

"In time I will tell you, but for now we must press on and continue on with your work".

"Ok", replied Tom, "I'll trust you on this one, but I'm not happy about secrets being kept from me".

"Secrets", stated Emre in a hushed voice, "secrets are the reason why you are on this journey, the journey to reveal the truth, the truth that will not only expose those who fear it, but those who have claimed Medad's life".

"Then my friend", said Tom, "we will continue for the honor of Medad".

"Yes for the honor of Medad", agreed Emre placing his hands gently in those of his friend's.

CHAPTER XVIII

The city left behind an indelible mark on the pilgrims of truth, weariness and fatigue taking their toll not only on the body but on the spirit too. The constant battle to find and seek the knowledge of others was a never ending voyage into the unknown; with one step forward they ventured two steps back. Frustration began to creep into their minds as did annoyance, annoyance at not being able to find the person they were seeking and their patience was wearing thin.

"I can't believe we've spent the last hour going round in circles", irked Tom who was irritated by their lack of progress. The staff at the museum had been less than helpful in tracking down the Professor of Byzantine Studies, first *THE ARCHAEOLOGICAL MUSEUM,* then *THE MUSEUM OF THE ANCIENT ORIENT*, followed by the *MUSEUM OF ISLAMIC ART*, then back once more to *THE ARCHAEOLOGICAL MUSEUM*, round and round they went in a never ending trap of circles, passed from pillar to post by people who seemed not to care about the men lost in the corridors of time.

"I know", snarled Emre, his patience wearing thin, "I'm frustrated by the whole process too".

The frustration was deeply genuine in Emre's voice for he, along with Tom, had spent what seemed like an eternity trying to locate the Professor of Byzantine Studies deep in the heart of the museum. The anger in his heart burning deep in his soul, he was trying to contain it within and so far he was doing fine, but he was walking the fine line between peace and rage.

"I just hope it's going to be worth this aggravation", protested Tom as they both ventured further into the catacombs of knowledge.

"You and me both", agreed Emre desperate for this quest to end.

The darkness that ran deep through the mazes of cognition, soon gave way to an oasis of light. In the distance an angelic figured appeared like a ghost from the shadows, the mysterious figurine seeing the two men appear walked forward to greet them.

"Good afternoon gentlemen", she said with a saintly smile, wondering who these two strangers were, "How can I help you?"

"We're trying to locate Professor Dubois, Head of Byzantine Studies", stated Emre.

"I'm Professor Dubois", replied the mysterious lady, "and you are?"

"I'm Emre Osman and this is my friend Tom Raust, I believe you are expecting us?"

Tom did not say anything, for the delicacy that his eyes fed upon took his breath away. The white freckled skin that decorated the beauty within, crowned off by a tiara of auburn hair flowing down to the shoulders with curls of vivaciousness.

"I am Professor Marie Dubois and your right *I WAS* expecting you, but your frightfully late gentlemen", explained the professor unhappy at the lateness of these men, "my time is very precious and I don't appreciate it being wasted".

"Then tell your staff to correctly point us in the right direction instead of sending us on a wild goose chase", interrupted Tom staring directly into the sparkling hazel eyes of the Professor.

Professor Marie Dubois looked directly back into Tom's pain laden eyes and saw that although they were filled with rage, she sensed a good man, only wishing to seek the answers to the many questions, she was sure he had, "Mr. err", she said trying to remember this stranger's name.

"Mr. Raust, Tom Raust", replied Tom on the verge of a cataclysmic breakdown.

"Mr. Raust, I'm sorry, I was not aware of the unhelpfulness of my staff, please accept my sincerest apologies", said the Professor offering an outstretched hand as an olive branch.

"Ermmm", stuttered Tom like a school boy asking a girl to the school dance, "Apology accepted".

He clasped the soft skin of the Professor's hand and it felt nice, for it had been a while since he had touched the flesh of a woman, the feel of skin on skin was overloading his senses with the warmth of embarrassment and he slowly broke off the engagement.

"This way gentleman please", a guiding hand prompted, directing them to the inner workings of the museum.

As they journeyed towards the offices of the professor Tom whispered to Emre," You didn't tell me the Professor was a woman".

"I didn't know", replied Emre under the stillness of his breath.

"Honestly?" pressed Tom.

"Yes Honestly".

The two men weren't as stealthy in their conversation as they needed to be, for on the face of Professor Marie Dubois, a smile broke out, a smile of mischievousness that coerced her into an inward laugh, for she had suspected (and not for the first time) that no-one had told these men that she was a woman, not only of great intellect, but of great wisdom too, and that occasionally put the male of the species at unease.

"Here we are gentlemen", prompted the Professor opening the door to her private chambers, "please come inside and take a seat whilst I arrange some refreshment for you".

"Thank you", Emre and Tom both said in unison, each one giving the other a raised eyebrow as they uttered the same words.

"After you", Tom said showing Emre the door in his eagerness to prove he was the alpha male.

"No after you", coerced Emre who was equally determined to show his politeness to their host.

"Men", muttered the Professor under her breath, "Why does their male ego always get in the way?"

The Professor left the *two little boys* to fight amongst themselves about who was going through the door first and went to acquire beverages for the weary travelers. When she returned carrying a pot of Turkish coffee and three cups on a silver platter, both men were sat inside, being quiet and well behaved, like schoolboys waiting for their principal to return.

"So what can I do for?" asked the Professor, closing the door behind her.

"We were hoping you could tell us about Constantine", politely queried Tom taking the tray from Marie.

"Thank you", said Marie appreciating the offer of Tom's help, "First, tell me what you know about the man".

Tom placed the ornately decorated tray on the desk and showed the Professor the book the priest had given him, whilst he was in Israel, "Only this".

"Please gentlemen help yourselves to coffee", she said opening the book with a look of slight surprise that concealed her bewilderment.

The two men did as they were told, pouring an infusion of Turkish Arabica beans into their cups, whilst waiting for their host to finish reading the book Tom had brought with him.

"So", stated the Professor handing Tom his book back before pouring herself a cup of coffee, "let us start from where your little book leaves off. According to scribes during the reign of Constantine he converted to Christianity from Paganism on his deathbed, this we now know not to be true. Records found since, have proved that he converted to Christianity before his victory at the *Battle of Milvian Bridge* in 312 AD".

"You said he was a pagan before his conversion, what type of paganism did he follow before his conversion?" asked Tom.

"There is much debate about that Mr. Raust, but it is wildly believed to be a form of *Mithraism*".

"Mithraism?" queried Tom who had never heard of this religion before.

"Around the 1st BC, the cult of Mithra was popular in Rome. It was first adopted by *Emperor Aurelian* who founded the cult of 'Sol Invictus' or *'The Invincible Sun'*. The Christian scriptures were burnt in 307AD by *Emperor Diocletian* enabling Constantine to merge the cult of Mithra with Christianity. This then enabled Constantine to become Christian but retain ties to the cult".

"For example Tom", said Emre interrupting the Professors lecture, "December 25th is assumed to be the birth date of Jesus when it fact, it is actually the birth date of Mithra".

"Very good Mr. Osman", the Professor said with a smile on her face.

Emre seeing he had gained a upper hand in proving who the man with the greatest intelligence was, turned to Tom and playfully stuck his tongue out, making Tom shake his head in disbelief. Tom was secretly pleased to have been given the opportunity to take his mind off the turbulent times that had persisted in following him on his travels, even if it meant being the brunt of someone else's practical jokes.

"Now this conversion of Constantine to Christianity", continued the Professor "was alleged to happen via a vision before the Battle of Milvian Bridge. One day before the battle, legends say, Constantine looked up to the sun and saw a cross of light before it with the Greek words *'Ev Toutw Nika'* which roughly translates to *'by this sign conquer'* or in Latin as *'in hoc signo vinces'*, after which he ordered his troops to adorn their shields with the *Chi-Rho*".

"Chi-Rho?" asked Tom who was puzzled by the term.

The Professor reached for a book that lay dormant on the desk that dominated the office and began to search. "This is a Chi-Rho", she said showing Tom the picture of the symbol.

Fig VI - CHI-RHO or LABARUM

"It's formed from the first two Greek letters of the word 'Christ', the Chi is the X part and the Rho is the other part", stated the Professor drawing a finger over each portion of the symbol.

"What about the battle?" Tom asked.

"Constantine won and marched triumphantly into Rome, ignoring the Roman alter to the pagan gods and headed straight to the Imperial Palace. Just how much Christianity was adopted after this is hard to say, as most officials were still of the pagan belief."

Just as Tom was about to ask another question, a loud and deafening explosion came from the internal workings of the repository, shaking the windows so violently and with such force that a small web like crack began to appear. The noise that followed the loud bang that preluded was superseded by that of the fire alarm ringing loudly throughout the museum.

"What the hell was that?" he asked Emre who was in the process of making his way to the door.

"Sounds like a bomb", came the reply from his friend who was ushering both Tom and the Professor from the room.

"A bomb?" asked the Professor nervously.

"A bomb", confirmed Emre, "We better get out of here in case there's a secondary device. Quickly Professor you lead the way out".

Tom shook his head in bewilderment, not at the bomb itself, but the fact that Emre knew immediately what it was and the possibility that a second one could detonate at any time.

What did Emre know that made Tom suspect that he was privy to first hand knowledge of who was behind the bombing of the museum? Tom decided that at the first opportunity possible he would interrogate what Emre truly knew about the manmade disaster that just took place in the museum. As the Professor lead the way through the maze of corridors and alleyways that were the life lines of the museum, they came to the room which housed the Vitruvian Man, or what was left of it, for this was the flash point of the explosion, rubble, masonry, broken timber, all strewn across the floor in a menagerie of manmade art.

"That's the Vitruvian Man room", yelled Tom with astonishment as his eyes lay upon the carnage that presented his eyes with a feast of mixed emotions.

"Was", corrected the Professor hurrying to the exit, "It was taken back to Venice yesterday. Quickly this way"

Soon they reached the outside of the building, gasping for air, gasping for breath, grasping for straws at what had just happened, "I can't believe what just occurred", exclaimed the Professor to her two fellow escapees.

"Neither can I", said Emre, who was stooped over struggling to breathe from the physical exertion which he had just under taken.

Tom whispered under his breath to his friend, "First Medad, now this. Is this purely coincidence or is the hand of evil that's placed upon *YOUR* shoulder?"

"I don't what you mean Tom", protested Emre defending himself from Tom's accusation.

"I think you know who did this, don't you?"

"I fear I might do", he confirmed with a solemn look on his face.

"And?"

"And they won't stop unless they're killed or their target is killed".

"My friend", whispered Tom to Emre, making sure that the Professor was not aware, "we better make sure it's them and not us then".

"How to your propose we do that then?" queried Emre.

"Simple", answered Tom with a devious smile on his face, "we give them what they want".

"Simple? Simple?" asked Emre, "nothing with you IS simple".

"That my friend is something I am counting on", Tom retorted with a look of guile on his face that announced to the world that he was ready to do battle with the perpetrator of the crime.

CHAPTER XIX

The enclave which was the fountain of knowledge, had become a think tank for the two generals, both locked deep inside the confines of the concrete bunker, each formulating a battle plan, neither one confident of the strategy they had formulated. Time and again the collateral damage was a burden neither man could live with, for the price of luring the enemy out into the open became a price to heavy on the alter of truth.

"I'm not entirely comfortable with the plan", Emre protested, the concern on his face matching the concern in his soul.

"I know", replied Tom scratching his head in hope that the stimulation would ignite a brain storm in his frontal lobe, "but what else can we do?"

Emre shook his head in disappointment, but he knew deep in his heart, that whoever was behind these events, he would not be flushed out of his hiding place without a devious plan being drawn up.

"I don't like it, I just don't like it", he irked as his attention was suddenly aware to the presence of a guest approaching the front door.

A gentle thud broke the silence, awakening Tom from his semi conscious state, "Who is it?" he fretted with a look on his face that suggested trouble ahead.

"Stay there a minute I'll find out", replied Emre as he disappeared through the doorway leading into the next compartmental slot in the house. The keep of the modern day castle opened slowly inward with a squeak of disgust as it greeted the visitor with an unnerving yawn.

Tom, who was listening to the conversation at the front door, hid from sight as his friend began to interrogate the visitor, afraid that this person was sent to kill Emre and himself, however his fears were soon pushed aside as a familiar face appeared in the confines of the library in which he stood.

"Professor", exclaimed Tom with a glee in his voice, "It's good to see you again".

"It's good to see you Mr. Raust, how are you?" greeted the Professor with a voice of concern that pierced his heart with the joys of a long lost friend coming home.

"I'm good Professor Dubois, real good and please call me Tom", said Tom with a genuine look of pleasure shining in his eyes.

"Ok Tom", the Professor smiled as an equal look of friendship penetrated the very essence of her being, "Please stop calling me Professor. It's a little contrived, call me Marie".

"Please, have a seat Marie", offered Tom showing the Professor a seat which had been his, "What can we do for you?"

"More like what I can do for you", replied Marie as she sat softly on the seat which Tom had given up for her.

"That sounds ominous", Emre said as he re-entered the room with a carafe filled with water and a stack of glasses in the shape of a vertical column.

"Not at all Mr. Osman", proclaimed Marie sensing a little bit of anxiety in his voice, "We never finished off our conversation before we got rudely interrupted"

"I wouldn't call a bomb blast a little interruption", pointed out Emre pouring water into the glasses from the translucent carafe.

"So what else is there left to know Marie?" asked Tom who was sure that there no more left to understand.

"Oh Marie now is it Tom?" quipped Emre under his breath as he passed a glass of water to his friend.

"Shut up Emre", replied Tom who was not entirely subtle as Emre was, for it reached the ears of Marie.

"Is everything ok?" she asked.

"Yes...Yes...Everything is fine, so what else is there left to know?" inquired Tom as he took a small sip of water from the glass which Emre had pressed in his hand.

"Tell me gentlemen have you ever heard of the *First Council of Nicaea*?" Marie asked posing a question of the two friends.

"Can't say I have", Emre stated.

"Neither have I", said Tom.

"In 325 AD", began Marie imparting knowledge on her two colleagues, "The First Council of Nicaea was convened by Constantine following a recommendation of a certain Hosius of Cordua, who was a prominent advocate of what became Catholic Christianity during the Arian controversy resulting in the split of the Christian Church during the 4th century".

"Arian controversy?" conceded Tom, "I'm not even sure what Arianism is".

"How can I tell you without over simplifying?" said Marie asking herself a question, "Basically Arianism was the first Christian heresy proposed in the 4th century by Arius".

"Hence the term Arian?" interrupted Emre asking the Professor a question.

"Yes hence the term Arian, however this man Arius stated that Christ was not truly divine but a created being".

"I bet that was not an entirely popular stance on religion?" Tom inquired.

"It wasn't. Arius and controversy, both walked down the same path, at the same time, making things even more heretic when he said,

'If the Father begat the Son, he that was begotten had a beginning of existence: and from this it is evident, that there was a time when the Son was not. It therefore necessarily follows, that he had his substance from nothing '", Marie said her lecture.

"Just for me", Tom implored Marie, confused by the ancient language used, "What the hell does that mean?"

"It basically means that God the Son was not eternal, but was created and subordinate to God the Father", she said trying to explain in layman terms what the controversial figure was saying.

"What's this all got to do with Constantine?" asked Tom with a look of intrigue in his eyes.

"Constantine convened the First Council of Nicaea to investigate the trouble brought about by the doctrines of Arius", said Marie.

"So this er council", interrupted Emre trying to force his way into the conversation, "was like an inquiry?"

"Basically speaking yes, an inquiry which between 250-320 bishops attended from every region of the Empire with the exception of Britain. It was the first council in history of the Church since the Apostolic Council of Jerusalem", Marie stated answering Emre's question with enthusiasm in her voice.

"So what was the outcome of this inquiry then?" asked Tom wanting to reaffirm his position as the dominant male in the room.

"According to records the agenda of the Council of Nicaea was to:

1. Answer the Arian question regarding the relationship between God the Father and Jesus.

2. The date of the celebration of Easter.

3. The Meletian schism

4. The validity of baptism by heretics and

5. The status of the lapsed in the persecution under Licinus.
The Meletian schism is a piece of papyrus which tells of the hardship which crafts folk and farming peasantry suffered during the early Byzantine era", Marie said taking sip of water from the glass which occupied her hand.

"And this Licinus persecution?" asked Tom.

"Licinus was a Roman Emperor which allegedly persecuted the Church until his defeat by Constantine, at the Battle of Tzirallum".

"So Constantine had a hand in stopping the persecution of the Christians by Pagans?" Emre asked Marie who had taken a great interest in Tom's quest for further knowledge.

"Apparently so", corroborated Marie answering Emre's question, "However don't let the Christians fool you into believing they were all about peace and respect of their fellow man".

"What do you mean?" asked Tom.

"During the 4th century when Constantine reigned the Roman Empire, Pagan temples were torn down, Non-Christian books got burnt and temple treasures were confiscated by '*Lay Christians*' who took advantage of anti Pagan laws, however what was worse, much worse than this insatiable appetite for destruction, was the slaying of thousands and thousands of pagans believers", Marie informed her two esteemed colleagues.

Tom was just about to pose another question of Marie, who sensing another inquiry was on its way, preempted the strike with a lightening quick reply "A Lay Christian is anyone who is faithful to the Christian belief and not a bishop or a priest".

Marie, seeing time was running short, got up from the chair on which she was sat and apologized, "I'm sorry gentlemen I've got to go and supervise the clean up at the museum".

"That's ok we understand", said Emre as he politely showed her to the door, "Thank you for your time".

"Not at all gentlemen, if there's anything you need, anything at all you know where to find me", she replied, leaving the safety of Emre's abode.

With the door closed firmly behind them, Emre rejoined his friend Tom back in the sanctity of the small office once again, "What do you think?" he asked.

Tom who by then had reclaimed his throne again, took a while to answer, "If these persecutions by the Christians really happened, then why does no one from the Church talk about it?", he said pondering the new questions in his head.

"Just because no one talks about it, doesn't mean it never happened", stated Emre trying to answer his friend's question.

"That makes sense", confirmed Tom in response to his friend's answer, "What doesn't make sense though is why people will kill just because the truth doesn't picture them in a positive light. I mean you can't rewrite history and undo years of oppression, if you've done wrong at least admit it".

"If people admitted they're wrong all the world's politicians would be out of a job", joked Emre trying to make the tension in the room a little lighter, for he could sense Tom's mood began to turn a darker shade of white.

"That my friend", agreed Tom, "would make the world a better place".

"It still doesn't solve our little problem though does it"?

"It might not, but then again it might, for I've just thought of an idea how to lure this assassin out into the open", said Tom with a devious look on his face.

"You have?" said a puzzled Emre, "How?"

"Just wait and see", promised Tom, "Just wait and see".

CHAPTER XX

The blend of espionage and a resolute fixating with doing what was asked, had become a powerful narcotic for Tom, he was hooked in its trance like grip, desperate not only for his next fix, but desperate in his need to fix what was wrong, not only with the world, but within his own life too and this made him dangerous, for the need to put what was wrong in order made him at times reckless, not only forsaking his own welfare but those he befriended too.

"I don't think she's going to appreciate being used as bait Tom", Emre remarked as the two men ventured forward to the meeting with the Professor. He was not entirely comfortable with the plan Tom had concocted, for it endangered not only their lives, but this independent, free thinking woman too.

"Can you think of a better way of luring this dangerous individual out into the open?" asked Tom who had been wrestling with the plan for the best part of the night, the tiredness in his voice, confirming what his body knew.

"I can't", replied Emre shaking his head at the discomfort he felt for using someone as *'bait'* to ensnare an individual of extreme violent tendencies, "but it certainly makes me feel very uneasy at the thought of you, not only putting our lives in danger, but that of the Professor's too".

"Why don't we just tell her then, that the reason her beloved museum was attacked by a wanton terrorist then, was because we are being perused by a dangerous God fearing anti-Christ ?", snarled Tom as he prodded the ethics of Emre with a probing question.

"I...I...I...I can't", bleated Emre astonished at Tom's provocation. Struggling to come to terms with his actions Emre knew deep in his heart Tom was correct in his hypothesis, for hadn't the two men ventured into the depths of the Professor's domain, then none of this would have happened.

"Then why don't we just stick with the plan then", bullied Tom slightly irate at Emre's lack of personal fortitude to correct the mistakes he had made.

"Agreed", muttered Emre, who had for once had been put in his place. The plan was simple in its efficiency, but complicated in assembling all the pieces together, for this was a plan of Tom's, which infused the master of a magician, with the cunning of a dangerous criminal into what they hoped would set free the chains of mystery and bring forth the power of knowledge that came with the entrapment of a dangerous killer.

"Ah there she is", stated Tom as the two men approached the familiar sight of the Professor who was sat at her favorite restaurant, partaking in the enjoyment of a small, but delightfully fruity glass of Bordeaux.

"It's good to see you", smiled Tom embracing his friend with a kiss on both cheeks.

"It's good to see you too Tom, and er you too Emre ", replied Marie greeting her two friends.

"Thank you for letting me interview you for my newspaper", said Tom sitting down in the seat next to Marie.

"It's my pleasure", Marie responded, and it genuinely was, for this was the first time anyone in the outside world took interest in her work.

"Will you both excuse me please?" asked Emre, "I've got some business to attend to".

"Sure thing", replied Tom summoning a waiter over for a glass of water with a slice of lemon for him to drink while he was engaging Marie in polite conversation.

"Ok", said Marie as Emre disappeared into the vastness of the city, "What do you need to know?"

"You're an expert in Byzantine studies are you not?" asked Tom.

"I am", agreed Marie who was slightly nervous at being interviewed by a newspaper reporter, even though it was someone she knew.

"What other areas of expertise do you have?" he gently prodded trying to get his interviewee to relax.

"I've got amongst other things a deep understanding of the Roman Empire, which is handy for my research on Byzantine studies, as both are closely connected", Marie said as her nerves slowly began to calm down.

"How so?" queried Tom.

"The Roman Emperor, Diocletian established the practice of dividing authority between two emperors, one in the western part of the Empire and one in the eastern, due to the vastness of the Empire".

"Diocletian wasn't he the one who executed St. George?" asked Tom recollecting the name from his notebook which the priest had given him.

"Yes he was", Marie said commending Tom's recollection of the event, and "He was also the Emperor who not only persecuted and executed St. George, but several other thousand Christians too".

"So what was Constantine's role in all of this?"

"Well", revealed Marie who was by now enjoying the experience of being interviewed, "Constantine was not only the first Christian Emperor, but he reversed the persecutions of Diocletian and with the other Emperor Licinus he issued the *'Edict of Milan'* in 313AD in which he proclaimed religious tolerance throughout the Roman Empire. He is also credited with turning Byzantium into a new imperial residence, renaming it Constantinople".

"Did he ever set foot in Rome then?"

"He did after winning the Battle of Milvian Bridge against Maxentius, putting an end to Maxentius' rebellion in 312AD entering the capital in October that year".

"So what was the significance of this victory then?" asked Tom who was intrigued by this side of Constantine he had not previously heard about.

"It gave him total control of both parts of the Empire and paved the way for Christianity to become the dominant religion".

"So it was a big to do then?" Tom asked Marie who by now was reveling in her role.

"Oh my God, yes", she exclaimed, "there's a triumphal arch in Rome commemorating Constantine's victory. He even completed the Basilica of Maxentius which Maxentius started and according to the fable found in the Golden Legends, there was a Statue of Romulus inside the Basilica which supposedly fell down on the night of Christ's birth."

"That's not possible is it considering the difference in dates?", Tom asked as his thoughts recognized a discrepancy in the passing of time .

"Well it is only legend Tom".

"You said it was in the Golden Legends", Tom stated searching for more information about the Statue.

"The Golden Legends is a collection of Saintly stories compiled by Jacopo da Varagine in 1260 AD, that went on to become a late medieval bestseller, it even contains the legend of your St. George in it".

"It does?" Tom asked in wonderment excited by the prospect of a clue possibly lurking in the confines of the ancient text book.

"Yes it does", Marie confirmed, "along with at least 130 more other saintly figures".

"So this Golden Legends is quite an important collection of stories".

"It certainly is, as sometimes the stories of saintly men are more truthful then the myths of mortal men".

"Speaking of myths of mortal men, do you know anything about the origins of Da Vinci's Vitruvian Man?" Tom asked, who was desperate to find out more information about the Vitruvian Man who had inspired him to seek the truth about the Da Vinci code.

"I know only a little about the work. It was created by Da Vinci in 1487 based on the works of Marcus Vitruvius Polilio's work in his Ten Books called De Architectura. I think it's in his third book, where he discusses the proportions of man, giving the actual dimensions of the human body, but don't ask me what they are Tom, because I don't know".

"Well", concluded Tom pleased with his afternoon's work, "I think we've got enough material here"

"That's good then", said Marie who was not only physically exhausted but mentally drained too, "I need to get some fresh air".

"I could do with stretching my legs too", agreed Tom as he stood up from the table, looking around in hope that Emre would soon appear.

The party of two left the safety of the restaurant into the wilderness of the jungle, and began to breathe in the freshness of the smog flavored air, lungfuls of carbon monoxide filling their lungs with a toxic mixture which made Tom cough.

"Keep coughing it will be your last", terrorized a voice from behind them with evil intent, "I've got a gun pointed at your girlfriend's back, so no sudden moves. Where's the Turk?"

"I...I...I...I don't know", Tom stuttered with disbelief uncomfortable at being used as an instrument to extract information from.

"I don't believe you", replied the stranger prodding the gun into Tom's coccyx, "I've been watching you and I've seen you talking to him".

"I...I...its true", Marie quaked, the fear in her voice echoing in the ears of the assassin, "He said he had business to attend to."

"If that is correct", snarled the voice from behind, "then you leave me no alternative but to keep you captive until the Turk makes an appearance".

"B...B...B...But why?" stammered Tom in disbelief.

"Because him and I have unfinished business. Now move slowly forward and a turn left when you reach the road end".

"And what if we don't?" asked Tom looking for a way out of their predicament.

"Then I'll be using your girlfriend for target practice", threatened the assassin prodding Marie's back with the gun in his hand.

"I suppose we don't have a choice then", murmured Tom to Marie under his breath.

"*NO YOU DON'T*", snapped the voice from behind who was irate at being given the runaround by someone he needed to *'talk with'*.

As the three individuals turned into the main road that intersected the city, the killer issued further instructions directing them to a delivery truck which stood silently on the side of the busy highway.

"Get in", he ordered once the coast was clear, bundling the two scared individuals into the back of the hauler before slamming the door shut and padlocking it once they were safely inside.

The truck shuddered forward as it lurched its way slowly into traffic. From within the confines of the portable containment unit, both Tom and Marie began to wonder what would happen to them. Whatever it was they both decided it was surely not going to be a pleasant experience.

CHAPTER XXI

Their bodies shook, their bones rattled, but their spirit remained intact. The appearance of a man who knew Emre, complicated things a little for Tom. He had not entirely known who the shadowy figure was and now his physical appearance, along with their kidnapping gave insight to the kind of man, this malevolent figure was.

"What do you think he's after?" pondered Marie as they sat huddled together in one corner of the truck's flat bed.

"I don't know", commented Tom trying to keep their morale in good shape, "but whatever it is, it's not a box of chocolates".

Marie laughed at Tom's spirit; she had never met a man as spirited and as free thinking as Tom. It made her relax, it made her happy and it made her begin to trust men again.

Man after man had come into her life, mistreating her kindness with broken promises of marriage, and physical abuse. Never again would she allow herself to be mentally or physically assaulted. But what about Tom? She knew very little about this new man in her life. Would he be like all the others before and mistreat her? Or would he be someone she could finally open up to?

"So tell me Tom", whispered Marie as the two banged against the truck's inner shell as it turned precipitously around a corner, "are you married?"

"Me? Married?" laughed Tom, "I'm afraid not. Divorced with two children".

"Oh God I'm sorry", apologized Marie placing her hand in Tom's, "I didn't know".

"That's okay", stated Tom pleased for the first time that someone was sorry for the breakup of his marriage, "What about you Marie?

Anyone special?"

Marie blushed a little, the blood circulating in her face failing to hide her excitement about Tom being unattached, "No-one special. Not yet".

"That's a shame", sighed Tom who was beginning to warm Marie's presence, "everyone needs somebody to love".

Tom was speaking from experience, for although he hated the breakup of his marriage, he hated the loneliness it brought with it too. He missed so many things that being in a committed relationship had given him, walks on the beach, sharing cotton candy at the fun fair, hell he even missed all the agony of clothes shopping during sale time at the stores.

"Everyone?" Marie asked, "Even the man up front ?".

Tom laughed as the eHarmony commercial played in his head, "Yes even him too. I think my ex-wife and him would probably get along well together".

"So what was she like?"

"She was 5ft 7, brown shoulder length hair".

"No you silly devil", Marie protested hitting Tom gently on the arm, "What was *SHE* like? You know personality wise".

Tom sighed, he was not entirely comfortable at remembering what Rachel used to be like before she discovered the lure of the credit card, but he decided maybe it was time to get it off his chest and put it where it belonged, firmly in the past, "At first she was fine, fun to be with. Even after our first child, she was still a joy to be around, but then after our second child, she changed. Her spending went way up, I couldn't physically satisfy her, and she became a different person".

Marie turned to look at Tom, who was beaten up like a boxer in the tenth round of a world championship bout, on the ropes with nowhere to hide, "Pretty tough I guess?"

"I suppose so".

"You really should see someone about all this crap you're carrying around with you".

"W...W...What", stammered Tom, "You mean a shrink?".

"Yes a shrink"

"I don't know. I think he would have his work cut out".

"You know I think you're probably right there", agreed Marie trying not to break out into hysterical fits of uncontrollable laughter.

Since the breakup of Tom's marriage, this had been the first time he felt comfortable in the presence of a woman, perhaps this was the beginning of a beautiful friendship. For a little while, at least, everything was fine, the demons of Tom's past were slowly being exorcised, Marie was finally beginning to trust a man again, but something was amiss, Emre was missing in action. Tom was beginning to suspect that this person he thought he knew and could trust, was not as he first appeared, however his thought's began to turn to that of a different worry for the truck that was carrying them off to God knows where, had begun its descent in velocity.

"This can't be good", commented Tom as the vehicle slowed to a halt. The driver's side door slowly creaked open, like a coffin lid being prised open, before the devil incarnate himself descended slowly to earth.

Much to their surprise, the passenger's door opened with the same bone chilling echo, that preceded their captor's exit and another, yet unknown individual walked around to join their unknown assailant at his side. "Shhh", whispered Marie as the two people began to chat, "I can just about make out what their saying".

"You're not going to kill them are you", asked a timid voice that Tom was sure he knew, but he knew not why.

"I have my orders", confirmed the voice of their captor.

"That was never part of the deal".

"I've changed the deal, hope I don't change it further".

A brief silence ensued, before the lock holding Marie and Tom was cautiously opened. The door to the outside world opened briefly and a small rubber hose inserted into the gap created. "What the hell', swore Tom as he witnessed a small plume of gas beginning to leave the mouth of the hose.

"Sleeping Gas", coughed Marie as large quantities of halothane began to fill the truck with a cloud of anesthetic.

"Hold your breath", ordered Tom but it was too late for Marie was beginning to slip slowly into unconsciousness, slowly he too began to feel the effects of the vapor entering his body as he drifted into a manmade induced coma.

Tom and Marie were now in great peril, they had succumbed to the might of a person hell bent on removing them from the face of the earth, and they were now in a sleep they might never wake up from.

CHAPTER XXII

The trap had been sprung, the noose around his neck had tightened, the quarry had fallen into the trap, or had he? For the question was now who had snared who? The deviousness of the assassin had caught the man who had sought to entrap him and the tables were turned, not only that, but his only means of escape, his friend, had been lost, lost in the shadows of an evilness so diabolical, that it was only a matter of time before the next victim would be terminated.

Tom and Marie awoke to the sounds of footsteps pacing up and down on wooden floor boards, creaking in agony with every burdensome weight it carried. "Ah, my guests are awake. Please tell me where the Turk is", prompted the stranger as the sound of his steps reverberated through the room.

"Who?" yawned Tom as the effects of the anesthetic began to subside.

"I'm not going to ask you again. For the last time, where is the *Turk*?" the assassin demanded slamming his hands down on the arm rests of Tom's chair.

"I've told you already, we don't know where he is", replied Tom, not entirely sure of his new surroundings, for the assassin had not only tied himself and his friend Marie to a pair of chairs, but they were blindfolded too, "What do you want with him anyhow?"

"He is an evil man who walks the path with Satan as his friend", taunted the assassin as his face invaded Tom's personal space, "All those who oppose the one true God, deserve to be punished".

Tom's heart sank, as he realized what this assassin was, a radical man of God, a man who thought he was doing God's work, a man who would not hesitate to kill, to take the life in the name of an omnipotent being, that Tom himself did not believe in.

"And who is this true God ?", Tom asked believing that if he engaged this individual in a free thinking debate on God, he would be able to not only save his own life, but that of Marie's too.

"You know not the true God?" sneered the assassin, "I ought to kill you now where you sit, heretic".

"Surely", stated Tom as he heard the cocking of a gun at his head, "if you kill me now you would be breaking one of God's laws?"

"What do you mean, heretic?" asked the perturbed man who retreated several paces backward.

"Isn't one of the Ten Commandments, *'you shall not murder'?*", Tom reminded his would be killer.

As the assassin heard Tom's remark, he sank slowly to his knees and began to slowly weep, "God, my God, I have forsaken you; I am not worthy to be called a Soldier in your name. Why must you torture me with these people who do not understand thy purpose for each one of our unworthy souls? *WHY? WHY? WHY?*"

"Let us go then", pleaded Tom, "and you will be doing God's work?"

"I'm sorry, I cannot do that", answered the assassin, "for my orders come from God's messenger".

"God's messenger, God's messenger?" Tom asked who was starting to get a little irate at this man's inability to free think for himself, "Who the hell is God's messenger ?".

"*SHUT UP HERETIC*", screamed the assassin firing a shot from his gun into the air, the smoke from the barrel producing a fine whispery cloud that Tom instantly recognized from his time shooting vermin on his Father's farm, "*SHUT UP*".

"Please, please let us go", Marie pleaded trying to reason with the deranged individual holding them prisoner, "We've done nothing wrong to you".

"*SHUT UP, YOU HEATHEN WOMAN*", screamed the assassin who was starting to become agitated at the two individuals incessant need to talk, "*YOU, YOU, YOU ARE THE ONE RESPONSIBLE FOR MY NEED TO BE HERE, IN THIS HELL ON EARTH*".

"I don't understand", replied Marie not entirely sure why this man held her responsible.

"You don't remember me do you?" he said questioning Marie's inability to recapture a past event.

"I'm sorry I don't", she answered.

"*YOU SHOULD DO*", screamed the assassin, "*IT WAS YOU, IT WAS YOU*".

"It was me who did what?" Marie asked in search of an answer from her tormentor.

"It was you", reminded the assassin lowering his voice, "It was you who pulled me from the river after, I jumped in".

Marie sat quietly in quiet contemplation and remembered how back in the summer of '85 she had gone back to her home in Paris, to visit her sick mom and dad. Her dad was ill with pneumonia whilst her mom was suffering from food poisoning brought on by eating under cooked chicken in a local restaurant. On her way to the hospital in the southern part of the city, she crossed a bridge that spanned the River Seine and on that bridge there stood a car parked silently, alone. She stopped and checked on the driver in the car, but alas he was not there, he had already taken himself to the center span of the bridge where he was bracing himself to take his own life.

Marie tried rushing to the suicidal man, but alas she was too late, for he was already in free fall to the water below. Quickly she rushed to the river bank beneath and proceeded to save the drowning man.

"*Fossor???? Fossor Dirichlet*", she remembered with astonishment as she recalled an event in her past.

"You know this lunatic?" Tom asked with bewilderment.

"*I'M NOT A LUNATIC, I'M NOT A LUNATIC*", Fossor screamed into Tom's face, "*SAY I'M NOT A LUNATIC, COME ON HERETIC, SAY IT, SAY IT*".

"Ok, Ok, You're not a lunatic", said Tom nervously doing as he was told.

"That's better heretic", replied the assassin removing the blindfolds from his two captive prisoners.

"Fossor", Marie exclaimed after the sociopath removed her blindfold, "What the hell happened to you?"

"Don't you recall?" asked Fossor, "*Don't you recall how you pull me from the river after I tried committing suicide? Don't you recall how the medical staff took me to hospital and treated my wounds? Don't you recall how after treating my wounds the medical staff certified me mentally insane? Don't you recall how after I was certified mentally insane I was locked away in an asylum? Don't you recall how after I was locked away in an asylum I found God through the staff there? NO, NO YOU DON'T, DO YOU*".

"And you blame me?" asked Marie staring into the face of her captor. It was a face of pure evil personified, a face driven by a desire to terminate those who opposed him, a face only a mother could love. Silver matted locks on his head caressed the sides of his face as it transformed into the tangled mess of a barbed wire beard. From his brilliant green eyes their came a stare that would kill. He felt and looked like the mad monk Rasputin; *healer, holy man, antichrist.*

"No I don't blame you, I *HATE YOU, YOU SHOULD HAVE LET ME DIE HEATHEN*", Fossor screamed, words of distrust at the focal point of his attention.

"Why? Just to make you feel better for losing your family in a car crash that was beyond your control?" Marie asked trying to understand the reasoning behind Fossor's rage.

"That was God's will", replied Fossor softening his tone after remembering the horrific incident, that took his family away from him.

"Crap", said Marie swearing at Fossor's inability to see logic when it was clearly staring at him in the face, "You told me after I dragged you out of the river, it was a drunk driver."

"Yes it was", replied Fossor a little tear forming in his eye, "but I didn't say the drunk driver was me did I?"

"No you didn't, and now, now you blame yourself for the accident don't you?"

"No I don't, I blame Satan for leading me into temptation", Fossor said wiping away the tears from his eyes, "that was before I found God, and now my friend's, it's time, time for you to find Him too".

"What do you mean?" asked Tom afraid to know what the truth was.

"It's time for you both to die", replied Fossor.

"B...B...But why", stammered Tom, "We've done nothing wrong to you".

"My friend, you are on a quest are you not? A quest to find the truth if I'm not mistaken?"

"Yes. Yes I am", Tom answered surprised at how this man knew about his voyage into the unknown.

"I'm afraid the truth must remain hidden, hidden from the outside world, for the mortals who inhabit this world are not ready to know the truth. For once the truth is revealed, man's understanding of his world will alter his perspective of things, and I'm afraid that just can't happen".

"Why? What are you afraid of?"

"I'm not afraid of anything", said Fossor who was not prepared for this reaction from Tom, "but you, you my friend are you afraid of anything?"

"Yes I am", confirmed Tom as he hung his head in shame.

"What are you afraid of then Heretic?"

"I'm afraid of failure, I'm afraid of not being loved, I'm afraid of not fulfilling my quest, I'm afraid", said Tom answering Fossor's question, but the last phrase in the sentence never got finished as Tom's head was planted firmly in the lower extremities of his captor, making Fossor scream with agony.

"Quick", Tom ordered Marie, "whilst he's down start rubbing the ties on the cross brace of the chair". As Fossor continued, to roll on the floor in abject pain the captive duo began to weaken the ties that binded them to the chairs on which they sat, and it wasn't long before they managed to free their hands from the prison in which they sat.

It was as this point that Fossor began to recover, and seeing his prisoners trying to escape immediately went for the gun, that he had dropped in the melee. "I don't think so", said Tom pushing the gun into the corner of room with one hand, whilst pushing his hand into the face of the surprised Fossor, with the hand free from removing the danger. Tom launched a giant upper cut that found its mark on Fossor's chin knocking him out cold.

"Is...Is...Is he dead?" asked Marie who was shocked by Tom's aggression.

"No he's only unconscious", said Tom untying the binds of their feet which were attached to the chairs on which they sat.

"Poor man", sighed Marie as she bent down to make sure he was okay.

"Poor man? Poor man?" queried Tom in complete bewilderment, "he just tried to kill us. He's also ...."

"He's also what?" asked Marie who unhappy with Tom's attitude to the fallen man.

"He's also killed a friend of mine in Israel".

"He did?"

"Yes he did".

"You're certain of that?" asked Marie who was surprised at Fossor's ability to kill someone.

"Yes it was Emre's nephew", answered Tom.

"Ah, I wondered how you two knew each other", said Marie getting up from her kneeling position on the floor.

"Speaking of which, I wonder where the hell he got too", said Tom as he searched the room with his eyes, looking for an exit from the prison which had contained them.

"Now you come to mention it, he was rather absent in his presence wasn't he?"

"Yes he was", said Tom with anger in his voice, "and when I find him, I'm going to kill him".

CHAPTER XXIII

The streets of Istanbul gave refuge to the hostages of a deranged sociopath, for in the shadows of the meandering paths they were isolated from the dangers he presented, even though they were lost, they were safe, they were safe in the knowledge that they were no longer in danger of being killed, but they were lost, lost in their own thoughts of what just transpired, neither daring to speak for the relief was too great.

Corners of disappointment, lead into alleyways of misery, for they were missing, lost in action, time and time again falling victim to hope of being found being dashed on the rocks of reality, where the shipwrecks of anguish were sinking deep into the seas of frustration.

"All of these alleys look the same to me", sighed Tom as once again they turned into another street only to find it was one they didn't recognize.

"It's starting to frighten me", confessed Marie who was afraid they might get lost in the maze of streets for all eternity.

"Don't worry", comforted Tom trying to put Marie's mind at ease, "we're bound to find a place we know soon". He hoped in his heart that he was correct in his assumption, for this trip through a place he did not know was tearing a large gaping hole in his self confidence.

"That's good", said Marie slipping a hand into Tom's searching for reassurance, he clasped it tight with a protective sleeve that encouraged Marie to become more self assure. Tom's assumption in finding somewhere, or someone, they knew, soon proved dividends, for the inner workings of the city soon lead them to a place they both knew as the paths of desperation gave way to roads of relief.

"The Column of Constantine", sighed Tom as they entered a place they both knew. The porphyry blocks were a genuine welcome vision of beauty for both, as they were fed up of being lost and isolated in a world and a culture they did not know, "What I don't understand", gasped Tom taking a breather, "Is, how the hell does he know Emre?"

"I suppose the only person who can answer that is Mr. Osman himself", stated Marie as she gazed towards the top of the structure, shielding her eyes directly from the sun's glare with a well placed hand on her forehead.

"You don't care for him much do you", Tom asked as he sensed the uneasiness in her voice.

"Something about him is a bit funny", Marie commented as she clasped Tom's hand a bit more firm to show her respect for his point of view.

"What do you mean?" asked Tom who was a little perturbed by Marie's remark of his friend.

"Well it was kind of funny how Fossor appeared just after Emre left", replied Marie who had noticed Fossor's appearance coincided with Emre's vanishing act.

"Now you come to mention it", stated Tom as the concerns about the legitimacy of his friend's hospitality started to nag deep within his mind, "It was kind of funny how he disappeared; he never said where he was going. He just said he had business to attend to".

"And what about the bomb blast at the museum?" Marie asked Tom who beginning to suspect that Emre was not entirely who he said he was.

"It was targeted at the Vitruvian man exhibit, which Emre and I went to several days before where I discovered....."

"What did you discover Tom", Marie asked who was a little puzzled at what he had found.

"I think I found a code in the picture", Tom murmured not entirely comfortable at releasing what he knew for fear of being labeled a *'crackpot'* by someone with greater intellectual prowess than he.

"You found it too did you?" confirmed Marie as she admitted about her belief in the existence of a secret message hidden within the Vitruvian Man.

"Yes I did, I saw that the".

"Hands were all different?" interrupted Marie as she gave insight to her little piece of detective work.

"Yes I did, they were all in the shape of Roman numerals, I wasn't quite sure about the IIII hand impression though, as I thought IV was the Roman numeral for 4".

"That varied through the centuries as IV represented Roman God Jupiter, whose Latin name is IVPPITER", commented Marie who had already researched the difference in Roman numerals.

"So IIII can be used to represent 4 then?" Tom asked Marie.

"Yes it can, so did you get 502, 7, 9 and 4?", Marie said answering Tom's question with one of her own.

"Yes, Yes, I did", said Tom, who was now genuinely pleased that someone else had seen the hands in different positions and he was not imagining it.

"The only thing is I couldn't determine what the numbers signified", Marie confessed hoping upon hope that Tom had cracked the message within the picture.

"I think I managed to solve it", smiled Tom as a smug self-satisfaction began to fill his persona.

"You did", said Marie her heart beating with excitement.

"Yes, yes I did", confirmed Tom, "what's it worth to you, to find out the secret message?".

"Oh I don't know", Marie smiled coyly trying to ease out the secret message in the picture from Tom, "my eternal gratitude".

"If that's the best you can do then, I might just keep the secret message to myself".

"How about one of these then?" Marie said gently placing a tender loving kiss on Tom's cheek.

"I'm not sure", replied Tom, "I might take a little more convincing".

"I'm sure this will cover payment then", said Marie as she pressed her two lips on Tom, taking him in a long lovers embrace.

"I'm sure it will", confessed Tom as Marie's lips left those of his own.

"So?" asked Marie, her curiosity beginning to get the better of her.

"So what", smirked Tom as a big smile tattooed his face with all the coyness of a brand new mother after giving birth.

"So what was the message?" Marie persisted playfully hitting him on the shoulder.

"Ok, Ok, I'll tell, just stop hitting me then", said Tom rubbing the spot on his shoulder were Marie had hit him.

"I'm all ears", Marie replied eager to find out the message in the painting.

"Well the key was finding out what the number 502 meant, after a little research on my part, I found it pointed to section 502 in Da Vinci's notebooks".

"Da Vinci's notebooks? Why didn't I think of that?"

"Because you're not as clever as I am", laughed Tom.

"I bow to your greater intelligence, oh master", Marie said playing along with Tom, "So what do the numbers 7, 9 and 4 mean then". "The 7th, 9th and 4th words in the paragraph", stated Tom remembering the code he had broken and the excitement he had at dismembering Da Vinci's encrypted message.

"And what were those words then?"

"*SHOULD TRUST WORKS*", responded Tom entrusting Marie with the answer to the puzzle he had solved.

"Oh my God", screamed Marie in delight at Tom's trust in her, "For real?"

"Yes for real" confirmed Tom beaming from ear to ear.

"Does anyone else know?" she queried.

"Unfortunately yes", sighed Tom his face of joy turning to one of disappointment.

"Let me guess", Marie said, "Emre?"

"Yes, and it was after I showed him the code that he started acting, well, a little strange".

"Well?" replied Marie, "what's your next step then?".

"I've always fancied a trip to Italy", said Tom

"I hear Florence is nice at this time of year", Marie said agreeing with Tom's assessment of the next step.

"Then Florence it is", agreed Tom as he put an arm around Marie and gazed upon the Obelisk that was a beacon of hope and knowledge for the next step in his quest.

CHAPTER XXIV

The foreignness of being a code breaker laid heavy in Tom's soul, for although he enjoyed the prospect of breaking a small part of a true Da Vinci Code, he was concerned too with what other messages were contained in other works of art. He was concerned too that maybe, just maybe, that other clandestine messages would reveal secrets that would alter not only his, but other people's ideas of the pillars of knowledge on which society was based, maybe this was his destiny and it was for a greater good that this quest for truth was given to him to undertake.

"If Emre", began Tom as they walked through the streets they knew, "is aware of this code now, do you think he is the only one?"

Marie was certain, that all though Emre appeared to be the only one in position of the key to cracking the code, she was not certain that he was the only one to benefit from its knowledge.

"I'd be surprised if he was", she said telling Tom not what he wanted to hear, but the truth. For she decided telling Tom the truth was something he deserved to hear.

"That's the way I figured it too", Tom sighed who was now running ideas of conspiracy through his head, "but for now, I think its best if we don't let on we know".

"I think", Marie consoled Tom, "that would be prudent".

Tom and Marie, silent in their communication between each other, made their way to Emre's home, thinking about Emre's subterfuge and the reasoning behind it. Their arrival at his home though soon presented more questions than answers; for as they approached they spotted Emre talking to someone they knew only too well.

"Quick", ordered Tom seeing who the person was talking to Emre, "get out of sight".

"Why?" asked Marie puzzled by Tom's reaction at seeing someone talking to Emre.

"I think your friend Fossor is the one talking to Emre", Tom stated. Marie, upon witnessing with her own eyes that it was truly Fossor talking to Emre in the open door of Emre's home, immediately did as she was told, taking a hiding position between a pair of overgrown bushes that lay dormant on the outskirts of the house which Tom shared with Emre.

"I don't believe it", she whispered silently to Tom who was spying on the two men deep in conversation, "What the hell is he doing talking to Emre?"

"I don't know", Tom whispered back, "but whatever it is, it can't be good".

"Yeah", replied Marie remembering the mental torture they had both endured at the hand of Fossor, "It was kind of strange too, how he kept on asking for the location of the Turk".

"Why have I got the feeling that was for his own amusement?" added Tom as his eyes watched with distrust the meeting of Fossor and Emre.

"You mean he did all that shit, just to please himself?" swore Marie in disbelief, as for the first time since they met, her anger started to get the better of her, "What is he, some mental psychopath or something?"

"Worse than that", admitted Tom as he continued his surveillance of Emre's home and the two men who stood outside, animated in conversion, "I think he's been brainwashed".

"Brainwashed by whom?"

"I don't know, but brainwashing usually suggests a cult".

"A cult?"

"Yes, Marie, a cult".

The pair of astonished code breakers, watched in horror as Emre and Fossor stood communicating with each other, both equally animated in their discussion with one another, although they could not be heard, Tom was sure both men were angry with the other for letting Tom and Marie escape. It wasn't long though before the conversation ran its natural course and was terminated by both men at the same time. The two men finished their communication with each other as Emre closed the door with a loud thud and joined Fossor, both men disappearing into the smoke filled city that hid their secret identities.

Tom and Marie watched the safe disappearance of Fossor and Emre, before they made their assault on the house. The front door however was firmly locked in place keeping unwanted guests out and its secrets within, "What do we do now ?", Marie asked Tom who was a little apprehensive at one, if not both men coming back.

"We break in", said Tom who was trying to pry the front window open.

"I don't think", Marie replied, but she never finished what she was about to say, for Tom had managed, either through luck or skill, to open the window and was beginning to climb slowly inside.

"You stay there", commanded Tom, "and keep watch, if you see anyone coming you know what to do".

Marie nodded as she witnessed Tom disappear into the confines of the house to search for clues of Emre's treachery. Tom immediately went to the one place he was sure Emre was keeping secrets from him, the office. He began to search high and low, looking through all the places he could think of looking for a clue, just one single solitary clue of his *so called friend's* treason, but alas to no avail for there was nothing there, not even a book out of place. Tom's patience was wearing thin when he thought he saw something on the desk he had not seen before.

"What the hell's this doing here?", thought Tom to himself picking up a leather bound bible from the desk, it's plain and simple design looking slightly out of place in the ornateness of Emre's office. He began to flick the pages of the holy book in search of something, anything that would give him an idea of what his friend was up to. As Tom reached the Book of Revelations he noticed small pencil markings contained within the margins of the scripture.

"1511,8,12,13,1512,7,3,48,49,1531,3,6,73,70,102,43"

"What the friggin hell are all these numbers and what do they mean?" Tom asked himself as he began to study the sequence of numbers. His brain began to contemplate what the significance of the numbers meant, but it was too slow to compute any meaning behind the numbers. Tom's mental capacity for thinking however was soon interrupted by the artificial call of a bird from outside. It was Marie's signal that meant danger approaching. Hastily Tom locked himself away in the study under the relative safety of the desk, just in time to hear the front door being gently swung open.

"You would forget you head if it was loose", Fossor laughed as Emre made his way inside.

"I know", shrugged Emre in disbelief, "I'd be lost without my cell phone too. The snag is I can't remember where I put the damn thing".

"Is it in the office?" questioned Fossor in hope that his comrade's portable communication device would be within easy reach.

"I don't know", sighed Emre, frustrated by his inability to focus on the task in hand, "I suppose I could have a look".

For a brief moment it seemed liked Tom's espionage was going to get him caught, as briefly the office door began to open like the trap door on a set of gallows. His heart began to race, his pulse began to quicken, his palms began to moisten, he prayed to anyone who was listening to get him out of the predicament he was in.

"Ah", stated Emre suddenly remembering the whereabouts of the lost item, "It's on the kitchen table".

Slowly he began to close the open door, the gentle thud allowing Tom to breathe a bit more normally, his body once tense from sheer panic, letting out a scream of relief, as Fossor and the now complete

Emre closed the outer door behind them. "Damn", he swore panting heavily, "That was too close for comfort"

Like a mole emerging from its hole, he began to reappear into the vacant house once more, the claws of his eyes searching for a hint that would assist him in deciphering Emre's hidden message. "I wonder", he said to himself picking up the Da Vinci notebooks from the shelf, "If it's another message encrypted using these".

He began to search the pages of the master's records in search of an answer to the clue contained within the Holy Scripture. Letter by letter, word by word he wrote down the broken code as quickly and as carefully as time permitted, writing down what he found in the small notebook that he always carried with him.

1511 - 8 = 1200 - 12, 13 = THE WEAPONS

1512 - 7 = 126 - 3, 48, 49 = ARE IN THE

1531 - 3, 6 = 8 JUNE (8 6?) = PLANE CARRY ON SPACES

"Oh my god", Tom said to himself, "he is not who he appears to be. I better quickly get to Marie and show her the message that I've found". He quickly tidied the office up, and cautiously walked to window, where he found Marie had vanished into hiding.

"She's probably" he thought seeing Marie was not where he left her," in the bushes we first hid".

Tom made his way cautiously to see if Marie was there, but she wasn't, she had completely vanished into thin air; he began to search for his lost friend when he felt a sharp pain to the temple and he blacked out.

The blurred vision that attached itself to his painful, but conscious stirring looked over him apologetically, "Oh my god. I'm sorry", came a voice as Tom tried to refocus his eyesight once more, "I thought you were Fossor and Emre coming back to kidnap me again".

"That's okay", groaned Tom rubbing the back of his head where

Marie had hit him with a rock she found laying on the dusty, earthen floor, "I think".

Once they were reunited in conscious awareness Tom showed the message to Marie who was as equally astonished, "This is worse than I feared", she explained, "This indicates that he is not only a dangerous man, but part of a larger organization for this takes planning, and logistical expertise"

"It was kind of ironic that I found it in The Book of Revelations too", Tom told Marie describing where he had found the secret message.

"What do you want do about Emre?" she asked.

"Hmmm", replied Tom who was beginning to think, "Maybe, just maybe we could possibly kill two birds with one stone".

"What do you mean?" asked Marie.

"Let me explain my idea to you as we go back to Column of Constantine and wait for Emre to *'find'* us", said Tom as he softly grasped Marie's hand with his. As they ventured back to the Column, Tom began to explain his plan, and although it was dangerous, Marie agreed with her confidant, that it would kill two birds with stone, not only would it expose Emre for who he was, but it would also give Tom opportunity to find out what really happened to his friend Medad.

The wait for Emre to show up at the Column of Constantine seemed like an eternity, but as time marched further on he made his appearance to the two long lost souls. "Tom", said Emre as the two men laid eyes on each other.
"Emre", replied Tom embracing his friend who he had not seen for some time.

"So what you been up to then?" he asked Tom.

"You know me and the Professor have been kind of busy", he said with a smile on his face as turned to the beaming Marie.

"Ah", sighed Emre who was jealous of his friend's blossoming relationship with Marie, "I understand Tom. So is there anything I can help you with?"

"Well Marie and myself, have found another clue and we need to go to Milan in Italy", replied Tom who wasn't surprised at Emre's offer of help.

"I can arrange transportation if you so desire", Emre said as the two men gazed upon the Column.

"That my friend would be most welcome", added Tom trying to play his part in making Emre reveal his true self.

"Consider it done", smiled Emre who was well and truly in Tom's plan. With the three of them walking slowly back to Emre's house, Tom's thoughts were only those of seeking revenge, not only for the loss of his friend, but the temporary loss of his freedom too, it was time he decided for Emre to pay the *pied piper*.

CHAPTER XXV

The blue skies above Istanbul left an indelible mark on Tom, for the city below had been at times hell, but for the most part it was a little slice of heaven. It had been a place where he tangled with the devil and won, he had also found an angel living in the cataclysm's of the past, someone who truly understood him and appreciated him for the person he was, but there was also a dark storm brewing beneath and Tom could sense the hand of evil trying to penetrate the goodness in his heart, but for now he was at peace with the world, and the world was at peace with him, he would however, soon have to take action on someone who was living in the shadow of fear, a doppelganger, a perpetrator of corruption and in his true self, Tom knew what he must do.

"You brought the stuff?" Tom whispered in Marie's ear trying to avoid Emre's suspicions being aroused.

Marie lent over and kissed him gently only the cheek, whispering as she did, "Yes I did".

"Ah, come on you two give it a rest will you", said Emre to his friends, not suspecting anything was afoot. He lent forward and took some peanuts from the glass bowl that lay on the small table, situated on the floor of the aircraft.

Tom blushed and apologized, "I'm sorry Emre".

"It's okay Tom, I'm just giving you a hard time", relented Emre as he munched his way through the peanuts that lay cupped in his hand.

"Could I ask you to get some drinks for us Marie?" Tom asked the lady in his protective custody.

"I certainly could", said Marie getting out of her chair and walking to the mini bar that sat directly opposite them, "What could I get for you?"

"Can I just have a water with ice please?", Tom replied as he engaged Emre in conversion to distract him from noticing Marie pouring a small amount of white powder into the bottom of Emre's drinking vessel.

"What about you?" Marie asked the target of the edible assassination.

"I'll take a Scotch and Soda please", Emre said answering Marie's request for his choice of poison not realizing what Tom and she were about to do.

"There you go gentlemen", she said presenting the drinks to her two esteemed colleagues.

As Tom and Emre both sipped their drinks, Emre slowly began to look a little flustered, beads of perspiration dripped slowly from his forehead and along the path that was carved out by his nasal cavities.

"Are you okay?" Tom asked Emre, "You don't look so good".

"I...I...I don't feel well", Emre replied as he began to loosen the collar of his shirt, trying to cool himself down.

"Well", replied Marie gloating over her victim, "You shouldn't, you evil man".

"I...I...I'm not sure I understand", stammered Emre as he got up and staggered around the aircraft fuselage, "W...W...What have you done?"

"We saw you talking to the assassin", gloated Tom as he watched Emre trying to reach up and open the overhead compartments, but he was too weak to do so, falling to the ground with thud.

"We also found your secret message in the bible too", remarked Marie as she bent down over Emre, "The weapons are in the plane carry on spaces". Instantly Emre's face turned pale white as he realized he had been snared in the trap of someone with greater intelligence than he. As the look of anguish appeared on his face he slipped slowly into the man made coma that Marie had prepared for him.

"We'd better tie him up quickly before he regains consciousness", Marie requested, admiring her handy work, "I only gave him enough to knock him out for a short space of time".

"Did you bring the?" Tom asked Marie.

"Handcuffs? Yes I did. Quickly put him back in his chair then we can shackle him to it", she replied. Tom picked up the dead weight that was Emre and positioned him in the chair so Marie could restrain the lifeless body of their former friend with the manacles she had brought with her. Once they were certain Emre was physically restrained, Tom went to overhead locker to see what he was trying to get to.

"Handguns", speculated Tom as he opened the storage locker to find out what was inside.

"Handguns?" Marie queried after Tom handed her one to examine, "So the code you broke was correct then?"

"Apparently so", Tom confirmed as he checked to see if the magazine in the gun contained bullets once Marie returned it, "These guns are fully loaded too".

"Who put these on board then?" Marie asked.

"I don't think we'll find that out until our friend wakes up".

"Hadn't you better have a word with the pilot about our change in plans?"

"Thank you for reminding me", said Tom as he placed a kiss on Marie's forehead. He went from the fuselage and into the cockpit of the aircraft, where he spoke with the pilot about a change in the flight plan. The pilot in return was only too happy as it saved him a great deal of money in refueling charges. Tom, once the plans were changed, returned to where Marie was and found Emre starting to come round from the coma his friends had put him in.

"Ahh my aching head", moaned Emre as he slowly regained consciousness, "What the hell? Where Am I?"

"You my friend", smirked Tom, as his face snarled into that of his former ally, "Are now *my prisoner*".

"You'll never get away with this Heathen", snapped Emre back at his captor, "I have friends waiting in Milan".

"That is why", said Tom with a look of satisfaction, "we are flying to Florence".

"*WHY YOU DOUBLE CROSSING*", shouted Emre who was frustrated at Tom's change of plans.

"Now, Now, Now", cautioned Tom brandishing a handgun in Emre's general direction, "I'd be quiet if I were you"

"T...T...Tom please", stuttered Emre pleading for his life.

"Please what?" Tom said questioning Emre's resolve to plea for his life.

"Please don't kill me", Emre replied, "I'll make a deal with you".

"I'll make a deal with *you*", said Tom as the handgun he was carrying made its way to Emre's forehead, "I'll let you live, if you tell me what I want to know"

"A...A...Agreed", stuttered Emre seeing Tom meant business, "W.W.What do you want to know?"

"First tell me who you're working for".

"I'm working for Fossor, Fossor is a contract killer, Fossor is a contract killer, and I'm working for Fossor".

"So who is Fossor working for?"
"I...I...I don't know, he wouldn't tell me".

"That sounds like Fossor too", confirmed Marie not caring too much whether Emre lived or died, providing the information they sought was forthcoming.

"Ok then", said Tom cocking the hammer on the gun, "I'll give you one chance, and one chance only, what really happened to Medad?"

"Y...Y...Y...You remember I told you Medad was in a cult ?", confessed Emre as little beads of complete and abject fear tumbled slowly down his face, "W...W...What I didn't tell you it was the C... C...Cult of H...H...Horus"

"The Cult of Horus? The Cult of Horus? Have you heard of this cult Marie?" Tom asked his expert on Byzantine studies.

"The Cult of Horus is a mythical cult that is supposed to be the blue print for the stories of Jesus", Marie responded answering Tom's question.

"N...N...Not mythical", interrupted Emre, "It really exists".

"Ok if this cult really exists, why was he killed then?" Tom said questioning Emre's knowledge of his best friend's murder.

"M...M...Medad knew too much", answered Emre

"Too much about what?" Tom probed trying to find out what Medad knew.

"I.I.I don't know, F...F...Fossor wouldn't say".

"In that case", said Tom moving his finger to the trigger, "You've outlived your usefulness". Tom squeezed the trigger on the gun, making the hammer snap on the weapon, as he did Emre screamed in panic and fainted out of sheer terror.

"Maybe I should have put the bullets in", he said to Marie with a smile on his face.

"No", Marie laughed, "That would have been the waste of a damn good bullet".

FLORENCE
ITALY

CHAPTER XXVI

The city of Florence, deep in the heart of Tuscany, lay on the River Arno which meandered its way from the birth of its conception in Mount Falterona, to the termination of its life at the entrance to the Ligurian Sea near Marina di Pisa. It was a breath of fresh air for Tom and Marie, not only was the city more European in its feel and it's way of life, but it was also a cultural smorgasbord too, for contained within the depths of the city, lay works of art created by such masters as Da Vinci, Michelangelo, Brunelleschi and Donatello to name but a few.

Tom's pleasure in being away from those who sought to kill him was evident on his face, as the recent discoverer of a code contained within the Vitruvian Man, he was eager to find new works of art to tempt his ego with the fruits of his newly gained knowledge. Marie seeing Tom's ecstasy was only too happy to feed him with a feast for the eyes, as she guided them both through the delights of modern Florence, making sure that neither suffered the pain of joy known as the Stendhal syndrome*.

"Now you've got a look at Florence", Marie said to Tom as the two travelers walked the streets of the Tuscan capital, "What would you like to do first?"

"I suppose", sighed Tom who was still in awe of the city, "the next logical step is to find out more about Leonardo Da Vinci".

"That can be quite easily done", Marie proclaimed as the two stood in the middle of the Historic Centre of Florence, "There's quite a lot of vendors around selling informational brochures to tourists". Marie scanned the horizon looking for a purveyor of information a

*(Stendhal Syndrome or Florence Syndrome is a psychosomatic illness that causes rapid heartbeat, dizziness, confusion and hallucinations when exposed to beautiful pieces of art or quite a lot of art in a short space of time.)

and spotted such a person selling the item needed. Without hesitation she left in hot pursuit and soon returned carrying a heavy brochure detailing the life and works of Leonardo Da Vinci with her.

"Thank you", exclaimed Tom who was not only surprised by Marie's ingenuity, but her grasp of Italian too.

"You're welcome", Marie yawned handing Tom the brochure. Marie was still a little groggy from the shenanigans that took place in the skies between Istanbul and Florence, and the fatigue was starting to encompass her body. She did not complain, not once, for the thrill of the chase had given her a new lease of life and she was enjoying every second of it.

They opened the booklet to the English part of the brochure and began to read:

"Leonardo Da Vinci was born in Vinci, Florence on April 15 1452, an illegitimate son of Piero da Vinci and a peasant woman, Caterina. He was educated under the tutorage of painter Verrocchio qualifying as a master in the Guild of St Luke, before spending the early part of his life in the service of Ludovico il Moro in Milan, before working for various patrons in Rome, Bologna and Venice.

Before his death on May 2 1519, aged 67 HE lived in his home in France given to him by Francis I, the King of France (12 September 1494 - 31 March 1547).

During his apprenticeship he was exposed to such people as Donatello, Uccello and Lucca Della Robbia, and assisted many other artists in their work, such as Francesco Rustici in his design of the northern gate of the Florence Baptistery.

Leonardo is mostly known for his works as a painter, the most famous of which are the Mona Lisa and The Last Supper, however his drawing of Vitruvian Man is thought to be more recognizable due to its use on the Euro.

Also known for his technological prowess, Leonardo conceived many modern day inventions before their creation e.g.: Helicopter, Parachute, Tank and Solar Power. He also aided in the development

and advanced the knowledge of anatomy, civil engineering, hydrodynamics and optics".

"Hmm", pondered Tom as he finished reading the booklet, "It would be interesting to see this Florence Baptistery and the northern gate on which he assisted".

"Are you thinking that there could be something significant on the northern gate?" Marie asked trying to understand Tom's reasoning.

"I don't know", replied Tom, "but it will be interesting to find out".

The parade to the Baptistery of Florence was a short one, but it was too long for Tom, for the anxiety of maybe finding another clue was too great for him to bear. His heart was racing, his head was pounding, his feet were aching, but unfortunately, as they found what they were looking for, his feet weren't the only ones to ache, for although a small piece of work above the northern door was reminiscent of some of Da Vinci's early work, there was nothing concrete, nothing definitive, nothing to point Tom and Marie in the direction they needed to go.

"That's disappointing", sighed Tom as the gloom in his soul enveloped his persona.

"Don't be too down hearted", Marie prompted her disappointed friend, "There will be set backs on the way. History is not only about finding the truth about the past lives of others; it is also about eliminating things we know not to be true. We've just got to find one tiny piece of the puzzle that will open the door to bigger and greater finds."

"Hold on a minute", commented Tom as he began to think about the topology of the Baptistery, "You did say open the door didn't you?"

"I did", conceded Marie uncertain of where Tom was going with his latest line of questioning.

"I've got a feeling that we could be overlooking something", he remarked as they went into the interior of the Baptistery.

"Such as?"

"I've got a hunch that the layout of the building itself could be a clue".

Tom went to where a collage of metal was formed into the branches of a tree, dangling the fruits of the written word in pictorial form for pilgrims to enlighten themselves, picking a ripe fruit before returning to the slightly suspicious Marie, her suspicions however where laid to rest when Tom illustrated what he thought a relevant piece of information with a pen he carried with him at all times.

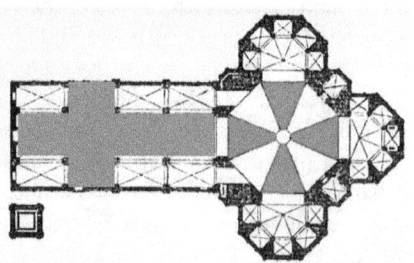

Fig VII – Topological Diagram
Of Florence Cathedral & Baptistery

"That's a key Tom", pointed out Marie as she bore witness to what Tom was illustrating with his finger, "It's a symbol not only of opening and closing powers, but knowledge and guardianship too, the only key I can relate this to is the papal crossed keys which were entrusted to Saint Peter".

"If there's one, does that mean another key exists?"

"You mean to complete the crossed keys? I'm not aware of one, however just because I'm not aware of one doesn't mean it doesn't exist"

"That's a pity. I was hoping you were going to tell me it was a key to unlock the next clue", sighed Tom with a heavy heart.

"Tell you what", said Marie trying to console Tom, "Why don't we do one of those cheesy tourist tours that run from here?"

"I'm not sure", said Tom who for the first time (probably due to him hitting a mental block) was lost for words.

"Ah come on", replied Marie pulling him by the hand to where the tour was starting, "It'll be a giggle".

"But...But..", Tom protested, but alas it was to no avail for he along with Marie found themselves along with part of a tour group about to depart from The Northern Gate .

"Hello ladies and gentlemen", commenced the tour guide with her usual spiel, "Thank you for taking this tour with us today. Now Florence was founded in 59 BCE for former Roman soldiers, by Julius Caesar who called the land on which Florence was built Florentina. It was a type of military camp with building plots of land laid out in the style of a chess board, with the main streets *'the cardo'* and *'the decumanus'* intersecting what today is known as the *'Piazza Della Repubblica'*, (which is today in the center of Florence). Florence is also in the middle of an important Roman road known as the *'Via Casa'* which comes out of the *'Via Flaminia' near* the Milvian Bridge".

"Excuse me er Miss", interrupted Tom who was not entirely sure what to call the female tour guide.

"Yes sir how can I help you?" she replied eager to answer his question.

"Is that the same Milvian Bridge over which Constantine defeated Maxentius?" Tom asked.

"Yes sir it was. You have a good knowledge of Roman history", she said praising his understanding of the Battle that took place.

"I had a good teacher", replied Tom smiling at Marie.

"Now this Roman road was important", the tour guide continued, "as it helped Florence expand as a commercial center. Emperor Dioclentianus made Florence the capital of Tuscany in around the 3rd century BCE".

"I was just wondering", Tom interjected as his curiosity got the better of him, "This Dioclentianus was he called Diocletian by any chance?"

"It's the same person", said the Tour Guide who was beginning to suspect that Tom was about to ask another question.

"The same one who beheaded St. George?" Tom queried.

"Yes, the same one. He also had St Minias executed the same way too. St Minias was Florence's first martyr after he refused to sacrifice to the Roman Gods, the Basilica di Minato al Monte stands near where he was put to death".

"I think", Marie told Tom, "we better leave this tour. You're starting to show me up".

"Yeah I think so too", Tom agreed who was slightly pleased with Marie's perspective on the probable outcome of the rest of the tour. "I think I need to go back to the hotel to rest, my head's starting to hurt".

"O.k., O.k.", smiled Marie, "Come on then Einstein".

As the pair of bewildered tourists left for the hotel, Tom began to think about all the knowledge he had gained because of Marie's expertise. He didn't think he had the understanding to comprehend everything she imparted on him, but to his surprise he did, and he did to its fullest extents. Whatever it was, she not only brought out the best in him, but improved him in more ways than he could imagine.

CHAPTER XXVII

The nomadic life style of Tom was not conducive to his mental well being. Weeks of living out of his small battered suitcase was taking its toll, for although he understood the need to follow the trail (wherever it may lead), he had not prepared himself fully for the exertion that the hours spent travelling between destinations would bring. Lands afar turned into European culture much too quickly. The limited opportunity he spent in two different continents, gave him very little time to fully absorb the atmosphere or the culture as much as he would have liked to. The shadows of a malevolent presence urging him to hasten his own presence in places he took pride in calling home, links to his home land had been severed. He knew deep in his heart, that if he tried to reach those people he knew, they too would have been placed in great peril, a price he decided that was much too costly to pay.

He sighed as he looked outwards towards the city of Florence from the balcony of his private suite in the Hotel Mona Lissa, his soul laden heavy with the burden of an expectant audience, the butterflies in his stomach no longer there, for the first time in this quest, his road forward was blocked and as much as he tried he could not see a way though.

"Don't burden yourself too much", comforted Marie sliding a protective arm around the visibly upset Tom, "The road ahead will soon present itself".

"I hope so", replied Tom unsure of which direction to take.

"I know so", said Marie who had more faith in Tom, than Tom had in himself, "I tell you what, why don't we go out for a drink tonight and just forget about the quest for now, there's a little bar around the corner I've been dying to try out".

"I...I...I", began Tom trying to explain the ghosts of past that still haunted himself. He had every reason to be frightened, the temptation to dive into the pool of excess, fresh in his mind. The promise he made to himself to get sober after spending a reckless night with a priest, still ringing loudly in his ears, but more than the sum of these two parts put together, he wanted to rid himself of all the demons that drove him to despair.

"Shhh", she hushed, placing a finger on Tom's lips, "Stop it".

Not for the first time since they met, Tom's breath had been taken away by this vision of beauty, the kindness, the tenderness, the respect she showed him, was a deep cleansing effect on the anguish he kept deep within, years of mistreatment at the hands of others washed away on the oceans of happiness.

"Okay, okay", smiled Tom with consolation, "let's go then".

As they walked hand in hand to the door of their a hotel suite, they noticed a small folded piece of paper slipped under the space between the lower edge of the barrier and the carpeted floor on which they stood, "I didn't notice that there before", conceded Tom picking up the note.

"Read it later", begged Marie, "I'm in dire need of a drink".

"Sure thing", promised Tom placing the cellulose pulp based message in the confines of his wallet.

Florence at night, was different to Florence during the day, no longer could the great works of art be seen, for they hid themselves in the veil of the night, the multitude of artificial sun's beaming down on other parts of the city, enticing the children of the night into reveling with other likeminded spirits. Taverns of sin entwining the modern day with the past in a coat of intoxicating debauchery, the modern day Romeo and Juliets decorating the gloom of the darkness with a warm glow of adoration.

The Cafe Slowly on the Via porto Rossa (Via Red Port) was a bar like no other Tom had been in, for it was not a place overrun by inebriated men brow beaten by their wives, but it was a place where intellectually spirited individuals came to theorize about art, science, and other mind numbing experiments of the soul. "Wow", he exclaimed with excitement, "This is really different".

"I thought you'd like it", Marie enthused with a sparkle in her eye, "Let's go and order drinks".

The bar was a laboratory of alcohol laden potions, poison bottles of all shapes and sizes lining the cabinets with a rainbow of enticing intoxicant liquids.

"Whata can I get you beautiful people tonight?" inquired the barman as Tom and Marie sat down on the leather upholstered bar stools.

"I'll have a glass of the house red please", ordered Marie who already knew what she wanted to drink. The red grapes of Italy, reminded her of growing up on a vineyard back home, in the southern western part of France. She spent many a happy time there, helping her parents cultivate the young grape plants into becoming the red musky liquid that was Bordeaux. As she got older, she took more interest in activities outside the confines of the family vineyard, lured eventually by the bright lights of Paris and the intellectual paradise that was the Sorbonne.

"Very good, and for you sir?" the barman asked Tom.

"I'll have a, er," stuttered Tom unsure what he should drink, when a little voice in his head spoken for him, "I'll have a vodka martini, shaken not stirred". Tom was a closet diehard fan of James Bond. From the first film Dr. No to the latest one released in the summer of last year, he loved them all.

He couldn't quite illuminate the reason for his affinity with the franchise. Perhaps it was the mystery? Perhaps it was the beautiful women? Perhaps it was all the gadgets Bond had at his disposal. Whatever it was that kept on bringing Tom back to the movies, year after year, in hope that the latest Bond release would out do the one before it, it was an experience that held Tom firmly in its grasp.

"Ha...Ha...Very a good Mr. Bond.", laughed the barman, "one a moment please." for a brief moment he disappeared concocting the prescriptions. Upon his return he carried in his hands two chalices containing the poison of choice, "There you go my friends. Enjoy".

"Hmm", savored Tom taking a sip from his glass, "I could get used to that". As he placed his glass down gently on the bar with a gentle clink, he remembered about the note in his wallet. He dove into his inside jacket pocket, pulled out the neatly folder paper, and read the message contained within, his eyes painting a picture of déjà vu that alarmed Marie.

"What's wrong?" she inquired noticing the change in Tom's demeanor.

"This", sighed Tom handing Marie the note that had been placed under their hotel room door.

You are in great peril,
Be careful
Signed

A .FRIEND

"What do you think it means?" she said returning the note to Tom.

"I'm not sure", Tom replied taking another large sip from his glass, "but whatever it is, it's not good".

"I think you could be right", confirmed Marie whose attention had been caught by the presence of two burly policemen entering the premises, "Look".

"Oh great, that's just frigging great", Tom replied answering Marie's call to witness the approachment of two law enforcement officials to their immediate vicinity.

"Raust, Mr. Tom Raust?", inquired the taller of the two speaking in his best, but slightly broken English.

"Yes I'm Tom Raust", Tom replied in earnest, "How can I help you gentlemen?".

"We need to ask you some questions down at the police station", the police officer said motioning his partner to guard the exit of the drinking establishment.

"A...A...About what?" Tom stammered not sure why the police would want to question him.

"That sir", stated the police official, "I cannot divulge. However Inspector Mancini, Chief of Police is eagerly awaiting your arrival".

"If he goes then so do I", Marie said interrupting the police officer.

"I'm sure we can facilitate your request", replied the police officer, "now please come".

Tom and Marie both followed the law enforcement officials, not entirely sure of the reason why they were wanted for questioning by the police, neither one however letting the other know how afraid they were, for they were sure the other was in need of their protection, protection against not only impending disaster, but protection against self pitying that would only lead to a reckless abandonment of their search for the truth.

CHAPTER XXVIII

Isolation for Tom was a 12ft x 12ft concrete interrogation room, the walls cold and damp with the past inquisitions of previous criminals, their confessions written in the stones of an Italian judicial system that would be the envy of most technologically advanced countries. The echoes of their crimes filling the prisons with screams of dread as their sentences were handed down, the shackles of justice their new master as their reigns of terror were stripped from them, losing all privileges and freedoms they had been given as free individuals; time was something they now served instead of time serving them.

In the dark recesses of his mind, Tom began to tread a path of self loathing, for he believed had he found something of worth at the Baptistery of Florence, he would not be in this God forsaken place staring at the walls of oppression waiting for the purveyor of justice to appear. He was getting more and more impatient by the minute, frustrated by every second he spent in isolation.

The dreariness of the containment unit was soon broken, as an imposing figure of a man entered the room carrying a cup of lukewarm coffee in one hand and his service revolver in the other, the scars of father time wounding his face with cuts of a deep resentment of the criminal fraternity. "Mr. Raust", stated the man as he sat down opposite Tom, "You are one illusive fellow."

"Who the hell are you?" Tom sneered deeply resentful of the man's remarks.

"Ah", remarked the mysterious figure, "You are a fighter. I like a man who fights for his freedom. My name is Inspector Mancini; I'm the head of the Guardia di Finanza here in Florence".
"Am I supposed to afraid of that?" quipped Tom preparing to give as good as he got from the Inspector.

The Inspector pondered for a minute as for the first time in his professional career here stood a man who was not afraid of him, this was something new, something he had not experienced before and it made him respect Tom a little more than he already did.

"That depends on how easily scared you are", he replied sipping his plastic cup that contained a somewhat diluted liquid that was suppose to resemble coffee. In his opinion that was as close as it came to even tasting like the best cappuccino they served at his favorite restaurant, but for now it was what it was, a dull imitation.

"I'm only scared of one thing", admitted Tom easing back in his chair.

"Oh and what's that?" coaxed Inspector Mancini intrigued by Tom's admission.

"My ex-wife when she hasn't received her allowance for the month", he snapped with a look of disgust at his adversary. Tom remembered the time when an irate attorney gave him an angry phone call. His wife had spent her allowance for the month within the first two weeks and now she was demanding more. "In return for what? Less time with the children", he sneered. Tom knew all too well what was coming, a ransom demand and he was right, the threat of seeing his children less was the ultimatum given, but this time he called his ex-wife's bluff and asked the court to intervene. Sixteen minutes was all the judge needed to condemn Rachel for dwindling the money Tom gave her, sixteen minutes of heaven, sixteen minutes worth its weight in gold.

"You poor devil", sympathized the Inspector acknowledging his pain, "I too have an ex-wife and all she does is siphon off the money from my pension fund, I'll be lucky to retire at all".

"What do *YOU* want?" barked Tom, who had already grown tired of the small talk that the Inspector was trying to engage him in.

"We found a man handcuffed to a seat in the charter plane you took", divulged the Inspector informing Tom of the man they had found shackled to a chair aboard the aircraft.

"Really?" Tom replied raising an eyebrow in disbelief, "What did he say, this *'mysterious man'*?"

"He said you and your girlfriend, drugged him, handcuffed him, and then diverted the plane from its prearranged flight plan from Milan to Florence".

"I suppose he never mentioned he had stowed away a loaded handgun in one of the overhead compartments?" Tom said leaning forward and snarling at the Inspector.

"Mr. Raust, please do not insult my intelligence, we found no weapons on board the aircraft".

"That's not surprising considering...." Tom broke off what he was about to say, for revealing what he knew about the incident may land him in more trouble than he was already in.

"Considering what Mr. Raust?" interrogated the Inspector sensing Tom was about to reveal he had taken the gun and disposed of it.

"Considering he's Turkish", pointed Tom thinking fast on his feet.

"And what's that got to do with it?" asked the Inspector not seeing the logic behind Tom's reasoning.

"Most Turkish men are not trust worthy", Tom justified, "They lie, they cheat, and they do anything to make a fast profit at someone else's expense".

"Now, Now, Now", replied the Inspector slightly angry with Tom's attitude, "You're just profiling all Turkish men, and not this one individual. Is that what this man did to you Mr. Raust? Did he try making a profit at your expense?"

"I'm not saying", retorted Tom crossing his arms in self defense.

"Come along Mr. Raust, you've just about admitted to kidnapping this man, in retaliation for doing something wrong to you".

"I'm not admitting to anything, *YOU HEAR ME, NOTHING!!*"

The Inspector was about to ask another question of Tom, when a knock at the door was followed by another member of Guardia di

Finanza bursting into the room, "I'm sorry to interrupt Inspector".

"Yes. Yes. What is it?" growled the Inspector annoyed at his subordinate's bad timing.

"There's a fire broken out at one of the hotels", said the junior officer.

"Which one?" queried the Inspector.

"The Hotel Mona Lissa".

"What's that got to do with me?" snapped the Inspector not entirely sure of the reason why he was being informed of the blaze presently making its way through the hotel.

"Someone was seen fleeing the hotel just shortly after the fire broke out".

"Suspected arson? I'm on my way then, place Mr. Raust and his girlfriend in the cells until I get back. I'm sorry Mr. Raust", said the Inspector apologizing to Tom, "but duty calls".

Tom could not answer, for he was in a state of disbelief, for the hotel in which Marie and himself were lodging, had been deliberately set on fire, not only that but the secret message they were given from a friend had warned them they were in peril. He was slowly beginning to suspect that foul play was showing its ugly hand once again, and that only meant one thing, Fossor.

CHAPTER XXIX

They sat contained, like animals in a cage waiting for someone, anyone to force open the cell door that held them within. Freedom only a few inches from their face taunting them, beckoning them with a finger of temptation, the temptation to break free from the cell by fair means or foul, but the foul stench of a killer on the streets, meant that whilst they were here, confined, they were safe, safe from the hand of a man who took pleasure in the killing of others, man, woman, child, they were all the same to him, viable, easy, targets of an unjust justice.

Whilst they sat thinking about this evil do-er walking the thoroughfares of Florence, they began to question everything they had come across during their stay in the Tuscan capital.

"What I don't understand", said Tom to Marie discussing their present predicament, "Is how the police knew exactly where we were, at exactly the right time we were in the bar, it almost seems like it was..."

"What? Staged?" Marie implied finishing Tom's sentence for him.

"Yeah staged", Tom agreed, the anxiety in his voice belittling his extreme worry that another hand was beginning to raise its ugly head from the pit of oblivion.

"If it WAS staged", Marie said as she began to pace back and forth in the prison cell, "Then why?"

"I don't know why", replied Tom unsure of the reasoning behind the conspiracy theory, "but I'm beginning to suspect that there's more to this than meets the eye".

For the first time in their hunt for the truth, Tom and Marie were unsure of the answers to the questions they posed, they were no longer sure of who was virtuous and who was depraved. The lines drawn, once separate were now blurred together making it difficult to identify who posed the greatest threat, Fossor, Inspector Mancini or some yet unknown adversary?

In time they would identify the correct person to ally themselves with, but for now they could only do one thing, and that was follow the path that lay in their heart. There was however, one question that remained unanswered, who was the writer of the note that was currently in Tom's wallet? Whoever that was knew of the impending disaster and the dangers that would, once more, step from the shadows into the light.

"Then there's the writer of the note too", said Marie as her pacing up and down, slowed to a stop.

"That's been intriguing me since we read it", commented Tom starring at the floor in search of inspiration, "How come Mancini never took it from us and what is the significance of the symbol at the foot of the message?"

Marie lost herself in Tom's questions, trying to find the answer to the questions he posed. The symbol was in the form of a triangle shaped mystical figure, that usually was a symbol for The Father, The Son and The Holy Spirit, however the mysteriousness of the symbolism contained within gave Marie no answers at all. In fact all they gave her were further questions she could not answer.

"I suppose", she stated contemplating the meanings contained within the symbols, "we won't know about the symbols without conducting further research, as for Mancini, either he's not the brightest button in the box or he's part of a bigger picture".

"That", confided Tom concerned with Mancini's lack of diligence to duty, "is something only time will tell, and unfortunately time is something we have plenty of".

Marie had to agree with Tom, time was an excess commodity that she wished she didn't have, she thought and worked better under tight deadlines. The impossible to her, became possible when schedules tightened like a noose around her throat, it made her more focused and more alive, she was in essence an adrenalin junkie that fed on the rush of living her life in the fast lane, but for now she was crawling along at a snail's pace and it made her uneasy with herself, second guessing every answer to every question that someone asked of her, she could not wait to feast at the table of adrenalin, for it was something she desired, something she needed and something she yearned for.

"How long do we have to wait before we are charged or released?" asked Marie desperate to aid Tom in his quest for the truth?

"Not much longer", stated Inspector Mancini parading to the cell door, swinging the key that would release them, around his index finger, "You are free to go".

"I don't understand", announced Tom as he turned to face his captor.

"That makes two of us", replied the Inspector, "The alleged victim of the crime had decided not to press charges, so tell me Mr. Raust truthfully, did you really kidnap him in retaliation for something he did?"

"Certainly not", answered Tom as the cell door was unlocked by a particularly irate Inspector.

"That's good", Mancini declared slamming the door shut behind Tom and Marie, "I'd hate to imprison someone who was innocent". "I did it to pay him back for killing Medad", he whispered softly to Marie who in return nodded in approval at Tom's actions in the skies between Istanbul and Florence.

Outside of the police station, the fresh air tasted like a fine Italian wine, sweet and full bodied, intoxicating the two freshly released detainee's with its delicate bouquet, the aroma giving fresh impetus to Tom's oxygen deprived brain.

"I think we should find out more about the man who designed the door, over which stands the carving in which Da Vinci assisted", said Tom eager to get back to the chase again.

"Lorenzo Ghiberti?" queried Marie who was surprised but delighted at Tom's resurgence for the quest again.

"Yes", said Tom, "Lozenger Chapati"

"Er you mean Lorenzo Ghiberti", Marie laughed.

"Yes him too", replied Tom who was slightly embarrassed at his inefficiency to grasp the name of the important Italian sculptor.

"I think", sniggered Marie trying to hide her laughter by placing her hand over her mouth, "that information could be found in the local library".

Tom who witnessed Marie's ineffective method of hiding her discretion, had to laugh too, for although he had been the brunt of her infectious laughter, he was secretly pleased, for there was nothing like seeing someone laugh, it made him happy, happy in the fact that he could make someone content, content enough that this woman would be happy to spend the rest of her life with him, and this made him more euphoric with every second that they spent together.

CHAPTER XXX

The Biblioteca Nazionale Centrale in the heart of the Tuscan capital on the Piazza dei Cavalleggeri (Public square of the Cavalryman), contained the secrets of an ongoing war, for line upon line of paper soldiers lay in their wooden trenches waiting for the enemy to attack. It would be a bloodless war but not a war without casualties, for all too often warriors of the written word would fall from grace never to be seen again. The grave yard of their broken comrades was a testament to the courage they gave in the line of duty, self sacrifice and heroism never once questioned, for although they readily gave up their secrets, they never gave up once, never questioned once, never looked the enemy in the face and ran away in cowardice, for they knew their duty and lived for the heat of the battle.

Tom and Marie selected their weapons of choice and sat down at the generals table to begin their foray against the enemies of ignorance.

"There's a lot of books here", commented Tom as the tower of knowledge lay somewhat precariously on the table at which they sat.

"I know", replied Marie overwhelmed by the copious amount of written works they had asked for, "I just hope there's something here to point us in the correct direction".

"If there's not then we just keep looking until we do", Tom said determined not to give up on his need for further information.

Book after book went into the heat of battle, each one falling a heroes death never to be used again, for a brief moment all seemed lost as the pile of the dead grew larger and larger, then like a shot from beyond the horizon a sniper's bullet found it's mark.

"It says here", commented Tom as he read the spoken words on the battlefields of knowledge, "that the Baptistery was considered to be originally a Roman Temple dedicated to the Roman God Mars, purported by the scribe Dante Alighieri, however this is wrong as the founder of this legend is Giovanni Villiani, blah,blah, blah, late 4th or early 5th century, blah, blah, blah, replaced another Christian baptistery in the 6th century, blah, blah, blah, used by important Florence families as a tomb, blah, blah, blah, Giotto, Andrea Pisano commissioned to design first doors in 1329. In 1401 a competition was announced to design a new set for the Northern Doors by the Arte de Calimala (Wool Merchant's Guild), seven sculptors competed, including Lorenzo Ghiberti, Fillippo Brunelleschi, Donatello and Jacopo Della Quercia, with the commission being finally given to Ghiberti".

"Why would the Arte de?" asked Marie trying to remember all the facts that Tom had just read to her.

"Arte de Calimala", corrected Tom reading the name of the guild he could barely remember himself.

"Yes the Arte de Calimala, be given the responsibility for deciding who was given the commission for the doors?"

"That is a very good question indeed", Tom commented closing the book, "They must have held a considerable amount of power or influence to be the ones to choose the designer of the Northern Doors".

"We need to find out more about this guild of men", said Marie to Tom as she pondered the reasoning why the guild were the ones to choose the artisan.

"First we ought to find out what a guild really is", stated Tom, "I don't think these books are going to really help us. Is there a computer near here we can use?"

"Yeah, over there in the corner", Marie replied pointing to a bulking looking, slightly out-of-date, computer.

"Let's get over there then quick", said Tom as he raised himself upwards from his chair. Tom and Marie hastened themselves to the modern day information system and began to search the libraries records for the knowledge they sought.

"According to the records contained here, guilds are an association of craftsmen of a particular trade (In our case the Wool Merchant's Guild). Early guilds were formed as a brotherhood of workers, similar to that of a trade union, some guilds held ritualistic traditions in order to preserve religious orders, such as the Freemasons".

"Does it say anything about the Wool Merchant's Guild?" Marie asked who now totally comprehended the essence of the guild and the part they played in shaping Italy during a specific time in history.

"Hold on let me look", said Tom his eyes scanning, searching for any particular records on the Wool Merchant's Guild, "Yep, it says here that the woolen cloth trade was responsible for the growth of the city as its leading form of trade. The merchants imported cloth from parts of France, Brabant and Flanders, then, through processes known only to themselves, created finished cloth from the raw materials they were given".

"Does it say why the Wool Merchant's Guilds were so important?" Marie quizzed Tom who was still busy searching for further information.

"Hmmm", pondered Tom studying the research material in front of his eyes, "They held communal post's during the late middle ages known as gonfaloniere, a position of civic power".

"So they were not only merchants, but public servants too?"

"Yes until the rise of the Medici family in the 14th century, who took control of the city for themselves".

"But what about the relationship to the Baptistery?"

"The Arte di Calimala were responsible for upholding the maintenance of the Baptistery, therefore they were the ones who commissioned Ghiberti to decorate the Northern doors".

"Does it say by whom?" Marie asked.

"I'm afraid not", said Tom who had already looked for a name, in anticipation of Marie's question.

"Ok then", sighed Marie who was a little disappointed, but not entirely surprised by the lack of information, "what about Ghiberti himself?"

"Born in Florence, blah, blah, blah, won the competition for the first set of doors, blah, blah, blah, set up a workshop, re-invented lost-wax casting, Michelangelo named scenes 'Gates Of Paradise', then commissioned to produce gilded bronze statues to be placed in Orsanmichele in Florence, one St John the Baptist for the Calimala, one of St. Matthew for the Arte di Cambio (Banker's Guild) and one of St. Stephen for Arte Della Lana (Wool Manufacturer's Guild). The Orsanmichele? Is that far?"

"Why?" asked Marie, "What are you thinking?".

"It would be interesting to see what these bronze statues looks like", said Tom as he began to shut the computer down.

"Are you thinking there could be a clue?" Marie inquired as her anticipation level went rocketing skywards.

"I don't know", responded Tom trying not to get his hopes up, "but I'm beginning to learn that we should leave no stone unturned".

"Then we should go there now then", said Marie already getting up from her chair, "before the night comes again".

Tom and Marie set out on their travels once again, in hope that something would aid them in their rescue mission, to rescue the truth from being hidden behind closed doors, for they both were sure that the truth, whatever it maybe, would not only change their own lives, but the entire world's perspective too. Whether that was good, or whether that was bad, only time and history would let them decide.

CHAPTER XXXI

During the time between the death of the sun and the birth of the moon, they hunted, searching for their prey, a rare breed of homosapien called St John that had been caught in Medusa's gaze. Influenced by Ghiberti's mastery, their lairs in which they nested had been camouflaged well. The modern sticks and stones that builders had found at their disposal were used to carve homes for the inanimate statues that stood guard over the Orsanmichele (*kitchen of St.Michael*) in service of the master of the religious structure.

The hunters took aim with the best weapons available to them, their eyes, and their central nervous systems, each one selecting a target and shooting them down one by one until they found the one they were searching for, St John.

"Here he is", stated Marie as she located the statue carved out of bronze by an Italian Artisan.

"Why do I get the feeling that there is nothing significant about this carving?" sighed Tom as his disappointment got the better of him.

"Maybe there isn't but don't forget he did other carvings too", Marie said trying to encourage Tom's disbelief to vanish into the skies above.

"Hmm", pondered Tom thinking about the statue that was standing before him, "You could be right, let's look at the other statues created by Ghiberti".

"Here Tom quick", enthused Marie pointing to the Statue of St. Matthew with a delicate finger of wonderment, "Wasn't St. Matthew one of the statues he created?"

"I seem to think he was", replied Tom as he joined the excited Marie at the base of the statue, "Why?"

"Take a look at this, there's two inscriptions here, one on the border decorating his tunic, the other in the open book in his hand", said Marie pointing to the two scribed messages on the statute.

"I think it says *OPVS VNIVERSITATIS CANSORVM FLORENTIE ANNO DOMINI MCCCCXX*", said Tom trying to read the smaller of the inscription, "What the hell does that mean?"

"My Latin's not that good", confessed Marie who knew exactly what it meant, but was far too modest to flaunt her knowledge, "but I think it means the work of the guild of bankers of Florence in the year of our Lord 1420. What about the inscription in the book?"

"I don't know I can't read it that well, it seems to be faded quite badly in places. Why don't you have a look?", pleaded Tom who was having trouble reading the inscription, either due to poor lighting, or poor eyesight he could not decide, but whatever the reason, to him it was illegible.

"Hmm", murmured Marie as she studied the words on the open stone book, "It seems like it's a passage from the gospel according to St. Matthew, probably from the way the book is opened, I would guess the first page, but I can't really grasp the language contained within".

"Why don't we go inside and see if there's a bible we can borrow?" asked Tom who was not prepared to give up without gaining more information about the passage quoted.

"That seems like a logical plan of action", said Marie as she clasped Tom's hand in excitement.

Tom and Marie entered the Orsanmichele in anticipation of finding something or someone who could assist them with their question, however the church was a desolate place, alone, and cold, with no one in sight to help them. They went searching for a bible, any bible; however all they could find were Italian versions.

"That's frustrating", sighed Marie slamming a borrowed copy of the bible she held tightly down on the pew in front of her.

"I wouldn't say so", replied an ominous, malevolent voice behind them, a voice so eerie, so chilling that the hairs on the back of their neck began to crawl with fear.

"F...F...Fossor?" stammered Tom as he and Marie turned around to see the face of evil smiling at them.

Fossor slowly sat down on a wooden pew directly behind them, his naked torso wrapped in the envelope of a half unbuttoned black trench coat, while a silver cross dangled like a garrote around his neck, moving in time to the vertical motion of his breathing. "What? You were expecting the Pope I suppose? How disappointing, and there was I thinking you and me could be friends", he smirked clasping his hands like in prayer.

"What the *HELL* do you want?" growled Tom sneering at the individual who had kidnapped them at gun point in Istanbul.

"Now, now Mr. Raust, you are in the House of God, please don't take the Lords name in vain", declared Fossor reminding Tom of the place in which they sat, "I get easily offended".

"Look", protested Tom placing his face near that of his enemy, "I don't care, I don't fucking care. So Fossor, what is it you are after this time? You want to kill me in this so called House of the Lord, then go ahead, I'm not afraid of you...*YOU, YOU, YOU, YOU SON OF SATAN YOU*".

Fossor just sat on his pew, unaffected, unnerved by Tom's little outburst, unimpressed and unafraid. There was no reason to be, for he was the one that held all the cards in an already stacked deck. The Soldier, The Assassin, The Righteous (in his own mind at least), knew already what Tom and Marie were seeking and where it would be sought. The contract to kill these two people had been given to him from his master to prevent the truth from escaping to the outside world, but he was not about to give up the thrill of the hunt so soon, for this little man, this little fly, this insignificant piece of human garbage that sat in the House Of The Lord (his Lord), deserved to be punished, and punished he would be, but not here, not now, it would be in his own time, on his own terms. "Mr. Raust look I come unarmed", attested Fossor as he opened the trench coat in which he sat, "I came to make you a one time, and I repeat one time deal only".

Tom looked hard at Fossor's naked chest, examining it closely for any sign of a concealed weapon, his eyes finding nothing but a small tattoo with the initials *"I.N.R.I"* on the skin above the position of his internal clock. "I'm not interested in any deals you offer", he uttered sitting back on the pew next to Marie.

"You've not heard it", warned Fossor closing his trench coat.

"I don't care", snarled Tom, "I'm not making any deals with, someone as twisted, and as warped, and as downright evil as you, you sick bastard".

"Frankly Mr. Raust", Fossor sighed in disbelief getting up from his position in the Church, "I'm disappointed, but not entirely surprised. Next time we meet Mr. Raust it will not be under pleasant circumstances. Here, take this", Fossor passed a folded piece of paper to Tom, which Tom reluctantly took, "Until next time we meet I bid you good bye and to you dear lady I say au revoir". Fossor blew Marie a kiss, taunting her with his suave, cavalier posture, making Marie turn her head away in total disgust. As Fossor left the Church, Tom hugged Marie, who in turn hugged him close to her heaving bosom.

She was frightened, scared to death, but she was not prepared to show Tom how scared she was, for she was afraid that Tom was more scared then she was, "W.W.What does the note say", she blurted as Tom left the safety of her comforting arms. For a moment in time, Tom was scared to open the note in case it contained something frightening; however curiosity got the better of him and began to read it aloud to Marie:

"Matthew 1 verses 1 to 3
The book of the generation of Jesus Christ, the son of David, the son of Abraham,
Abraham begat Isaac; and Isaac begat Jacob; and Jacob begat Judas and his brethren;
And Judas begat Phares and Zara of Thamar; and Phares begat Esrom; and Esrom begat Aram;"

"I don't understand", exclaimed Marie as she listened to the bible quote that Fossor had unexpectedly given them, "What's he trying to do?"

"I don't know", said Tom who wasn't sure whether he should be frightened or thankful, "but I don't trust him one iota".

"Good", Marie replied agreeing with Tom, "Neither do I. However he has answered one question for us, but posed us another one".

"He has, hasn't he? What the hell has the book of the genealogy of Jesus Christ got in connection with the guild of bankers?"

"Maybe they know the secret of the genealogy of Jesus, but I don't suppose we can confirm that either way until we do some more digging in the archives", stated Marie standing up from her sitting position on her pew.

"Where are you going?" Tom asked as Marie left the pews on which they were sat.

"I'm going to look at the tabernacle", said Marie.

"The taber what?" quizzed Tom as he got up and proceeded to follow Marie.

"The tabernacle", Marie laughed as Tom joined the quest to see to the religious icon.

"What the hell is a ...." said Tom pausing for Marie to correct him again.

"A tabernacle?" Marie corrected trying to hide her laughter from Tom. She knew he secretly didn't object to her laughter especially at his expense, however she thought this was more serious and it needed a serious response, "A tabernacle varies from religion to religion, for example in Catholicism, a tabernacle is a box in which the consecrated bread and wine are kept".

"So what about this one?" asked Tom, his eyes fixed on the beauty of the artwork in front of them.

"I don't know", confessed Marie, "I've not seen one as beautifully decorated as this one before".

"It is beautiful is it not?" asked the saintly figure of a priest as he approached them from within the inner sanctity of the church.

"It certainly is Father, my friend here was just asking me about tabernacles", Marie told the priest as he moved closer towards them.

"In Florence my child, tabernacles are part of the history of art and as such are thought to be first hand authentication of the religious feeling of the town", replied the senior priest of the church, "They were built by the people of Florence to fight against the heretics and also to fight off the plague, however whatever the purpose they were built for, the main purpose was to protect their loved ones from the evil that threatened their lives".

"What about this one in particular Father?" asked Tom.

"This one of the Madonna and Child, was painted by Bernardo Daddi, as for the Tabernacle itself, I believe that was done by Andrea Orcagna somewhere between 1355 and 1359", the priest replied answering Tom's question.

"Orcagna, Orcagna? Where have I heard that name before?" Marie said trying to recollect the name Andrea Orcagna from her past.

"He was Master of Works, during his time working on the rose window and mosaic decoration in the Cathedral of Orvieto", came the priest's reply, who was only too happy to impart his knowledge on the two young children in his church.

"Of course it is", said Marie smacking herself gently on the forehead, "Thank you father you've been most helpful".

"Not at all my children, may you go in peace with the Lord's protection".

"And with you", replied Marie as she clasped Tom's hand and pulled him towards the door of the church.

"I presume you're in a rush to get somewhere?" asked Tom as he was dragged towards the exit.

"Yes", confirmed Marie almost breaking into a run, "We're going to see the Cathedral of Orvieto".

"*OH WE ARE, ARE WE*", echoed Tom as they disappeared through the door. He knew when Marie got excited, she was onto something, this he hoped, could be the break they were looking for. They were due for some good fortune, and some good luck in keeping Fossor at arms length, for once, he hoped, his prayers would be answered.

ORVIETO
ITALY

CHAPTER XXXII

It was a 100 miles and a 100 minutes of hell, hell in a rickety, run down train that swung you from side to side, your bones being beaten to a pulp as it ran over rails on its journey between two of Italy's most famous cities, Florence and Rome, however their own journey would terminate in Orvieto a city in the south west of Umbria in the center of the country, but for Tom it was a chance to rest his weary head. Marie had already succumbed to the temptation of fatigue and was currently asleep in his protective arms, he however was taking in the sounds of the trip, the noises of the trains wheels ringing in his head, as his gaze was fixed on his own reflection in the window that was dark with the sights of the nocturnal visions of the countryside.

For the first time in his life he felt needed. Others in his past life used him to enrich their own existence at the expense of his own, but with Marie he felt different, for she completed him, she trusted him, but most of all she loved him, she loved him unconditionally, with all his faults and traits, she was the first person in his entire 40 plus years as man living amongst strangers, who took him for what he was and that made him feel alive.

Orvieto could not come too quickly for the two weary travelers, for although the journey was necessary it was tiring, tiring to a point where mistakes and errors in their computational skills would manufacture results of a catastrophic nature. Their decision to rest up for the night was probably the correct judgment call, for neither Tom nor Marie had slept properly for a couple of days and both were in dire need of a decent night's sleep.

The Grand Hotel Italia was ideal, for it was only a stone's throw away from the cathedral, panoramic views of the city projected from the rooms they offered, graciously brushed by the oils of life onto a canvas of rich architectural works of art, the frame of the night hanging resplendently in the galleries of the central Italian city.

Marie awoke to find Tom was already awake, gazing at the skyline of the new city they had taken residence in. She smiled as she thought about all the trials and tribulations they had undertaken, and the pride she had in the blossoming relationship between herself and Tom.

Marie respected his views on everything they had come into contact with, the trust between the two was an unbroken bond and it made her feel like she was reborn once again. Her past life with an abusive husband drifted away on the seas of adoration when she was with Tom, he made her feel good about herself again, agreed there had been other men in her past, but he was different, he was everything she needed in a man, intelligence, humor, but more than anything else, he was totally trust worthy, someone she could rely on.

She joined Tom as he continued his journey amongst his inner thoughts. "Do you ever pinch yourself and wonder if this is all a dream?" she asked placing an arm of adoration around him.

"All the time, all the time", he sighed as he continued further inward in his thoughts.

"I don't just mean the city, I mean you and I", she said falling under the spell of city's charm.

"That's what I thought you meant", he replied as he turned to look at Marie's face, "for the first time in my life, I feel complete and that makes me ...."

"What, scared?" Marie asked as she too turned towards the face of the man, who gave her inner peace, peace from the demons that haunted her past existence.

"No", he replied, "It makes me very happy, so happy that I want to tell the rest of the world, that this person here, by my side breathes life into my once lifeless existence, giving me hope and fulfilling my every need".

"Good", she replied kissing Tom's forehead, "because I feel the same way too".

"But we hardly know one another", Tom sighed astonished by Marie's remarks, "How do you? How do we know?"

"It's been decided for us", Marie commented as she turned to face the panoramic view of the city, "We've paid our dues, and now it's our time to be happy".

"I'll be even happier when I find out what the purpose of this stinking journey is", replied Tom who was frustrated by the deviations that other people placed in his way.

"In time Tom", Marie comforted with words of kindness that came forth from her sweet but honest lips, "All the questions you have will be answered".

"I hope so", Tom shrugged breathing a huge sigh of disappointment.

"You know, you really should have more self confidence in your own ability".

"It's been battered to pieces by other people in my past, with any I had left getting stolen from me by my ex-wife in the courtroom", remarked Tom remembering all the times in his past when people washed away his self belief, with words that would destroy most saintly people's trust in humanity .

"Those people are not important any more, what's important is what's here and now, and what's here and now is someone has total confidence in your ability to do what is being asked of him and uncover the lies of the past, that, for whatever reason, have been hidden from the rest of the world".

Tom knew that Marie was right, it was time to bury the ghosts of his past, and get on with life, for life was for living not for dreaming about the past and the nightmares contained within.

"You're right", he smiled as his gaze became transfixed on the Cathedral in his sight, "I've been living in the past too long, it's time to get on with my future, and that includes you".

"Moi?" giggled Marie pretentiously as she pointed towards herself, "You mean little old me? I'm not sure I deserve that honor".

"Your right, perhaps you don't", Tom chuckled sensing an opening to lighten the mood they found themselves in.

"I'm always right", Marie said catching on to Tom's humorous reply.

"Since when?"

"Since the beginning of time".

"I didn't think you were that old".

"I'm not", Marie said playfully hitting Tom on his shoulder.

"Oww stop it that hurts", he replied rubbing the spot on which he had been hit.

"You're a lot of fun", Marie commented placing her hand in that of Tom's, "I like that".

"Good", laughed Tom, "That's the way I'll always be too, even when least expect it".

"I think", Marie started beginning to snare Tom in a trap of words.

"What? What?" Tom replied in anticipation.

"I think it's time to go and getting ready, then do some work", Marie continued ensnaring her victim in a carefully planned dictionary based noose.

Tom and Marie left the vision of the city behind in their wake, as they went off to plan their day's events, in hope that whatever they discovered within the walls of the cathedral would be worth their voyage into these unknown parts of the Italian landscape.

CHAPTER XXXIII

A plague of tourists, descended like locusts into the central Italian town of Orvieto, choking the thoroughfares with a disease ridden sickness. Souvenir shops took the brunt of the full frontal attack as mementoes were stripped from their display cases with the infestation sweeping everything up in its tornado vice like grip. The old and the young, were not the only ones to fall prey to the foul smelling odor that encapsulated the hamlet in its ritualistic meanderings, for all were easy targets as the fever that held its victims in a hypnotic state did not care about age or belief, it only cared about satisfying it's cravings for the pawning of the victims souls in return for trinkets of a faraway place.

Tom and Marie waited for the plague and the disease ridden to move on to pastures new before they ventured into the midday sun, "I'm pleased they've all gone", said Tom to Marie as they trekked their way to the Cathedral of the city.

"Me too", she replied with a sigh of relief, "I thought they were never going to leave".

"Hold on a minute", said Tom as he stooped down to look at some garbage, some careless wanderer had left behind.

"What is it?" Marie asked as Tom picked up the paper trail at his feet.

"It's a visitor's guide to the Cathedral", stated Tom as he examined closely the document in his hand, "and there's a section in English too".

"That's a stroke of luck", Marie said as the two treasure seekers continued forth onwards to the Cathedral.

The winding, narrow passage ways that they had journeyed through, gave way to the symbolic place of worship as Tom and Marie found themselves dwarfed by the magnificence that was the Orvieto Cathedral, "Oh my God", remarked Marie as her eyes transfixed her stare on the manmade structure, that stood firmly in front of them, it's victims held enchanted in a hypnotic like trance.

"Wow", exclaimed Tom, as he too was drawn into its vice like grip of the outstanding architectural brilliance, "In my whole life I've never seen anything like this before, it's simply astonishing".

They ravished the building with their eyes, as they took in all that it was pleased to offer them, the construction, the artistic decorations, the beautifully sculptured figurines, each one raping their senses with a visual decadence so wonderful that even the sun in the sky marveled at the feast before its eyes. Marie who had left the planet earth and was in permanent orbit around the cathedral spire had to be brought back down to earth with a gentle nudge from Tom.

"Ermmm Oh? What? Er? Yes totally", she stuttered, a little ashamed of being brought to her knees by the sights that her eyes feasted on, "What does it say in the book?"

"According to this, it took almost 300 years to finish construction of this dedication to St. Mary. Pope Nicholas IV laid the flag stone in 1290 before entrusting the work to chief-mason (capomastro) Father Bevignate di Perugie, whose blue prints were drawn up by Arnolfo di Cambio (the chief Architect of the Florence Cathedral). In 1309 architect Lorenzo Maitani was brought in to solve several design issues, most of which revolving around the load bearing aspects of the Cathedral. After his death in 1330 (a little time before the dome was completed), his responsibilities became that of his sons. Andrea Pisano followed in 1347 as Master of Works, before he too was succeeded by Andrea di Cione, better known as", said Tom reading the script from the book, he got to a certain part in the history of cathedral when, upon recognizing a name she knew, Marie interrupted Tom's preaching.

"Orcagna?" she said.

"Yes Orcagna", Tom confirmed, pleased that Marie was now fully cohesive, "The mosaic for the facade and the rose window are ascribed to be his input to the overall design of the cathedral".

"So those are the two things we should really be concentrating on", Marie stated as her thought's went to those of the works of art undertaken by the master in question.

"I think", prompted Tom as the thoughts in head started churning around his frontal lobe, "we ought to check out both sides of the rose window, both the exterior and the interior, depending on what lies underneath the window on the inside, we could possibly find another clue".

"I wouldn't get your hopes up", Marie said trying to keep Tom's expectations realistic, "Remember what happened at the Baptistery of Florence?"

"I totally understand", replied Tom who was battling the demon inside him that wanted to find more knowledge than was presented to him, "We should start on the outside first. What about these decorated columns?", said Tom pointing to the columns that lay upright on the exterior wall.

"Hmm", said Marie as she began to study the columns one at a time in order, "I think the first one is scenes from Genesis, see God giving life to man and the creation of Eve, this second one I'm not entirely sure about, but I believe it's the Tree of Jesse with Messianic Prophesies, now this third one contains stories from the New Testament".

"I'm sorry", interrupted Tom, "The Tree of what?"

"The Tree of Jesse", Marie replied who was sure Tom was about to ask a question pertaining to art work on the column, "Why?"

"Is the tree of Jesse anything to do with Jesus?"

"I don't know, why what are you thinking?"

"Well the Bible of St. Matthew that he had in his hand at the Orsanmichele was to do with the genealogy of Jesus and if I didn't know any better I'd swear that the Tree of Jesse is referring to the Tree of Jesus".

"What are you saying Tom?" Marie blurted out alarmed by the sequence of events that brought them to the place in which they stood, "Are you saying this is a quest for the descendants of Jesus?"

"I'm not entirely sure", Tom sighed who was a little frightened by the thought of finding hidden messages of Jesus' true bloodline, "but if it is the purpose of our quest, then that means not only will Fossor try and stop us, but other people will rally to his aid and keep the secret hidden".

A frightened Marie then turned to Tom and said quietly under her breath, "Perhaps Fossor is working for those people who wish the secret to remain hidden, in which case Tom, this thing has gotten a whole lot more serious".

"I don't like this, I don't like this at all", Tom confessed grabbing his trusted friends hand, "We've got to find out more on this Tree of Jesse as it could have enormous implications on the reasons for our quest".

The thought of a true bloodline of Jesus had scared Tom and Marie, for if it was as they feared, a secret worth killing for, then this meant other people were aware of its existence too, and these people would not hesitate to take the life of another just to keep the secret dormant in the annals of time.

CHAPTER XXXIV

Fingers of masonry swooped down from ceiling like stalactites, permeating the floor with an awe inspiring presence. The alternating rows of alabaster and travertine decorated the walls with the jacket of a prisoner's uniform, as wooden struts traversed the aisle with a minimalist attitude. Arch ways lead the procession to an alter like structure surrounded by frescoes of a time gone by, however all was not well in the house of God, for the silence was being broken by the anguished sighs of a man's voice crying out in abject agony.

"What was that?" Marie whispered as she and Tom walked through the door to the interior of the cathedral.

"It sounds like someone's being tortured", replied Tom who was unaware, that his unfortunate choice of words were most profound, for as they walked slowly down the shaft of light that decorated the aisle, a vision of horror would not only penetrate their eyes, but their very souls too.

"OH MY GOD", screamed Marie as she laid her scarred eyes on the torturous aspect that presented its horrific vision to them both.

"What the hell", Tom swore as his eyes met for the first time, a wooden crucifix braced between two columns, on which was nailed a man, a man he thought he knew, but he was uncertain, uncertain because this individual had been sacrificed on the alter of pure evil.

"An apt choice of words Mr. Raust", said Fossor with an evil look in his eyes, as he walked towards them with a malevolent purpose, his torso wrapped in the uniform of a Benedictine monk supporting his recently shaved head," Very poetic don't you agree ?"

"Are you completely insane?" Tom hissed as his eyes swooped to see his enemy standing in front of him.

"Not at all Mr. Raust", Fossor said as he looked upwards admiring the work created by his own hand, "I'm just doing the will of my master, my lord, my savior. Pity he was a good spy too, but he out lived his usefulness". The groans of the man on the crucifix slowly tapered off, as the life essence was drained from his soul, the last feeble attempt at life exhumed from his corpse by the grim reaper. Fossor grinned in contentment at seeing his handy work producing a more than satisfactory outcome.

"Who... Who... Who was he?" Marie asked timidly struggling to remove the new born lump from her throat.

"Don't you recognize the man, you should do, he's the one you imprisoned aboard on *MY PLANE, WITH MY WEAPONS*", Fossor screamed in disapproval, "but what's done, is done".

"Em...Em...Emre?" gulped Tom as his eyes began to fill with rage at the sight of his former friend's purgatory. Even though Emre had done him wrong, this was no way to treat his former friend and confidant, "*WHY YOU!!*" Tom charged at his adversary with all his might, but Fossor eluded him and struck him squarely on his cheek with a side swipe from the back of his hand.

"Now, Now, Mr. Raust", Fossor said grinning with an evil intent, "This time I come fully prepared, next time I won't be quite so lenient", as he finished gloating over Tom, he slipped a jewel incrusted sword that he was secretly carrying in the sleeve of his tunic.

"The Shahi Sword?", Marie puzzled in bewilderment, eyeing the weapon in the palm of Fossor's hand, "How did you?"

"I just liberated it from its owner", Fossor laughed running his hand over the weapon, the sharpness of the blade making a small incision. Fossor seeing this, smiled at Marie and ran his mouth over the wound, torturing her with a look that would kill, "Now I've got your attention, it's time for you both to join your friend here".

"Why", asked Tom slowly rising to his feet, "Why now?"

"Because my friend", snarled Fossor, "you know too much".

"You actually mean we are correct about our assumption in the purpose of our quest?" Marie said witnessing the snarl in Fossor's voice echoing that of his demeanor.

"*There shall come forth a shoot from the stump of Jesse, and a branch shall grow out of his roots. Et egredietur virga de radice Iesse et flos de radice eius ascendent. A rod out of the root of Jesse and a flower shall rise up*", Fossor quoted remembering the lessons he had been taught by his master in the confinements of the mental institution.

"I don't understand", admitted Tom as he slowly got to his knees rubbing the side of the cheek where Fossor had struck him.

"The Tree of Jesse as you have probably seen on the front of the cathedral confirms what Matthew began with the words, '*the book of the genealogy of Jesus Christ, the son* of David, the son* of Abraham*'. Jesus indeed was a son* of David, who in turn was a son* of Abraham", stated Fossor releasing the secrets of his masters' teachings.

"So that means what? The birth of Jesus is not the immaculate conception but a cover up of biblical proportions?" hypothesized Marie astonished at what Fossor was telling them.

"Correct my dear lady, but now unfortunately for you", Fossor sighed, his thoughts turning to the thrill of the chase, "The history lesson is over, it's been fun".

"What do you mean fun?" Tom demanded scarcely believing what his ears were listening too, "You kidnapped us, you held us at gun point. We barely escaped with our lives".

"Now if I remember", Fossor corrected, pointing the sword at Tom's face, "You escaped by hitting me where no man should hit another man, then you knocked me out cold, so don't play the innocent Mr. Raust. You're no better then I".

"I'm not even close to being as nasty as you", an angry Tom

*(Son is often used to denote the word descendant).

reminded Fossor. "I don't go round killing people, because they've *'outlived their usefulness'* ".

"Unfortunately Mr. Raust,   killing is my business, and business is good", Fossor said tormenting Tom with the weapon in his hand.

"So it's a business?", queried Marie as her eyes locked on those of their captor, "So whose paying you?"

"I'm sorry, but due to a confidentiality clause on their part, I cannot divulge that information, however, needless to say it's a necessary service that I offer, and these people have put a price on your heads".

"Whatever their paying, I can double it", Tom promised just to see if Fossor would be paid off.

"Mr. Raust, it's not the money, it's the ethics, I'm sure you understand, being an ethical man, once a contract is signed, I cannot go back on my word".

"How about my word then?" bellowed a loud voice from the back of cathedral.

"Come forward then my friend and show us your face", a puzzled Fossor asked of the mysterious stranger.

Footsteps echoed their way softy on the marble inlaid floor, nearer and nearer, not rushing making the hit man wait for him, for whoever this person might be, they were not afraid, in fact far from it, they were more used to being the one who intimated.

"I'm sorry I don't know who you are", an intimated Fossor said, slightly concerned at this interruption.

"No you don't, but I know you", a mysterious voice answered.

"Inspector Mancini?" queried Tom recognizing the stranger in the midst of this chaos.

"Ah, an upholder of the law ", Fossor commented as he drew his sword under the chin of Tom, "I presumed you're armed, kindly place your firearm on the floor".

"I'm sorry I can't do that", revealed the Inspector removing a gun from the inside of his coat.

"That wasn't a request. That was a demand", snarled Fossor.

"I know", Mancini stated unafraid of the assassin, penetrating the assailant, with a cold, hard stare of invincibility.

"*WHAT DO YOU MEAN YOU KNOW?*" screamed an irate Fossor, "*HAVE YOU ANY IDEA WHO YOU'RE MESSING WITH?*"

"No and I don't really give a shit. So drop the weapon and the hard man act", ordered the Inspector moving his gun into the firing position.

"*THIS IS YOUR LAST CHANCE*", Fossor yelled, his voice echoing through the cathedral's theater like structure.

"That's what I figured".

"*AND?*"

"You do what you got to do, and I'll do what I have I do".

"*OK*", Fossor uttered in an angry retort, "*DON'T SAY I DIDN'T WARN YOU*". In an act of pure aggression, Fossor pulled the hair of Tom taut, making his neck exposed, seeing that his hostage was now prone, moved his arm, in which the weapon was held, slowly backwards in a arch (almost similar to that of a golf swing).

For a brief moment he hesitated giving the Inspector just enough time to get a shot off, wounding the astonished Fossor in the hand which contained the weapon.

"*AAAAAAHHHHHH*", Fossor screamed in pain as the injury caused him to drop his weapon on the floor, the blood from his hand slowly began to fall to the ground in time with gravity. Fossor, wounded, seeing for once he was outnumbered, released from underneath his tunic a flash bang grenade that blinded all in its blast radius.

"God Damn It", swore the annoyed police chief as the smoke began to clear, "Where the freaking' hell has he disappeared to?"
A befuddled, but still aware Tom, saw that the wound caused by the Inspector had left tiny droplets in the form of a path towards where the baptismal font lay asleep, "This way Inspector", he pointed, leading the way the crimson path of hemoglobin drew a line on the cathedral floor.

"What the hell", cursed a disgruntled Inspector, "He can't just have vanished into thin air".

"He hasn't", Marie exclaimed examining the font, "There's got to be a secret compartment somewhere here", Tom and the Inspector watched in amazement, as the determined Marie ran her hands over the font, searching for a mechanism that would reveal a door to the underworld, "I can't seem to find it", she uttered in disbelief.

"It's got to be here somewhere", Tom remarked as he climbed onto the ledge of the font. Beginning his more frantic search around the precipice he went feeling, looking, hunting, hunting for something, anything that would reveal Fossor's secret door to the world underneath, his frustration began to grow as in turn his efforts remained fruitless.

Just as he was about to climb down from the font his eyes focused on the statue of Jesus holding a staff in his hand. He pondered for a moment, wondering if maybe, just maybe that the mechanism was the statue itself.

"I'm going to try the statue", Tom told Marie, as she and the Inspector looked on with anticipation. He slowly guided his hand towards the staff the statue was holding, and slowly, very slowly, began to push. To his surprise it began to move as a mechanical sound echoed throughout the building, as he did the roof of the miniature church began to slide slowly down, revealing the entrance to an underground network of tunnels.

"Ok", ordered the Inspector, "Let me go first".

"What about Emre?" panted a slightly out of breath Tom.

"Who?" inquired the Inspector uncertain of who this Emre person was.

"Him", Tom answered pointed to the man nailed to the cross.

"Here", replied the Inspector handing Tom his hand gun, for although he didn't want to see Fossor escape, he knew the body of Tom's fallen comrade would need taking care of, "Take this, but please, be careful".

"Thank you", said Tom clasping the weapon in his hand, "Let's go Marie".

Marie and Tom disappeared down into the underground system that took Fossor as its prey, they were not sure what they would find, but they were sure that where ever it was leading too, they would discover what became of their wounded adversary.

CHAPTER XXXV

The subterranean citadel that lay underneath the teraformed crust of the world above, held its own secrets, secrets of a time when escape routes contained within the polymorphic layers would aid those seeking refuge, for not only did it provide means of escape from tormentors, it also sought to confuse them. Tunnels ran into dead ends, chasms opened into vast arrays of nothingness and walkways devoid of light intersected paths leading to sanctity and thoroughfares that went deeper and further into the unknown.

A small trail of blood illuminated the pursuers' path, as they went in search of man who had not only betrayed his best friend, but his own sanity too. The display of madness he had shown was driven by desire to kill those who had come to close to a secret that others wanted kept hidden. Agreed he knew what the secret was, but he did not care about the reasons why, for in his own mind at least, it was a viable mission and that meant protecting the secret at all costs, even if it meant losing his own life.

Tom and his accomplice Marie knew this, for they were certain the mental capacity for rational thinking of their would be assassin had ceased to be. Compassion, humility and respect for his fellow man were traits that had turned over to a darker master. As they continued to follow the path created by Fossor's hand wound, Tom turned to Marie and said, "I think there's more to this then we originally thought".

"What do you mean?" she replied as they turned another corner that lead them closer to a deranged man.

"Do you remember when we asked Fossor who was paying him?" queried Tom.

"He said something about a necessary service that he offered, and those people have put a price on our heads", Marie paused for a moment before she realized what Tom was pertaining too, "He said these people, that means there's more than one".

"And who has enough power and influence, to hire a hit man to kill those who seek the true blood line of Jesus, and is religiously biased ?", Tom questioned Marie as they stopped in their tracks.

"The church?" Marie remarked in disbelief, "Surely you can't be serious".

"I am", said Tom as he looked down upon the ground to witness that the trail of blood had ceased to exist, "*SHIT! SHIT! SHIT!*", as he swore he pounded the rock face of the passageway with his fist, causing a little abrasion to appear on his knuckles.

"What's the matter?" Marie said grasping Tom's arm, preventing him from striking the rock face again.

"The friggin trails run cold", Tom cursed as the anguish filled his eyes with a burst of abject failure. He slumped to the ground as his emotional state of mind relapsed into a wallow of self pity, tears of frustration mixed with those of sorrow, flooded down his face as the need to release his anguish took the better of his self preservation.

Marie sat down beside her fallen hero and comforted him, "What's the matter?" she asked trying to pinpoint the source of his misery.

"I'm, I'm", Tom stuttered trying to explain to the nurse of his soul his fall from grace, "I'm just fed up of being stuck on this stupid quest, being chased by this, this, this madman, with no end in sight. When will it end?"

"Soon my prince, soon", Marie comforted placing Tom's head on her shoulder, "We must continue though before others join the cause of our enemy".

The wound in his self belief to do what was asked of him was similar to the physical wound endured by that of Fossor, for he too was bleeding, bleeding from a lack of self-confidence in the form of tears of woe that fell from grace like fallen soldiers in the heat of battle. The nurse at his side began to treat his injury with kindness and the loving touch of a human being who totally understood the pain and anguish he was going through, "So, So, So what do we do now?", he sighed removing the dead from the fields of his scarred face.

"We'll see if there's a way out of here", Marie said picking herself up from the cold ground that she was sat on.

"I think", Tom answered as he too, stood upright, "that could be the way to go". He pointed to a small shaft of light at the end of the labyrinth, from where he was certain they could ascend upwards. Hand in hand they slowly meandered their way to the source of the light and found something most unusual, for they had joined a small fraternity of underground tourists being lead in procession by an orator of knowledge, impairing her wealth and expertise on to those less experienced than herself.

"Throughout time, Orvieto's most basic need for an ample supply of drinking water had been problematic, a problem that had caught the attention of the Medici Pope, Pope Clement VII. It was during the sack of Rome in 1527, by the Spanish King and Holy Roman Emperor, Charles V, that Pope Clement VII escaped from the ravages of the ongoing struggle disguised as a fruit vendor into the city of Orvieto. Determined not to be caught by the Emperor, Pope Clement VII set about fortifying his position in the city. He hired an Italian architect by the name of Antonio da Sangallo the Younger, who had also been chief architect of St. Peter's Basilica in Rome, to draw plans up to dig up a new well to aid the city's water supply in case of siege by outside forces. As you can see by looking upwards Antonio managed not only to succeed, but succeed in a way that was most efficient by having carts go down one way, and up the other. Are they any questions?"

"Yes", replied one tourist in the group, "Is that the same Pope Medici whose father was assassinated during the Pazzi conspiracy?"

"It is indeed", replied the tour guide, "Giuliano de Medici, father of Pope Clement VII, a Knight of Rhodes and Grand Prior of Capua, was assassinated by the Pazzi family, who were patrons for Filippo Brunelleschi's chapter house, although they were not the ones to instigate the plot, they were the ones to carry it out".

"Why did they kill this Medici man?" Tom queried as his mind began to formulate another hypothesis in his head.

"Men. Lorenzo Medici was also killed in the same attack. It was all to do with the power struggle between the Medici family and Pazzi family over who was to control Tuscany. Any more questions?"

"Why is this called the Well of St. Patrick?" inquired a second tourist.

"It was called the Well of St. Patrick or the Pozzo di San Patrizio, because it is similar to that in design and appearance to the cave of the Irish saint", the tour guide replied, "Any more questions? No? Let's proceed upwards and outwards then".

"Why did you want to know about the assassination for?" Marie asked Tom not entirely sure of his train of thought.

"I think I might know the reason for Fossor's rampage", replied Tom quietly, so no-one could hear. As they ascended from the depths of the well, to the beauty of the city above, Tom explained his thoughts on the killing spree of Fossor. The possibility that Fossor could be under contract to someone who was related, or be related himself to either the Medici's or the Pazzi family was a thought that entered his mind, and to him it made perfect sense, a lifelong revenge attack by either family's descendant, that would end centuries waiting for the day when vengeance would finally be claimed.

CHAPTER XXXVI

The daylight that broke their entrance onto the surface of the city mirrored their state of mind. The darkness that had clouded their judgment broke free and left behind nothing but clarity, the free thinking that had held its two unwilling prisoners in a state of debauchery, had returned to tear down the barriers that had shut inspirational thought in the dark recesses of the mind. Now clear and free thought flowed like salt from a shaker, as ideas of a morbid realization told a story, of more than the assassin's hand in the death of innocent people.

The lifeless body of their former friend being transported out in a body bag met their return to the cathedral with a stare that brought Tom and Marie back down to earth. The coroner that was now in charge of finding the cause of death was in deep conversation with Inspector Mancini. What the discussion was about remained anonymous to them both, for neither could lip read Italian and to be quite honest neither one really cared, they only cared about one thing, the pursuit of the truth and those who sought to hide behind the veil of lies.

Seeing Tom and Marie approach without the scarred Fossor in their possession the Inspector shrugged his shoulders in disbelief as they answered his body question with the shake of their heads, the attitude in their body language however denied that of their missed opportunity to capture the wanted criminal.

"No joy?" queried the Inspector with a look of disappointment when he had finished giving orders to the coroner.

"Sorry", apologized Tom handing the undischarged weapon back to its rightful owner.

"Don't worry", the Inspector replied patting Tom on the shoulder, "We'll get him sooner or later. I've got to head back with the body. Are you going to be okay?"

"Yes we're going to be fine, thank you Inspector", Marie answered as she put a loving arm around Tom, "What about the Shahi Sword?"

"It's back in protective custody now. The Iranian government is going to be pleased to get it back, it's been *'unofficially'* missing for several months now", stated the Inspector.

"Why do you think he stole it in the first place?" asked Tom trying to figure out (in his own mind), the purpose behind the theft of the Imperial Sword.

"I presume he was trying to initiate more tension between Muslims and Christians. Whatever the reason it's now back in safe hands, now if you don't mind I've got official business to attend to. Here's my card, so if there's anything you need, anything at all, please don't hesitate to call", the Inspector stated thrusting his business card in the hand of Tom. As the Inspector left with the body of the deceased Emre in tow, Tom and Marie's attention was drawn to the matter in hand, finding the next clue and continue their pursuit of the truth.

"So Einstein, what's the next step then?" Marie said caressing Tom's ego with a gentle remark.

Tom didn't answer for he was deep in thought as his eyes scanned the front of the Cathedral, the statues began to speak to him in a way they hadn't before, in a way he was beginning to understand the language they spoke, "The statues of the angel, the winged lion, the winged ox and the eagle what do they represent?"

"That's a good question", Marie commented trying to answer Tom's question, "I believe the Angel is the symbol of St. Matthew, the winged lion the symbol of St. Mark, The Ox, St. Luke and the St. John the Evangelist the Eagle".

"Do you by any chance know who they were the patrons of, because I suspect there's a clue that relates all these saints together", Tom asked engaging Marie in a conversation he hoped would gain then further advancement down the path to the final truth.

"You're not asking much", Marie complained, "St. Matthew is the patron of accountants and Salerno, St. Mark the patron of Barristers and Venice, St. Luke the patron of Artists, Physicians and Surgeons, now St. John the Evangelist, not to be confused with the John The Baptist, was the patron of the Knights Templar and is currently the patron of The Freemasons".

"The Knights Templar?" an astonished Tom queried in bewilderment, "The same Knights Templar who were the original protectors of the Holy Grail?"

"The alleged Holy Grail", corrected Marie, "Yes those Knights Templars".

"You know", Tom said observing Marie's knowledge of the Saints and all things related, "there's one thing that puzzles me about you".

"What's that?" chirped Marie as she welcomed Tom's comment.

"Your knowledge of the saints, and the bible, it's a little unsettling", he replied.

"My father was a religious zealot", Marie said with a heavy heart, "we had to attend church every week, as well as being forced to attend Sunday school".

"We?" said an observant Tom, "You mean there's more than one of you?"

"I've got a brother somewhere", a solemn Marie stated, "He's a military man, so I've got no idea where he is right now".

"I'm sorry", a disconsolate Tom apologized to Marie for causing her distress in a time when he needed her more than she needed him.

"It's Ok", Marie said grabbing his hand in comfort, "I get a letter when he feels the need to unburden himself from the troubles of a life in the armed forces, still he's got his military buddies to lean on when tragedy occurs. Where now, now I got you".

"That you have", comforted Tom rubbing his fingers over Marie's hand, he paused for a minute before remembering something

"Something's just occurred to me".

"What's that?" asked Marie who was in need to take her mind from her past, and the heartache that her absent sibling brought her.

"Inspector Mancini said he knew Fossor. I wonder why?" Tom pondered as his eyes turned to that of the cathedral.

"Hmm", puzzled Marie pondering Tom's apt observation, "You know you've got a point, that was kind of strange, I wonder if these two met previously".

"I don't think so", said Tom his brain churning over new conspiracy theories in his head, "Fossor said he didn't know him. Whatever it is Mancini has the upper hand".

"That he does", Marie said a little surprised by Mancini's prior knowledge of Fossor, "But right now, we've got to get an upper hand on this clue, there's an internet cafe within walking distance"

"Ok", said Tom his hand still in union with Marie's, "let's go then".

The cathedral disappeared from view, as Tom and Marie went searching for a search engine, a vast knowledge lay in wait, just a few minute's walk and a few keystrokes away, the anxiety in their hearts hastened their journey to the internet cafe as the passage of time that accompanied them seemed to fly fast like an eagle in flight. The desire to find a clue in the statues and the bas-de-relief's on the front of the city's capital religious icon, overwhelming their need to slow the pace of their footsteps.

"Here we are", Marie said as she opened the door to the terminal of terminals, "I'll just go book a computer for us".

"Not before time", Tom remarked as a few particles of water began to splash the ground with a transparent paint scheme, "it's just starting to rain".

The internet cafe was a social point for the intellectual, but socially devoid scholars, all more eager to ride the crest of a wide world web than take in a movie or spend time with their peers. Tom looked at them with distrust, for in his eyes, anyone who lived in the faceless chat rooms was a social outcast, a misfit, who society couldn't pigeon hole, and that put him at unease with those who chose this life style.

"You're not entirely comfortable are you Tom", Marie said observing his darting eyes, moving side to side in his head.

"It's not that", he commented, "I just don't get this whole faceless dating scene".

"There's nothing to get", Marie said as she sat down on a chair in front of an illuminated computer, "it is what it is. Ok what do you need to know?"

"Let me see", said Tom as he began to write on paper beside the computer.

St. Matthew	St.Mark	St.John	St.Luke
Accountants	Barristers	Templar	Artists
Salerno	Venice	Freemasons	Physicians Surgeons
Genesis	Messianic Prophecies	New Testament	Last Judgement

"Is there anything on St. Luke and the Last Judgment?"

"The Last Judgment is the final and eternal judgment by God of all nations after the resurrection of the dead and the Second Coming", Marie read from the computer screen.

"Can you check the quote of the second Coming?" asked Tom.

"Book Of Revelations Chapter 20, parts 12 to 15, 'And I saw the dead, small and great, stand before God; and the books were opened: and another book was opened, which is the book of life: and the dead were judged out of those things which were written in the books, according to their works.

And the sea gave up the dead which were in it; and death and delivered up the dead which were in them: and they were judged every man according to their works.

And death and hell were cast into the lake of fire. This is the second death. And whosoever was not found written in the book of life was cast into the lake of fire'"

"What's this book of life?" Tom asked not entirely certain whether it was metaphor for something else, or indeed it truly was a book.

"It's supposed to be a register of those who are worthy of life, those whose names do not appear are sentenced to death".

"Doesn't give us anything really does it? Ok how about a reference to St. Luke then?"

"There is no direct reference to St. Luke in the Last Judgment; however St. Luke was used as a reference for the Last Judgment".

"Who wrote the Book of Revelations in which the Last Judgment appears?" Tom queried.

"Ahh", said Marie pinpointing a good source of information, "John the Evangelist wrote the Book of Revelations in the New Testament. It also states that the Book of Life is mentioned six times in the Book of Revelations".

"So there is a connection between the statues of St. John the Evangelist and that of St. Luke. St. Mark is the patron of Venice correct?"

"Yes correct", confirmed Marie understanding the link between St.Mark and Venice.

"So we've got Venice, Book of Revelations, and Last Judgment. Hmmmmmmm. What's the connection? What's the connection?", Tom pondered as he sat deep in thought.

"Hold on a minute", Marie spluttered in excitement causing everyone in the place to stop what they were doing and stare at Tom and Marie in disgust for breaking the silence, "There's actually a St. Mark's Basilica in Venice, which contains a Poor Man's Bible".

"What the hell is a Poor Man's Bible?" queried Tom puzzled at the term used.

"It's basically a bible in a pictorial form, it's called a Poor Man's Bible because the majority of poor were unable to read or write, so it was a good way of spreading the bible's message without having to read it yourself. There's one in St. Mark's Basilica called the Pala d'Oro (or the Golden Pall, a Pall is a cloth used to cover a casket at funerals) and on which there is?"

"A picture of St. Matthew?" Tom asked in eager anticipation.

"A picture of St. Matthew", a gleeful Marie stated, "You were right Tom there was a clue, and the clue points to this Poor Man's Bible in Venice".

Tom and Marie, especially Tom, were ecstatic, for they had their next destination, a place, a physical item, which they could study and hope upon hope find the next clue in their pursuit of the truth.

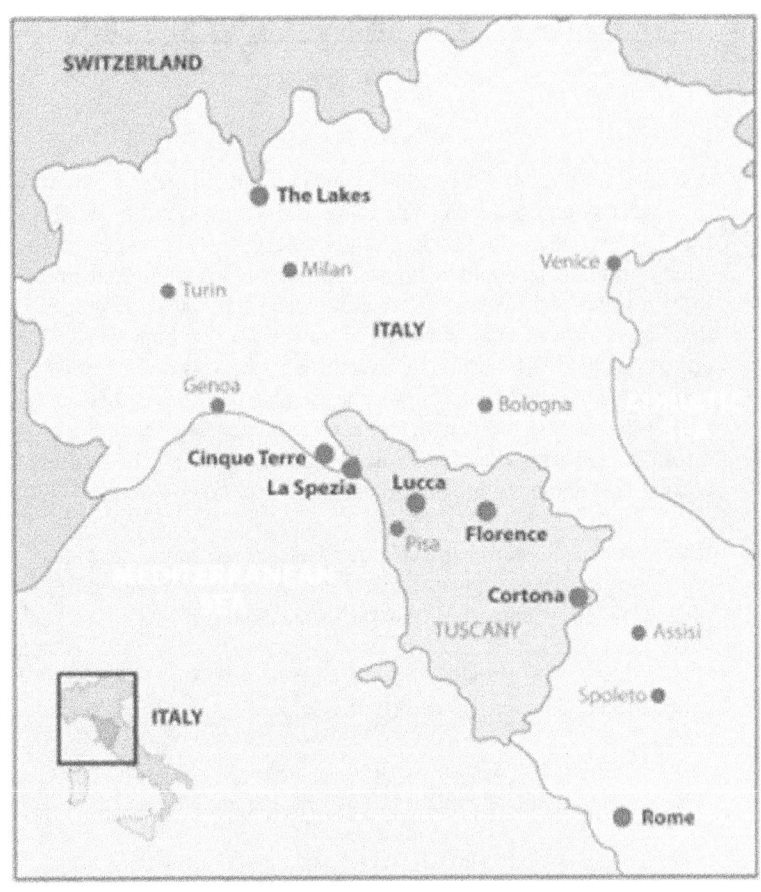

TUSCANY
ITALY

CHAPTER XXXVII

A small little church, in a small little non descript village, in a part of the Tuscan countryside which no one (unless they were hopelessly lost) visited, was the perfect hiding place for a man of Fossor's talents, for here he could be himself and devote what time he could to his master and his master's bidding. The religious ceremonies that he performed daily without fail, underlined his brain washed attitude to his work and that's exactly what he was brainwashed, brainwashed by someone who was the member of a society that held great power and wealth, enough of each to influence the thinking of a man, a man who would without hesitation, kill in a split second and not care about the life he had taken.

His entrance to his chosen place of rest signaled the verger out of his hiding place, who was pleased to see the return of his commanding officer, "Good Afternoon Mr. Fossor sir, pleasant trip?"

"Not really Lucio, I had a slight mishap as you can see" Fossor confided showing the concerned Verger his wounded prehensile extremity.

"Oh my, how did that happen Mr. Fossor?" inquired the Verger.

"Hunting accident Lucio", replied Fossor, "Can you have some water sent to my quarters so I can take care of it".

"Certainly Mr. Fossor. Oh Mr. Fossor sir before I forget, there's someone waiting for you in the confessional booth", answered the Verger.

"I don't usually take confession at this time of day", Fossor reminded the Verger, who was usually more adherent to his daily routines than at times he was.

"I'm sorry Mr. Fossor sir", apologized the Verger, "but he was most insistent".

"Thank you Lucio, I will see him straight away then. God Bless You", Fossor said as he made his way to the structure where sins were forgiven, leaving the Verger to undertake his master's bidding.

The unimpressive structure that lay in one corner of his church, had the shadow of a man sitting waiting, waiting for Fossor to come in and forgive the sins that he had undertaken.

"Forgive me Father for I have sinned", confessed the mysterious man as Fossor entered the priest's side of the confessional booth.

"How many days since your last confession my child?" asked Fossor.

"My last confession was during the feast of St. Peter".

"During the feast of St. Peter you say? You must be very troubled, my son. Why don't you unburden yourself with the message you carry ".
"My sources tell me, that the two you seek are currently in transit to the town of St. Mark's bones."

"Thank you my son. Have you any other sins you wish to unburden yourself from", Fossor said understanding the nature of the hidden message.

"The police man you have come across is from the House of Medici".

"Ah, an old enemy", Fossor snarled as he recognized the name of his family's executioner, "Thank you my child, you may depart now".

"One last thing Father", prompted the man who hid in the shadows, "My Master wishes to inform you, that failure is not an option and to remind you that the consequences, should you fail to carry out his wishes, will be the termination of your contract".

"Thank you", replied Fossor as the gravity of his mission set in, for the details set in the contract were specific, either the two specified in the contract would be terminated or he would. For a brief moment he sat motionless, pondering his next move, a move that would either mean the fulfillment of the contract or the end of his own life. He left the safety of the confessional booth, and set off slowly towards his own private quarters in need of nutrients, not only physical nutrients but nutrients for his faith, for the first time since he could remember, his faith had let him down, for the first time he had failed those who contacted him and this would be the last time, for he knew that those who employed him would not except failure.

The plainly decorated room that was his own private quarters, was very dark, for there was no light source that illuminated the shadows and that suited him. He thought better when the light was not influencing his judgment, the only light he cared for, was the light of truth that impaled his heart with a stake of pure devotion to the Lord. As he entered the room he saw a bowl of water placed that his manservant had put in the room on his bed side table, a towel by the side, and a small silver chalice of red wine. Lucio always went above and beyond the call of duty that was what he expected, it showed Fossor how devoted to him he was, at times it made him feel a little uneasy, but for the majority of the time he was pleased.

Fossor sat on the corner of the bed, leaving the door ajar for light, and opened the top drawer of the bed side table, where he found a small first aid kit, a bible and his own personal hand gun, a small Luger that contained a magazine with 3 bullets in the handle of the weapon.

Taking the bible in one hand, and the first aid kit in the other, he prayed to his Lord to give him strength, not only to heal himself, but to give him the strength and the guile he needed to kill those two under warrant of death.

As he completed his prayer, he opened the first aid kit and removed the tweezers from protective cover that held the medical equipment in safe, clean, storage. Slowly very slowly, he dug the tweezers into the gaping wound, an instant hit of pain struck as the instrument triggered the nerve endings sending impulses of agony to his brain. He gritted his teeth through the anguish as the bullet from the Inspector's handgun was removed from his hand. Seeing the foreign object detached from the break in the skin, he began to stitch it closed with the needle and thread contained within the medical kit.

Fossor examined the bullet closely with an all seeing eye, angry, not at the Inspector, but at himself for being allowed to be hurt by the enemy of his forefathers, "You my little friend", Fossor cursed the bullet, "Are most annoying, you've caused me to lose my prey, you've caused me to fail my master, you've cause me to fail my Lord, as penance you will be fed into the belly of the beast". He leaned forward to the bedside table for the silver chalice that contained the blood of Jesus, paused for a moment to blaspheme those who had done him wrong, before he placed the bullet in his mouth, and with a mouthful of the wine his friend Lucio had brought, swallowed the projectile into the pit of his stomach.

"Are you okay?" inquired the concerned verger peering into the private chambers of his master.

"Yes I'm fine, my faithful friend", replied Fossor with a smile on his face, "Come we have much work to do".

"Oh good", stated Lucio as he anticipated Fossor's instructions with baited breath, "Another hunt?"

"Yes my friend", answered Fossor placing an arm on the shoulder of his verger, "another hunt".

Lucio grinned with malice as the prospect of a safari into the shadow jungle to capture big game sent his pulse into overdrive. It wasn't the first time Fossor had relied on his ingenuity in luring their quarry out into the open and he hoped in his heart that it wouldn't prove to be the last either.

VENICE
ITALY

CHAPTER XXXVIII

Another city, another time, another dead end? Tom wondered if the city of Venice would actually lead them another step closer to the truth, or whether it was just a wild goose chase, he was beginning to suspect it was the latter but he was open to the thought that this could be the real deal, in which case what was wrong with Jesus having a true bloodline? He didn't have any thoughts either way so he decided to consult the fountain of all knowledge in such areas, his partner in crime, Marie.

"So Marie", Tom said as the two of them walked the streets of Venice, taking in the sights and sounds of the wonders of the Italian city, "just suppose there's a blood line of Jesus alive today, what's the implication, I mean what's the bigger picture?"

Marie realizing Tom was asking a hypothetical responded, "If there is a blood line of Jesus, then that means he had a partner, if he had a partner that means he probably never died on the cross, if he never truly died on the cross then who did? Did someone else die on the cross instead of him? If so then that means Jesus is not the true Messiah, in which the whole of the western world's knowledge on religion has been based on a lie".

"So this could be possibly exposing the whole of religion as a complete fabrication made up by someone?" Tom asked, as the implications of the quest dawned on him, "If so then why?"

"Let's look at it like this Tom", Marie said continuing her hypothetical response to Tom's question, "Who would have the knowledge of the lie and would profit from the myth of religion being based on the lie?"

"The only people I could think of would be", he stopped in his thoughts for the gravity of the situation became apparent, "Would be the church".

"And which church has been the most dominant in shaping man's ideological thoughts and beliefs?" Marie said lowering her voice.

"You surely don't mean?" asked Tom who stood still in his tracks and waited for Marie to confirm his suspicions.

Marie nodded and confirmed what Tom had concluded, "Yes the Vatican".

"So what do we do now then?" a little disturbed Tom queried.

"For now", stated Marie as her role as not only a confidant, but an intellectual equal, "we continue to follow the trail of evidence and that means we head off to St. Mark's Basilica".

"Times a ticking then", said Tom understanding Marie's logical progression of events, and it was for their progression down the path they had chosen was being followed closely, not only by Fossor, but Fossor's employer, for they were frightened, and they had good reason to be frightened, for if these two individuals revealed the truth, then they would have a lot of difficult questions to answer, for with every new clue Tom and Marie discovered they moved a step closer to the truth.

"So if the truth gets revealed", asked Tom as they entered St. Mark's Square, "what happens to the church?"

"That", replied Marie, "will be the $60,000 dollar question, but you should think too about what happens if the truth doesn't get revealed".

"The lie perpetuates, and they continue to worship a false god", stated Tom, "which ironically sounds a bit like what they have accused other people doing, through the passage of time".

"And the good thing about this", Marie argued as they walked slowly through St. Mark's Square, "is they've got no one to answer to".

"Isn't that a little dangerous?", a perturbed Tom asked.

"It's more than a little dangerous", she concluded, "It's very dangerous. Think about it, you've got no one to answer to but yourself, you could basically get away with anything you wanted to".

"Even murder?"

"Even murder", Marie stated as a rock pigeon fell head long into the concrete only a few feet from them, "What the hell?"

Shortly another one did the same thing running head long into the concrete, then another, followed by another and soon dozens upon dozens of rock pigeons were dropping like flies from the sky above. Like a plague of locusts they fell onto St. Mark's square, falling to their death at the feet of scared tourist's running for cover under the safety of the Procuratie Nuove and Procuratie Vecchie. Tom and Marie followed the lead of everyone else, and darted the barrage of avian missiles into the protective safety of the buildings around them.

An eternity passed before the reign of terror ended, thousands upon thousands of dead and dying birds lay in the square, piled up like rotten corpses like victims of the bubonic plague as it swept its way through Europe during the 14th century. People stood and stared at the carnage in front of them, disbelieving what occurred, the Venetian pigeons that were an iconic symbol of Venice lying in ruins at their feet.

"It's a sign from God", screamed a distraught woman overcome with emotion at the sight of death all around, "It's a sign from God.

Tom turned to Marie who was visibly shaken by the biblical event that just happened "F...F...Fossor", she cried in emotional distress, "F...F...Fossor did this".

"Are you sure?" Tom asked placing a comforting arm around Marie, trying to alleviate the anxiety she was feeling.

"Y...Y...Yes I'm certain of", stuttered Marie trying to calm down her pulse and her breathing to a more normal level, "He...He...He thinks he's God".

"If your right, then that means he's here in Venice, watching us, watching every move we make".

"We...We...We better move on then".

"Are you sure Marie?" inquired Tom who was more concerned for his friend's welfare then the quest in hand.

"Yes, I'm sure", she confirmed as her breathing return to a more normal level, "Every minute we spend here gives Fossor extra time and more opportunity to eliminate us from the equation".

Cautiously they circumnavigated the field of the dead as through the corridors of the massing throng they moved, joining the triage at St. Mark's Basilica for the visibly shocked innocent bystanders of the massacre that just took place. Tom and Marie just wanted to escape, escape to a sanctuary whose visual sights would lift their spirits and forget about the events that just unfolded before them.

"The Pala d'Oro", Marie confirmed as they found the relic they were searching for. The golden brilliance and the ornate decoration of the artistry took their breath away, for a small portion of time, neither one spoke to the other, lost in the golden glow that emanated from the Poor Man's Bible.

"Wow!", exclaimed Tom in wonderment.

"Double Wow", agreed Marie fascinated by the intricate carvings that scarred the artwork with a hand of delicate precision, "That is truly awe inspiring".

"All we've got to do now is find St. Matthew in it", Tom reminded as his eyes began to search for the Saint that the statues in Orvieto foretold. Time after time they found an image they thought resembled that of St. Matthew, but it wasn't until they found one in particular, a bearded man reading a book with a halo of what appeared to be small pearls, that they became convinced that this piece of art contained another clue.

"There are some letters in the book he is holding", Marie said staring intently at a group of minuscule letters.

"What are they?" Tom asked anxiously.

"I think", Marie answered, "they could be, *L,I,B,E,R,G,E,N* or *H,E,R,A,T,I,O,N* or *H,* the N's are very difficult to read, I and S".

"*LIBERGENERATIONIS*? Is that an anagram?"

"*LIBERGENERATIONIS*? No, No, It's not an anagram its two separate words Liber and Generationis", Marie responded with a combination of bewilderment and excitement, "It's Latin for The Book of the Generation, or the genealogy of Jesus Christ".

"So what we suspected is correct then?" Tom asked Marie as the two of them took in the gravity of their discovery.

"It appears so", affirmed Marie daring not to believe what they had found.

"So we've got the correct piece of art, so where's the next clue?" Tom queried, "Is that all there is on that particular panel?"

"I'm afraid so", apologized Marie as she restudied the panel looking for another clue, but to no avail.

Tom thought for a moment, before he asked "If it's not on the front, it's got to be?"

"On the back", Marie answered in excitement. She was pleased Tom had not given up so easily this time, and she was delighted he was beginning to think outside the box. As Tom and Marie ventured around the back of the canvas they found a wooden container within which they found a detailed painting bearing a ship sailing with a saintly man at the helm, at the bottom the words "*MAGR. PAULUS CU LUCA. ET IOHE FILIIS SUIS PINXERUNT [HOC OPUS]*" were signed.

Fig VIII - The painting of St. Mark returning his own body back to
Venice on the rear of the Pala d'Oro

"I know this work of art", Marie commented as she observed the detailed work of art in her view, "Its a representation of a story in the Golden Legends in which St. Mark appears on a ship carrying his own dead body in transit from Alexandria to Venice. The translation at the bottom reads *'Master Paul with his sons Luke and John, painted [this work]'*".

"This gives us Matthew (on the Front), Mark (on the rear), Luke and John the four writers of the New Testament as well as Paul", stated Tom as his eyes were transfixed on the painting, "and this Golden Legends book we've come across this before. Once could be explained as an accidental coincident, twice tells me we need to find out more about this Golden Legends book".

"I agree", remarked Marie who was in total accord with Tom's plan of action, "If we ignore this now, we could be missing out on an important part of the puzzle".

Tom and Marie left behind the Pala d'Oro as well as any suspicions about a coincidence in the knowledge of the genealogy of Jesus, for now they were certain that this was the task they had been given to investigate. Whether it was good or whether it was bad, remained to be seen, for now they were happy in the knowledge that they had found messages that corroborated all their previous clues, that there was a true bloodline of Jesus.

CHAPTER XXXIX

With every step Tom and Marie took, they seemed to edge just a little closer to their ultimate goal. Inspector Mancini wished that he had the same luck too, for nothing about the dead man they found in the Orvieto Cathedral made sense. Questions by the score, answers by the few. How did one man get the torture device plus the weight of the intended victim and raise the crucifix to a vertical base? How did he manage to cordon off a part of the Cathedral without anyone noticing?

Then there was the coroner's report too. That was making no sense at all. It was a report that also held many mysteries, mysteries that did not make sense. The victim had been flogged, poisoned, and then physically attached to the crucifix with nails that were of a unique design, for each nail used to attach the murdered man's appendages to the cross contained a letter. The nails for the hands were engraved with the letter I, the nail for the left foot was engraved with an N and finally the right foot with a letter R. Then the poison used itself, was something he hadn't seen or heard of before, arsenic laced with phosphorus. Why on earth would someone use a poison that hadn't been around since the time of the Renaissance?

Nothing made any sense at all. The only thing Inspector Mancini was certain of, was that there had been more than one person involved in the death of this man, and he was determined to find out who that was. He let out a breath of despair as he went back and forth from the coroner's report to the crime scene photos, hoping that something would inspire his malnourished brain, nothing came to pass so he banged his head repeatedly on the table out of total frustration. He was just about to call it a night when something caught his attention, something he had not noticed before.

"Dio, voi spola italiana stupida'", he swore as for the first time his mind produced a thought of pure genius, "The letters on the nails, it spells out I.N.R.I., that's usually found above Jesus' head on the cross, but why put them on the nails instead? I've got to find out more about these letters".

The cogs in his brain, turned the cogs in the computer on his desk, he looked at the results that it presented him and to his surprise it gave a long list of answers, "I've got to put it into context with the rest of the clues", Mancini thought to himself as his eyes darted up and down the screen, the trouble was not one of them really stood out, until one appeared to him that made his skin turn cold in fear.

"*I.N.R.I - Iustum Necare Reges Impious , It is just to exterminate or annihilate impious or heretical kings, governments or rulers, used by the Jesuits to induct novices into the order*", he paused in his reading when he read the warning notice that accompanied the text, "*WARNING - Jesuits are considered highly fanatical and must be viewed with extreme caution. It is acknowledged that this extremist faction of the Church has killed in order to protect their faith*".

Slowly the implication of the death of the man Tom knew began to sink in, as did the realization that everyone connected with the ritualistic killing was in deep peril, "Fucking hell I've got to warn Mr. Raust. It is more serious than we thought" he swore leaping to his feet, his hastened departure from his office noticed by everyone in the station, including his superior officer, who shook his head and went about his own affairs. He knew that once Mancini got the sniff of a clue, he was like a bulldog, not one to let go until the perpetrator had been brought to justice.

Inspector Mancini hurried himself to the car lot where his own car was at the front of the queue, waiting for him to tear off in search for Tom and Marie, however this time something was amiss, for as soon as he entered the vehicle Fossor appeared from behind the rear seat. "Hello Medici" he quipped with a menacing look in his eyes. Mancini only had time for a brief obscenity, before he was anesthetized by his enemy with a swift veil of ethyl ether to his face.

Time seemed to pass quickly for Mancini, for as soon as he was asleep he was waking up, waking up to the sight of a naked Fossor kneeling before two flags, one yellow and white, the other a black

*(Translation – "God you stupid Italian cop")

flag with a dagger and red cross above a skull and crossbones, as he knelt Fossor renewed his dedication to his faith, "*I, Fossor Dirichlet, Now in the presence of Almighty God, the Blessed Virgin Mary, the blessed Michael the Archangel, the blessed St. John the Baptist, the holy Apostles St. Peter and St. Paul and all the saints and the sacred hosts of heaven, and to you, my ghostly father, the Superior general of the Society of Jesus, founded by St. Ignatius of Loyola, in the Pontificate of Paul the Third, and continued to the present, do by the womb of the Virgin, the matrix of God, and the rod of Jesus Christ, declare and swear, that his holiness the Pope is Christ's Vicergent and is the true and only Head of the Catholic or Universal Church throughout the earth; and that by virtue of the keys of binding and loosing, given to his Holiness by my Savior, Jesus Christ, he hath power to dispose heretical kings, princes, states, commonwealths and governments, all being illegal without his sacred confirmation and that they may safely be destroyed*".

Fossor arose from his place of dedication and turned to see Inspector Mancini fully conscious, "Ah the Medici has awoken from his sleep".

"I don't know what you're on about, you lunatic", snarled the bemused Inspector uncertain of his surroundings.

"You are Medici are you not?" queried Fossor.

"I'm not", Mancini reiterated.

"YOU ARE MEDICI", Fossor shouted in the face of his foe.

"WHAT THE FUCK IS A MEDICI?" Mancini yelled unafraid of the deranged man in front of him.

"YOU ARE DESCENDANT OF MEDICI, MEDICI IS THE HOUSE OF MY FAMILIES EXECUTIONER", Fossor shouted with venom into the eyes and the soul of Mancini.

"I'm what?" Mancini asked.

"You are descendant of Medici; my master has proof of your bloodline".

"So there is more than one of you?"

"We are more than one. We are infinite".

"Infinite in your stupidity", snapped Mancini at his tormentor's brainwashed attitude.

"If we are stupid, then how is it we captured you Medici?"

Mancini did not answer, for Fossor was correct he had been captured by this extremist of the church, the worrying thing was, it was all a little too easily done.

"No reply? I thought not", stated Fossor as he gloated over Mancini's indisposition, "You police are all the same, stupid in your wisdom, far too predictable, far too easily caught. As we speak right now Medici, my manservant Lucio is causing a little distraction for your little friends in Venice."

"My friends in Venice? You mean Mr. Raust and Miss Dubois? What have you done to them?"

"Let me just say Lucio had definitely put the cat amongst the pigeons", an evil laugh echoed in the privacy of Fossor's dominion fully aware of the biblical event that Lucio, his verger, had just undertaken for his master. Poison in the bird seed that the tourists fed the Venetian pigeons initiating the sequence of events leading to the plague descending on St. Mark's square in Venice.

"What do you want?" Mancini asked.

"What do I want? I want to kill you, but alas my master in his infinite wisdom has other plans for you, but for the mean time you are my prisoner, so get comfortable Medici, we're in for a wait, short or long, depends on how quick your friends are at putting the pieces of the puzzle together".

Inspector Mancini could do nothing, but hope and pray that Tom and Marie were wise enough not only to figure out what they needed too, but also wise enough to sense that danger was fast approaching, for he was certain that once Fossor cornered them, the outcome would be that of certain death for either Tom and Marie or Fossor himself. He hoped that it would be the latter, for he was under the impression that there was more to this than meets the eye.

CHAPTER XL

Secrets once hidden from the world, were now revealing all, mysteries unsolved now became all too clear as they gave up their messages, messages that lead to other portals that contained more hidden Arcana, for every clue solved another one replaced its predecessor, but as they became knowledge to those who sought it, further down the path of enlightenment they went, until one hidden secret gave them more than one alternative. They had come to a crossroads in their quest, choosing the wrong path might lead them to a dead end, choosing the right one would enable them to pursue their pilgrimage.

"I'm not sure which way to turn", Tom admitted to Marie as they sat in The Bibliotheca Nazionale Marciana (National Library of St. Marks) located in the city of Venice, "We've got the book, I'm just not entirely sure whether to open the book and read, or find out more about its author".

"What does your gut instinct tell you?" Marie quizzed Tom as they sat pondering their next move.

"My instinct tells me we ought to find out more about St. Paul in this book, as he was the odd one out", Tom answering the question best he could.

"I don't understand, what do you mean he was the odd one out?" Marie asked not entirely sure of Tom's logical progression.

"You remember the Pala d'Oro had Matthew on the front, and the painting of Mark on the reverse, with Master Paul alongside his son's Luke and John as the creators of the piece of art?" Tom queried Marie.

"I do", affirmed Marie.

"Well Matthew, Mark, Luke and John, were the four evangelists who were supposed to have written the New Testament in the bible, where as Paul was never a part of it, so why mention him?"

"That's a good point, why mention him at all? Maybe he's the connection to the next clue".

"That's what I figured", commented Tom as he slowly opened the pages of a copy of The Golden Legends, "If I'm wrong then at least we can come back to Jacopo de Varagine, the original scribe of the book". One by one he turned the pages of the book to St. Paul, to his and Marie's surprise a small, neatly folded piece of paper lay in the crease of the book's spine.

"What's that?" Marie asked as she saw the mystery that lay before their eyes.

"I don't know but I intend to find out ", answered Tom placing the paper between his thumb and forefinger, "That's strange."

"What is?" a bewildered Marie inquired.

"This paper's a little warm", said Tom as he unfurled the paper to reveal a message contained within.

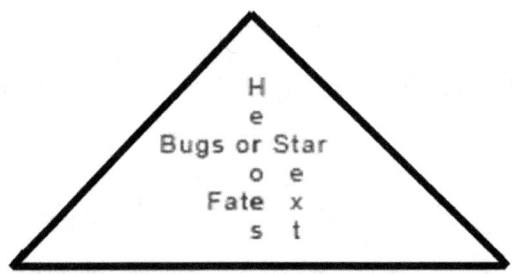

Fig. VIII - The secret
Message Tom and Marie found in the Golden Legends

"This makes no sense at all", commented Marie as Tom handed her the piece of paper, then for a little while her cognitive reasoning sprung into life as it began to recognize the pattern shown, "Hold on a moment we've seen this before".

"We have? Where?" said Tom astounded by Marie's statement.

"On the back of the warning note we got whilst we were stopping in Florence", she replied as her eyes began to search further for more clues.

"What the hell is going on Marie?" a disturbed Tom asked.

"I don't know", she answered, "but what I do know is this is not the hand of Fossor. This is someone else. Who? I don't know. Friend or foe? Impossible to say, but they must be watching us, for they left this paper in here deliberately for us to find".

"So we are on the correct path then?"

"I assume we are, otherwise we wouldn't have found this. This is all very bewildering".

"So what do we do?" Tom quizzed, his eyes transfixed on the pyramid puzzle in front of them, staring, thinking, lost within the confines of his own mind.

"I think you better solve that before your mind explodes", Marie commented noticing Tom was in deep thought over the appearance of what could be another puzzle for them to solve.

"Oh my god I'm sorry", he apologized as he began to stop receiving messages from beyond the grave. He often went into a trance like state when he was thinking; it made those around him slightly uncomfortable as he just stared off into space. His brother Jack, as a young boy, would often laugh and say he was receiving communication signals from an invisible alien space craft overhead. So he pretended he was getting plans of a secret invasion force that started by taking over the minds of the owner's of the corner shop not far from their home.

"So what you thinking about then Einstein?" Marie asked once Tom returned safely to Planet Earth.

"I was just wondering", he replied communicating his idea to Marie, "If this pyramid puzzle is a form of a test".

"A test?"

"Yes a test".

"What makes you say that?" Marie pondered a little uncertain at Tom's wayward statement.

"The first time this shape was in the form of a warning letter about the impending disaster at the hotel. The second time its, here, in this book, in a library in Venice. I don't think it's malicious. I believe it's sent to challenge us".

"If it is a challenge, then what does the message say?"

"I believe", Tom answered, "it's a form of an anagram. Take the words *Bugs or Star* for instance, if you unscramble those letters you get the word Strasbourg".

"What about the other three words in Strasbourg then?"

"You mean Heroes Fate Text?"

Marie nodded, waiting for Tom's analytical engine to provide the details that she was certain it would give them.

Tom contemplated the meaning of *'Heroes Fate Text'*, the power of his brain producing enough heat to turn water into steam, "Street of the Axe" he stated as vapor began to release his thoughts into the purified stratosphere.

"Street of the Axe, Strasbourg?"

"I believe so".

"So does that really exist then?"

"I don't know", confessed Tom uncertain if the Street of the Axe really existed in the French city of Strasbourg, "There will be only one way of finding out though".

"If it really is the Street of the Axe, Strasbourg", stated Marie as she looked on the nearby bookshelf containing maps of major cities of the world, "Then the Street of the Axe will be in French".

"Which is?"

"Which is Rue de la Hache", translated Marie bringing over a city map relating to the French city in question, before laying it flat on the table in front of them.

"Ah here it is", noted Tom pointing to Rue de la Hache on the street map, "It's not far from the cathedral either".

"I wonder if that's significant." Marie said as her thoughts went racing ahead like a locomotive on full power trundling its way through the countryside.

"Why don't we find out", Tom speculated searching through the pile of books in their possession, before allocating the resource material they needed, "*Strasbourg Cathedral was erected by Saint Arbogast in the latter part of the 7th century*". Tom paused in his tracks as once more the number seven surfaced its way into the equation.

"What is it?" Marie interjected wondering why Tom had stopped quoting from the book he held in his hands.

"Seven", Tom muttered in disbelief, scarcely believing the prominence of the number in his quest so far.

"I'm sorry", Marie replied, "For a minute I thought you said the number seven".

"I did", confirmed Tom before explaining the reoccurrence time and time again of the number in his journey so far. July 7th 2007, 7am, plane seat G7, hotel room number 412 (adding up to 7), time and time again the number seven forced its way into the equation and was beginning to unsettle him a little.

Marie shook her head in disbelief at Tom's love/hate relationship with the number seven. It made no sense to her either; it did however make her suspect that all this had been preordained by those who had prior knowledge of their quest. Who and for what reason would remain a mystery until their quest was fulfilled, "What else does it say on the Strasbourg Cathedral?" Marie prompted trying to get Tom back on track.

"Oh my God yes", he apologized forgetting about the number seven (for a little while at least), "*'Strasbourg Cathedral was erected by Saint Arbogast in the latter part of the 7th century on the base of a former temple dedicated to the Virgin Mary. Charlemagne replaced the first Cathedral with that of a more impressive structure in the 8th century. Recent excavations revealed that the Carolingian Cathedral had three naves and three apses '*".

"Is that it?" sighed Marie who was secretly hoping for more information than was given.

"I'm afraid so", shrugged Tom slightly disappointed by the ineffectual tangent they just went on, "What do we do now?"

"For now we continue on processing the information we have in front of us on St. Paul, but we do so with one eye on the truth in front, and one eye on our enemies in the back", Marie said warning Tom not to get too complacent.

Seconds, turned into minutes, minutes into hours with Tom and Marie not making any head way getting more frustrated as each second they spent analyzing the data in front of them, not getting any where fast, making mistakes and losing precious time.

"I don't think there's anything here", Marie complained to Tom as she re-read the St. Paul's story in the Golden Legend.

"Maybe, just maybe", stated Tom as he lay back in his seat with head cupped in his hands "we're taking this too literally. Is there another St. Paul that isn't a book?"

"There's an alter to him and St. James in the St. Marks Basilica, there's also a Basilica of St. Paul outside the Walls in Rome, there's", said Marie but she never finished what she was about to say, for it inspired Tom to formulate yet another idea.

"In the Golden Legends, St. Paul is a Hermit, and hermits usually live alone don't they on the outside of society? I'm just wondering if it's trying to tell us to look at the Basilica of St. Paul Outside the Walls", said Tom as his thoughts turned to that of this Basilica in question.

"I think we've got a book somewhere here about ancient Basilica's in Rome", Marie said as she began to search the pile of books that lay in front of them, "Ah here it is, St. Paul's, St. Paul's, where are you, ah here we are. *The basilica is one of four churches considered to be the Great Basilicas of Rome (the other three being, St. John Lateran, St. Mary Major and St. Peter) was built by Emperor Constantine over the burial place of St. Paul after he was executed. The four major or four papal basilicas along with St. Lawrence Outside the Walls, are often referred to as the 'five patriarchal' basilicas of Rome. St. Lawrence Outside the Walls is one of the seven pilgrim churches of Rome, the remaining 2 basilicas being minor are Santa Croce in Gerusalemme, (The Basilica of the Holy Cross in Jerusalem), and the San Sebastiano fuori le mura (Saint Sebastian Outside the Walls), although this was replaced in the year 2000 by Pope John Paul II by the Santuario Della Madonna del Divino Amore.*"

"I've got an idea", stated Tom as he went to a computer located in their vicinity, "let's see if the location of the Basilicas produce a pattern".

"What are you thinking?" a suspicious Marie asked.

"I've got a feeling that they could be in these locations for a specific reason", replied Tom as he settled himself down into the driver's seat, "First let us put in the location of the four major ones, Peter and Paul, John and Mary, then we'll do the three minor ones, Lawrence, The Holy Cross and Sebastian".

As he entered the information into the computer, Marie reminded him about St. Lawrence being one of the five patriarchal basilicas too and that he needed to join it up to the four major basilicas. Upon finishing the data entry Tom and Marie sat back in amazement at the picture that was upon the screen.

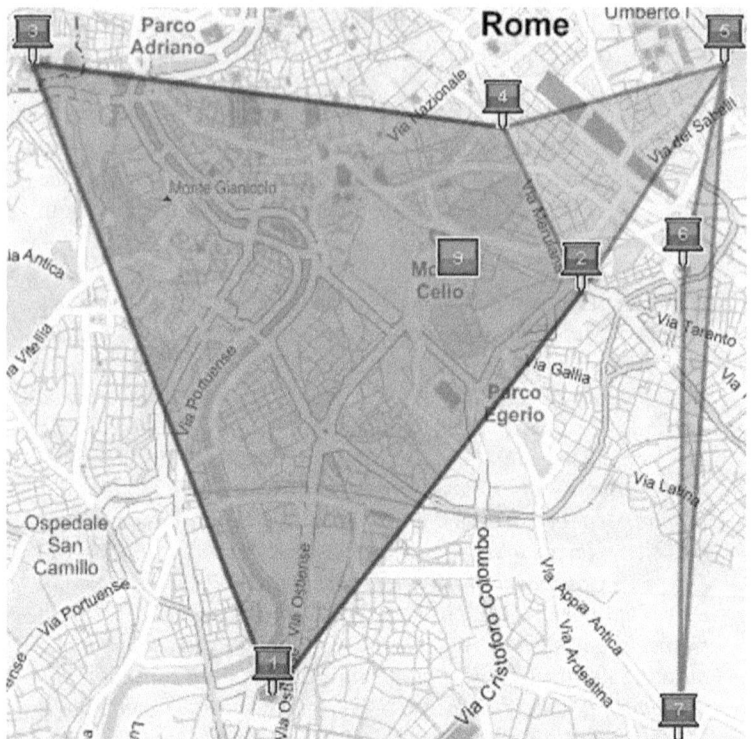

(Key : 1 - St. Paul, 2 - St. Mary, 3 - St. Peter, 4 - St. John, 5 - St. Lawrence, 6 - Holy Cross of Jerusalem, 7 - St. Sebastian, 8 - Directly under 9, 9 - Five Patriarchal basilica)

<u>*Fig IX* - PATTERN PRODUCED ON TOM & MARIE'S COMPUTER SCREEN</u>

"That's an axe isn't it?" Marie echoed with an air of disbelief.

"Yes that is an axe", confirmed Tom as he too looked on in disbelief, not daring to believe what they had discovered, "What's the symbolism behind it though?"

"It's got several, from destruction and creation, to the execution of military duty, but the one that has the most significance is that during Roman times it was bundled together with white birch rods called a Fasces to represent a symbol of power, usually over life and death", Marie answered as she recalled the purpose behind the symbol of the axe from her text books, "I seem to recall too, a legend belonging to the House of Sforza with regards to an axe. It is all to do with their rise from camp to Duchy. *'The tale goes one day a troop of mercenaries were riding between Ravenna and Bologna, when they came upon a peasant lad cutting wood near his native town of Cotignola. Seeing this young peasant boy they asked him to join their company of mercenaries, his response was a bit unique to say the least, he threw his axe into the branches of an adjacent oak saying "If it stays, I will go"'*, needless to say the axe stuck and the Sforza went forth to found a line of Dukes. Now the Sforza family is important not only in the history of Milan but in the history of Leonardo Da Vinci too".

For the first time in the quest, since Istanbul, Leonardo Da Vinci's name appeared. Whether it was significant or not was open to debate, but there it was and it was something that neither Tom nor Marie could ignore, especially as from the echoes of his existence there came a cry to *'Trust the Works'*. Maybe it was time to do just that, trust the works and follow the path to the place of his most controversial work *The Last Supper.*

Yet there still was a nagging doubt in Tom's mind about the mysterious appearance of the pyramid clue in the Golden Legends book, a nagging doubt that he had, that not only this was a quest for the Bloodline Of Jesus, but a test too, a test to see if he was worthy, worthy of what and by who ? Only time would tell, and that was something he was sure they had plenty of, time.

MILAN
ITALY

CHAPTER XLI

The winds of war that had once swept through the Lombardy plains, were now blowing the winds of change, no longer were the Guelph and Ghibelines drawing blood from each other's offspring. The savages of war turned into the savages of modern day living, gone were the days when brother turned on brother, sons killed fathers, mothers their daughters, peace finally conquered all those with a bloodthirsty heart, for here in Milan, that most infamously famous Italian city, people cared not for the past, but were instead preoccupied with the trappings of life in a modern metropolis, as they fed their hunger for an existence fed on fossil fuel led chariots.

However all was not as it first appeared in this bustling city, for in the Sforza Castle there lay a tower called The Tower Of Bona di Savoia (named after Galeazzo Maria Sforza's widow) and in this tower there was a man hiding, a man whose purpose was to serve and protect his master by whatever means possible, if it meant taking the life (or lives) of those who got too perilously close to undermining the power of the leader of his faith.

"Don't worry", comforted Fossor as he parted the hair of his captive audience with a knife in his possession, "One way or the other it's soon going to be over".

All the prisoner could do was mumble an obscenity, for he was bound and gagged to a chair that was dominant in the center of the room in which they rested.

"Cat got your tongue?" tormented Fossor as he lent forward into the face of the surprisingly calm Inspector Mancini, "You're lucky you wasn't that stupid Turk. I took not only his life but his soul too. Maybe, just maybe, when I've killed those two meddling individuals, I will kill you too", as he venomed the last word of his threat Fossor slammed the sharpened blade through the hand of Mancini, making him scream out in abject agony, "See how it feels Medici?, See how the pain washes over the sins you have committed and cleanses the evil from your feeble body? See how as you scream, the screams of your forefathers cry out in pain too?"

Fossor's demonic possession was now complete, for years of brainwashing had lead him down a path that he had never once contemplated until that fateful night when divine providence and the help of a complete stranger placed him in the hands of the creator, someone who molded and gave birth to this monster of a man. He slowly turned and went to the arch way of the tower that watched over the city beneath and viewed all in his sight with a piercing look of distaste, for his hatred of modern day life was only succeeded by his hatred of those seeking the knowledge which he sought to protect.

"Such a waste", he sighed as Milan sprawled out in front of him, "Such a pity too. It would have been nice to *'convert'* a few more lost souls too. They've no idea how great the joy is of being able to fulfill my true calling in life. What do you say Medici?" he slowly looked over his shoulder with a smile of malice echoed the evil intent in his heart, "Of course you wouldn't understand would you? You don't know your true bloodline do you? You don't know what I know do you? You don't know that you were secretly adopted at the birth of your conception to protect the line of your forefathers? A secret that others have died to protect, a secret that others have killed to extinguish, and now, here you sit, in front of your families victim, begging for your life, how ironic that the tables have been turned Medici".

Fossor's gaze upon the city turned slowly to that of his victim, witnessing the distress that the knowledge he had just imparted upon the unknowing Mancini, "You really didn't know did you? Let me help you out *'old friend'* ", as the last word of his tortuous remark travelled from his brain to his mouth, he quickly removed the foreign object from the hand of the Inspector, "You see", he commented as he smelt the victim's blood on the blade of the knife, "It was never about you, it was always going to be this, you and I, sitting together, mano-a-mano, so to speak, it was always going to be me sitting here holding you at knife point, issuing you threats while you listen bewildered at the history of your family, for you have no idea how long, I'm sorry we have waited for this. Who am I? Who are we? I am descendant of the House of Pazzi, the noble

House of Pazzi, my forefathers were the Pazzi family accused of conspiring to murder Lorenzo de' Medici and Guiliano de Medici in the year of our Lord 1478, but you see the accusers were wrong, so very wrong indeed, for although they did indeed carry out the murders, they were not the instigators, those instigators belonged to the House of Salviati, the papal bankers in Florence. Unfortunately for me and unfortunately for you their line could not be found, so I got the next best thing, YOU, a true descendant of the Medici family, your family should have been wiped out and the Pazzi family should have been the rightful rulers of Florence, BUT NO, YOU MEDICI JUST WOULDN'T DIE WOULD YOU? Still not to worry, we're going to alleviate that little problem soon, real soon".

His promise rang true in the ears of Inspector Mancini, who for the first time since his capture, he fully understood the motives behind his kidnapping, he didn't agree with it, but he fully understood, power, money and greed, all adding to the circumstances that brought himself and Fossor together in this isolated part of the Sforza castle.

Fossor ran his finger along the knife, collecting more blood of Mancini before placing the crimson red finger in his mouth, "Kind of Ironic", he professed swallowing the blood from the knife, "How we sit here in this icon to Milanese rule, a structure to one of the most powerful families ever to grace the lands of Lombardy, when my family has had to endure centuries of distrust and ridicule, I tell you Medici, it stops right here, right now. From this day forward we will stop at nothing until all those who betrayed us have been brought to justice and rightfully claim what is ours. No one and I repeat no one is going to stand in our way", he paused a little pause, wiping more blood from the knife onto his lips, "and not even your little friends can stop me".

The smile on Fossor's face issued the challenge, a challenge that anyone's interference in his own quest for justice would be met with a swift blade to the heart, his narrow mindedness blinding his reasoning. In his heart he was doing what was right, correcting centuries of falsehoods, but in his soul he had just crossed the line from purity to defilement, a line no one returned from, not even those under jurisdiction of a higher authority.

From the depths of his soul, torment began to take over his body like a cleansing rain, washing the damned below, "Your interference has forced me to change my plans for a holy war that would see my master in charge of a New World Order. Trust me Medici it will happen, sooner or later it will happen".

Slowly and purposely he walked over to a small wooden table, which lay alone and forlorn in the corner of the tower. Picking up a jar containing an armored arachnid he ambled his way back to a visibly disturbed Inspector Mancini, "Heterometrus Longimanus. The Black Asian Forest Scorpion native to southern Asia. They inject their venom into the prey until they are paralyzed or dead from a stinger that holds a poison, a toxin that acts on nerve cells. It's not dangerous to the human species but it does make you feel quite uncomfortable. Come here my little beauty".

The glass prison cell which contained the scorpion at bay, had its lid removed, "See how beautiful it looks?" he continued extracting the scorpion by the tail, "What do you think Medici?".

Fossor dangled the scorpion directly over the fear ridden face of Mancini, taunting him with the snipping pincers trying to slice the skin open like a can of sardines, before opening his own mouth and placing the arachnid inside. He held the animal inside for a brief moment, watching Mancini squirm in disgust, before his teeth crushed the outer surface of the Scorpion's outer casing killing it immediately, the viscera swallowed into the pit of his stomach, before dropping the carcass to the floor below.

"This is what I should do you", he snarled his teeth coated with the scorpion's remains, "I should have your flesh rotting in my body, whilst your bones lay scattered on the floor", he paused in his tirade before continuing, "See ? See what you made me do? You made me kill a creature of the Lord. Damn you heathen. DAMN YOU. DAMN.YOU. DAMN YOU".

Quiet solitude followed the anger outburst of a man whose mental stability was in question, he was not psychopathological, he was fully aware of what he was doing and what he was capable of, instead he had his thoughts tampered with, by someone whose motives were more than scrupulous.

Fossor, the glass jar still in his possession, dropped to his knees in anguish and prayed for forgiveness, "Forgive me Father for I have sinned. I have taken your name in vain. I am weak of the mind and of the flesh. I am not worthy to be called a soldier in your service. Please guide me and help me in doing thy work and help me to stop those who seek to tell untruth's about thy name. Give me the fortitude to do what is being asked of me and to perform without question the will of my master". He paused in his incantation, listening carefully to the voice that spoke to him, "I understand and it will be done".

Up from his kneeling position he rose in resurrection of his soul, pondering the word from *'God'* and what form it should take, his eyes glazed, not blinking, and never moving. The hypnotic trance like frenzy he had put himself in, soon wore off and stood in front of Mancini with the glass jar in his hand, waiting purposely for the next instruction from the voice in his head.

"Yes my Lord", he uttered removing the shackle from Mancini's wounded hand. The blood still dripping down from the injury Fossor had caused was running like water into the jar which previously held the condemned scorpion within its translucent wall. Seeing the container was full he placed it on the ground, before gently reshackling, with great care and attention, Mancini's bonds once more.

He stood in front of Mancini, who was still visibly shaken by the *'scorpion incident'*, picked up the glass jar containing the blood of his enemy and took a little mouthful of the hemoglobin wine, gargling it like mouthwash until he was satisfied with the vintage.

For a brief moment the claret jug dangled over his head like a guillotine ready to slice the head of an aristocratic nobleman, before he allowed its contents to fall onto his shaven head below, showering him self with crimson water singing the Hymn "Onward Christian Soldiers" as he did.

> *"Onward, Christian soldiers, marching as to war,*
> *With the cross of Jesus going on before.*
> *Christ, the royal Master, leads against the foe;*
> *Forward into battle see His banners go!*

Onward, Christian soldiers, marching as to war,
With the cross of Jesus going on before.

At the sign of triumph Satan's host doth flee;
On then, Christian soldiers, on to victory!
Hell's foundations quiver at the shout of praise;

Onward, Christian soldiers, marching as to war,
With the cross of Jesus going on before.

Brothers, lift your voices, loud your anthems raise.
Like a mighty army moves the church of God;
Brothers, we are treading where the saints have trod.
We are not divided, all one body we,
One in hope and doctrine, one in charity.

Onward, Christian soldiers, marching as to war,
With the cross of Jesus going on before.

Crowns and thrones may perish, kingdoms rise and wane,
But the church of Jesus constant will remain.
Gates of hell can never 'gainst that church prevail;
We have Christ's own promise, and that cannot fail.
Onward then, ye people, join our happy throng,
Blend with ours your voices in the triumph song.
Glory, laud, and honor unto Christ the King,
This through countless ages men and angels sing.
Onward, Christian soldiers, marching as to war,
With the cross of Jesus going on before".

(Written Sabine Baring-Gould 1865)

Mancini sat spellbound at the torment that was second nature to Fossor, wondering in hope that this was as far as the torture went, for he was unsure how much more he could stomach.

CHAPTER XLII

Time and distance had elapsed between Tom and Marie's journey between Venice and Milan, enough to recognize that this would probably be the last link in the chain of events that would lead them to the truth; they also recognized too that this meant they would eventually end up with Fossor crossing their path. If that was the case then, they had to ready themselves for the battle of their lives and hope that the outcome would be in their favor.

"I don't like it", said Tom to Marie as they sat discussing the absence of their enemy in a restaurant which lay on the Naviglio Grande canal, "He's been too quiet for too long".

"I agree", replied Marie, "And that usually spells trouble, I seem to think he's plotting our demise".

Marie was more correct in her assumption then she realized for that was exactly what Fossor was doing, and he was a lot closer than either of them knew, for he sat in the same restaurant, watching every breath they took.

A lobster, fully cooked his meal for the evening, lay precariously on a ceramic platter, engulfed by a sea of green leaves, lemon wedges and clarified butter. His eyes darting back and forth between the sea creature in front and the prey that lay off in the distance, took little time to reflect on the loss of his childhood. Fossor had been the victim of a heinous crime by the family priest, a trip to the coast organized by the church had turned from a theater of joy into a theater of sexual deviance for the depraved. He tried to live a life of normality, ending up with the typical family, of a wife, two children and a family pet, but eventually his past caught up with him and he slowly spiraled into the depths of his own hell, losing his job, his family and eventually his mind.

The tiger began stalking its prey, waiting for the moment when the trap would be unleashed and the prey would be caught, he paused for a moment watching his quarry in discussion before he summoned a waiter to his table.

"Yes sir", answered the waiter, "How can I help you?"

"Send a bottle of your finest red wine to the couple over there with my compliments", Fossor stated as he discretely pointed to Tom and Marie sat in his line of sight.

"Very good sir", the waiter replied, who disappeared off into the background of the busy restaurant before promptly returning with a fine claret that he lay on Tom and Marie's table, along with a fine pair of drinking vessels.

"What's this?" queried Tom as the unexpected gift was presented to Marie and himself, "We never ordered this".

"That's okay sir, it's the compliments of the man sat over there", the waiter motioned with a hand the direction of the table in which Fossor sat, "Enjoy".

Tom looked towards Fossor eyeing him with a look of disbelief as their eyes met, Fossor seeing that their gift had been received, lifted his glass in utter contempt that made Tom swallow hard as a lump in his throat appeared, "Fuck me, he's here".

"Whose here?" Marie asked as she poured herself and Tom a glass of the fruity yeast driven beverage.

"Frigging Fossor", said Tom quietly taking a large sip of the wine that Fossor had presented them.

"You've got to be kidding me", squeaked Marie as she turned around to witness Fossor's presence in the restaurant. Fossor seeing Marie turn around blew her a gentle kiss from the lips that only recently held the blood of Inspector Mancini on them, "How the hell did he know where we were?"

"I can only assume that he had someone follow us, the question is what we do now?" Tom asked Marie, but the lady in his company could not answer for the menacing figure of Fossor had presented itself at their table.

"Can I join you?" Fossor inquired his head tinged red with Mancini's blood.

"If we said no, you would go ahead and do it anyhow", conceded Tom grinding his teeth with anger.

"You know me too well Mr. Raust. Miss Dubois how lovely it is to see you again", Fossor replied sitting down as a chair was brought forth for him.

"Go to hell", stormed Marie unhappy at the reappearance of their nemesis.

"Now, now, that's no way to treat an old friend. Speaking of which, you ought to be careful what you say, for I have your friend Mancini held captive in the Sforza Castle. Very apt don't you agree?" said Fossor tormenting the two totally shocked individuals in front of him.

"M...M...Mancini. Why?" stammered Tom in astonishment.

"Well I presume you solved that last clue otherwise you wouldn't be here. So naturally I thought it just, to bring Mancini here to witness your demise at the place where you fail", snarled Fossor.

"If you've done anything to hurt him, I'll, I'll", Tom retorted as the frustration of hearing an acquaintance captured began to sink in.

"You'll what?" interrupted Fossor, "Bore me to death with your almighty speech on you doing what was asked of you? I don't think so. Anyhow I only did to Mancini what he did to me, an eye for eye, a tooth for a tooth, a hand for a hand"

"What did you do to him?" a distressed Marie asked.

"Don't you worry your pretty little head Miss Dubois. He's fine where he is. For now", answered Fossor pouring himself a glass of wine from the bottle in front of them, "Very good vintage don't you agree?"

"Ok Fossor, what the hell do you want?" demanded Tom his rage beginning to surface.

"That's what I like about you Mr. Raust, sharp and straight to point. If only everyone was more like that, the world would be a better place".

"It would be better off without you", corrected Tom as he directly looked into the eye of their tormentor.

"Probably so Mr. Raust, but at least I'll have the pleasure of watching you die first", Fossor pointed out taking a small sip of wine from his glass.

"What do you mean?" Marie asked, her eyes dilating in fear once more.

"Underneath my coat is a bomb strapped to my body, which I will not hesitate to use if you fail to meet my demands", warned Fossor as he opened his coat slowly to reveal the inner workings of an explosive device underneath.

"Are you totally mad?" queried Tom noticing the naked torso of Fossor underneath was painted, with what he suspected was dried blood.

"Not at all Mr. Raust. Now what I suggest we do is get up slowly from the table and proceed to leave. From here we are going to walk along the footpath until we get to the bridge", demanded Fossor with an air of authority.

"And what if we don't?" Tom inquired wondering why they should follow the instructions of this deranged individual.

"If you don't then I'll explode the bomb now, killing dozens and dozens of innocent bystanders. The choice is yours Mr. Raust".

"You don't leave us any choice".

"I thought you would see it my way", said Fossor with the smile of a child on its birthday, "Shall we go?"

With Fossor at their back, Tom and Marie left the relative safety of the restaurant and proceeded to walk the green mile that lead them to the bridge that spanned the canal, for the first time since the beginning of their quest, things were not going well for the two intrepid travelers, not only did they have Fossor motioning them towards their inevitable demise, but Mancini was held captive, presumed wounded in the line of duty, the cavalry this time was not forthcoming.

"To the center span please", demanded Fossor as they made their way onto the bridge.

Tom and Marie followed the orders and slowly trudged their way to the center of the bridge, which they were sure would be their last vision of their mortal time on earth, as they did they clasped each other's hand in hope that salvation would yet undermine Fossor's plans.

"How very touching", Fossor said the irony in his voice masking the hatred he had for Tom and Marie, "How futile. Any last requests?"

"I suppose not killing us would be off the agenda?" Tom asked in vain hope to put off the execution.

"You assume correctly, any other requests?" Fossor snarled as his patience was beginning to wear thin.

"Just one", prompted a voice from behind them, "How badly do you want to live?"

Fossor turned around to see Inspector Mancini standing in front of him, ready to pounce. The time between Mancini's question and Fossor's reaction was not quick enough, for Fossor's body was flying through the air as Mancini threw him over the side of the bridge.

"Inspector Mancini", cried Tom watching the Inspector fall to floor holding his hand in pain, "How?"

"The curator of the Castle, found me, released me, and I followed... I followed Fossor to the restaurant where I saw him meet you", commented the Inspector gasping for breath in between the sharp attacks of pain in his hand, "Make...Make sure he's dead".

Tom ran immediately to the side of the bridge to witness Fossor clinging to life as his feet dangled towards the water below, "Here give me your hand", ordered Tom as he reached out a hand in friendship.

"I can't", whimpered Fossor struggling to hold his grip on the structure which he had tried to demolish with Tom and Marie on it, "This is the path I have chosen. You walk the path laid in front of you; mine has come to an end. I hope that once you have found what you are seeking, you put the knowledge to good use".

"I will", promised Tom, "You have my word on that".

"Then I go in peace. Good bye Mr. Raust", with Fossor uttering his final word he let go of his grasp on life, plummeting to the watery grave below. Tom seeing that his enemy was no more, returned to assist Marie in taking care of their wounded friend, for the first since Istanbul they were finally free, free of the evil nature of Fossor, but yet he still felt threatened, for he sensed that Fossor was only a pawn in someone else's game, a game that he intended to win, whatever the cost maybe.

CHAPTER XLIII

The noose around their neck had been removed, no longer was the threat of a man after them part of the equation, they were free to go and do as they please without having to constantly look over their shoulder, but yet they still felt a little uneasy. The sense of still being watched would not elude them and rightly so, for they were not alone in this quest and they never were, for in the shadows a secret watched their every move. They would in time show themselves, but not yet, not until the final solution had been found, then and only then would they make their presence known.

With their nemesis no longer around, Tom and Marie no longer felt the pressure of being pursued; they felt relaxed and more comfortable not only with each other, but their surroundings too. Their greatest wish was more time to enjoy the cities they had visited, to take in the culture and the architecture without the need to seek the clues of a past existence they had contained, but alas it was not meant to be, for they understood the gravity of the situation they found themselves in. They recognized that although Fossor was gone it wouldn't be long before another killer was dispatched to hinder their progress, so they pressed on and sought more evidence of a link to a past.

"Where do you think we should start?" Marie asked Tom as they stood side by the side outside of the hospital where Inspector Mancini was being treated for his wounds.

"I think we ought to start at the beginning", replied Tom as he looked towards the city stretching out in front of them, "We need to find out more about the Sforza family".

"That seems quite logical", agreed Marie, "Where to first then Einstein?"

Tom laughed at Marie's pet name for him, he liked it, it was comforting enough but not too comforting that he got complacent with it, "Probably the Sforza Castle, the home of Sforza family will be the best place to begin".

"You mean the place where Fossor held Mancini captive?" queried Marie, not entirely comfortable at going to the spot where an evil deed of great magnitude was done by one man to another.

"Yes, I know it's not the best place to go under such circumstances, but I believe it's the next logical step", Tom said trying to comfort his slightly distressed friend.

"Ok", Marie replied, "Let's take a taxi there; I'm too tired to walk".

Tom agreed with Marie and they climbed aboard a pure white taxi which sat outside the hospital waiting for the next patrons to arrive. The ride from the hospital to the castle was their first opportunity to grab a breath in their relentless pursuit of a secret they hoped would be worth waiting for, they hoped it would last longer that it actually did, but they knew that once their destination was reached, their quest would begin all over again.

Upon reaching their destination, they left the comfort that the ride had brought them, and they preceded to journey backwards in time, into the Castle that bore the Sforza family name. They hoped that whatever circumstances brought them here, fate would provide them with the tools needed to further their pursuit of the knowledge which eluded them. Fate would smile on them quicker then they realized, for a guided tour was just about to start from the courtyard in which they stood.

Tom and Marie listened intently as the tour guide described the history behind the Castle in which they stood, "*The Sforzesco Castle is one of Milan's most beloved historical sites, originally built in the middle of the 14th century the Castle belonged to Galeazzo II Visconti, a prominent member of the Visconti dynasty and ruler of Milan, however his most famous contribution to the history of Milan is a form of torture known as the quaresmia, which included flogging, then the drinking of water, vinegar and slaked lime, then the loosening of the limbs, dismemberment following the removal one eye from the head, it goes on to finish with being hanged from a cart and put on a wheel, it is called quaresmia because it is supposed to last for forty days, with many people dying before reaching the fortieth day. His successors Gian Galeazzo and Filippo Maria went* on with the building process and built a tower in each corner of Visconti square planned designed structure. Filippo Maria, the last descendant of the Visconti family died in 1447 and because he had no legitimate heirs, the castle was demolished with the stones used to restore the town walls. In 1450, three years after the demolition Francesco Sforza, a great leader and warrior married Bianca Maria Visconti, Filippo Maria's illegitimate child and sole heir of the Visconti dynasty, making Francesco Sforza, Duke of Milan. The Sforza Castle was rebuilt on the ancient foundations of the Visconti Castle, as a retreat for the new Duke Of Milan, as you can see from the towers there is a family crest on several of them, bearing a man-eating-serpent eating a child, legend has it goes back to a 5th century fable about the family founder slaying a child devouring dragon, however historians tend to believe it was painted on the shield of a Saracen leader named Voluce, who was killed during the first crusades by an Italian named Ottone, under the Christianity heraldic laws, Ottone could adopt the slain man's symbol, now Ottone was the first Duke Of Milan, so Visconti was originally his title, as Viscount is Italian for Count or Duke, he later retired to the Abbey Of Clairvaux when he died in 1295".

"Pity I kind of like the dragon slaying legend myself", Tom whispered to Marie.

"Why's that?" she replied softly.

"It was St. George in Israel that started me off on this quest", Tom softly spoke to Marie, delicately holding her hand. "It was also what led me to you".

Marie blushed a little, as Tom lent forward and kissed her softly on the cheek, "I think", she said trying to hide the embarrassment from Tom, "I think we need more information on this Franceso Sforza person. I also seem to think he's either directly or indirectly responsible for some of Leonardo Da Vinci's artwork in Milan".

Tom turned to Marie and whispered to her, "Okay then Einstein let's go and get more information on this Franceso Sforza person, I'm sure there's an expert somewhere here we can ask, without been given the usual touristy garbage".

Tom and Marie, ventured off into the deeper confines of the castle in great spirits, hoping that someone would assist them with their need for the founder of the Sforza dynasty, for they suspected that someone as important as he, would be the catalyst to open Pandora's box, a box which would unlock the secrets of a bloodline of historical importance.

CHAPTER XLIV

The musty smelling catacombs that led to the office of the curator, echoed with the reverberations of past struggles between good and evil, as the voices of centuries lost to old age tried to speak to the living, the walls draped with cobwebs of innocence. Time cared not to remember those who had perished building the legends and tales of a period in history when death was a carefree release from the agonies of a tormented existence, upon which their blood was used to worship false gods and prophets who sought to gain riches from the misery of others. Tom and Marie had become wary, and rightly so of those who claimed to be doing the work of God, for they were the ones who put a price on their heads, a deed that broke one of the most sacred laws of religion, thou shall not kill. They were certain too, that if one law was broken they had sacrificed several more to justify their own existence, and that made them dangerous, very dangerous indeed.

As they sat waiting in the curator's office for the curator to turn up, they began to think very hard and long about the meaningless death of all those people they had come into contact with, Fossor, Emre, and Tom's friend Medad. What did they all have that made others kill to maintain their silence? Was it to keep the Bloodline of Jesus secret? Was it because they knew too much? Whatever the reason it made no sense, no sense at all, maybe in time it would, but for now the veil of death hung over their heads waiting for a time when clarity transformed the darkness into light.

"Mr. Raust, Miss Dubois, my name is Annunziata Montagna, I'm the curator here, how may I be of service to you", asked the curator greeting her two guests.

"We're doing some background research on the history of Milan for my newspaper", explained Tom as Miss Montagna sat down in her chair.

"Good, Good", she replied, eager to assist where she could, "I'm only too pleased to help, what would you like to know?"

"We would like to know more about the founder of the Sforza dynasty, Francesco Sforza", Tom stated producing his notebook from somewhere on his person.

"Let us begin at the beginning then Mr. Raust shall we? The Sforza family, a ruling family during the Renaissance, (the name Sforza is a derivative of the word sforzare meaning to exert or to force) was founded by Muzio Attendolo, a mercenary solider from the historic region of Romagna who served the Angevin kings of Naples".

"I'm sorry", interrupted Marie politely, "Who or what precisely are the Angevin kings of Naples?"

"Angevin is the name applied to the residents of Anjou, which used to be a province in the Kingdom of France. It was also used to describe three distinct medieval dynasties. The First, also called the House of Plantagenet ruled England between 1128 and 1485, The Second, a branch of the Capetian dynasty was founded by Charles, Count of Anjou lasted from 1246 to 1435, and finally The Third which ruled Naples from 1350 to 1480", Annunziata replied answering Marie's question, "Now to continue. Francesco Sforza, who ruled Milan for the first half of the Renaissance, acquired the title of the Duke of Milan from the extinct Visconti family in 1447".

"How precisely did he acquire the title?" Tom asked wanting to know more about the title adopted by Francesco Sforza.

"That is a very good question Mr. Raust, one that might take a little explanation", Annunziata stated, "However I will do the best I can. When Filippo Maria Visconti, the last of the Visconti's bloodline died, the Duchy of Milan went to Alfonso of Aragona".

"Who?" interrupted Tom as his curiosity got the better of him.

"Alfonso V of Aragon was King of Naples, from 1442 and also a knight of the Order of the Dragon", answered the curator who was pleased about this newspaper reporter's need to expand his horizons. Tom on the other hand was now a little perplexed for the Order of the Dragon was a group of Knights he had not come across, he had heard of The Knights Templar, The Knights Hospitaller, but never about this Order of the Dragon. He suspected that it may not be significant, but he had learnt from past experiences never to underestimate even the littlest clue. Tom decided not to press the curator for more information about this Order for he was wary of her own motives, although she may be an innocent party for Tom, discretion was the better part of valor.

"Now this title was given to Alfonso", continued the curator, "through the last will and testament of Fillippo, the problem with this was that the title was suppose to revert back to the Holy Roman Empire as decreed by their laws, upsetting Alfonso's supporters The Bracceschi . With support for both Alfonso and Francesco Sforza in its ascendancy, several leading citizens called for the foundation of the old republic once more. The night after Bracceschi took control of the castle, a new republic called the Golden Ambrosian Republic was formed, and the Bracceschi were driven out of Milan by Francesco Sforza, who was already commanding the Milanese troops in the service of the last duke. In doing so he proclaimed himself master of the Ambrosian Republic and Duke of Milan".

"And that's how Francesco Sforza got the title Duke of Milan?" a slightly suspicious Tom wondered aloud.

"Yes", replied the curator who was beginning to suspect that Tom was not really totally honest with her.

"I think we've got enough information. Thank you for your time", he replied as he stood up and shook the curator's hand.

"Not at all", the curator politely said, "it was a pleasure to be of assistance. Whilst you're in Milan, Mr. Raust you ought to check out the Santa Maria delle Grazie built under the orders of Francesco Sforza where the Last Supper is. It's a marvelous piece of architecture".

"Thank you we will", said Tom as Marie and himself left the curator's office. Tom was beginning to suspect that not everything was what it seemed. He was beginning to smell the foul stench of treason raise its ugly head. Why? He didn't know, but he was learning to trust his instinct, and his instinct told him to be cautious, for when people gave up information too easy, there was usually a price to pay, and he was tired of being the one to bear the brunt of the burden, for it meant that someone close to him would ultimately perish at the hand of someone's evil intent.

CHAPTER XLV

The lies etched in the annals of the past were slowly eroded by the secrets revealed in the future. Would history forgive those who had tainted the past not only with the falsehoods, but the blood spilt in servitude to those who sought to maintain the hidden truth? Was the price of revealing the truth a burden too great not only for those it effected, but mankind as a race? Not one person really knew the true cost, not one person should dictate what history was wanted to be, but what history truly was. It was time to stop living a life of lies and let the people decide, if they wanted to live with the lie then that was their prerogative, however if they wanted to know the truth, then that was their right too, for living with a lie was worse than knowing what the truth really is.

For Tom and Marie the realization that the truth, once found, would alter their perspective on absolutely everything they knew, but they realized too that if the truth had been told from the start then it wouldn't have to be kept under lock and key in the art work of those who knew it. They wrestled with their conscience more and more as they got further into the maze of clues and questions that each one presented.

"You do realize that when we find whatever it is we're supposed to be searching for, life will never be the same?" Marie asked Tom as they sat in yet another library, staring at yet another pile of books.

"The thought had crossed my mind", he admitted as the moral maze unwound in front of him, "but I look at it like this. We've been sent on this journey for a reason. Someone somewhere wants us to locate the missing piece of the puzzle they can't and that makes me want to repay their faith by unveiling whatever it is we're supposed to find".

"That makes a lot of sense", Marie said patting him gently on his hand, "I presume we're here for a reason?".

"We are", affirmed Tom, "I want to find out more about the Santa Maria delle Grazie. I was kind of perplexed why the curator was eager to point us in that direction".

"You suspect foul play?" Marie said wondering why Tom had mentioned the fact.

"I suspect nothing, but I've come to learn that with this bloodline of Jesus, nothing is as it first appears", Tom replied arguing his reasoning behind not entirely trusting the curator.

"So", queried Marie staring at the column of books in front of them, "Where shall we start?"

"Firstly we need to clarify what the curator told us about Francesco Sforza and the Santa Maria delle Grazie", Tom said as his eyes went up and down the title of books at their disposal, before he locked on one that caught his attention. He slowly removed the knowledge holder from its brethren and proceeded to locate the information he desired, "According to this book he ordered a Dominican convent and a church where a previous chapel dedicated to St. Mary of the Grace stood, the architect is thought to be Guiniforte Solari although there is much debate about the authenticity of this story".

"Hold on a minute did you say Dominican convent?" Marie asked a little unsure why the church would be dedicated to a specific religious order, "Why do you think that would be?"

"I'm not entirely sure", stated Tom as his thoughts went on a different tangent, "The only reason I can think of is, is that it was done to protect the family from the Inquisition as the Dominicans were the order present at the Inquisition and", he never finished what he was about to say for he recollected something else about the Inquisition, "I'm sure that the Knights Templar had the Dominican Order friars at their trial too"

"I don't think this is coincidental", Marie said as the excitement in her voice built, "and usually where there's Knights Templar, there's usually the fable of them being the protectors of the bloodline of Jesus".

"Do you think that the Dominican order where given the secret by the Knights Templar before their trial?" queried Tom.

"I suppose that's possible", Marie answered, "It's feasible that's the reason they were at the trials in the first place, probably at bequest of the Knights Templar themselves".

"Then there's this Order of the Dragon too".

"You mean the one Alfonso V of Aragon was supposed to be a member of?"

"Yes", confirmed Tom as he began searching for reference material pertaining to the Order of the Dragon, "The Order was a chivalric order for selected nobility, created in Hungary by King Sigismund in the year 1408. The Order requires those of its clan to defend the cross and fight the enemies of Christianity. Based on the Order of St. George famous inductees have included, Henry V of England, King Alfonso of Aragon and Naples and the most famous of them all, Vlad The Impaler".

"That's really bizarre, considering Vlad was an extremely ruthless individual", stated Marie surprised at the induction into the Order of the Dragon by one of history's most barbaric men, "You know all this information surrounding this Order of the Dragon and the Dominican Order could potentially be a golden discovery".

"Hold a minute", pondered Tom as a word Marie spoke triggered of an alarm in his head, "Did you say Golden?"

"Yes I did, why?" Marie responded in excitement for she knew that Tom was about to suggest another thought outside the box.

"The author of the Golden Legends, Jacopo da Varagine was he a member of the Dominican Order of monks too?"

"Hold on let me look", Marie said as she looked at one of the text books in her possession, "YES HE WAS".

Tom looked at Marie with a smug look of satisfaction that boasted he knew already what the answer was, in response to his boast Marie playfully hit him on the shoulder, "You brat you knew he was".

"I didn't", Tom replied in earnest, "I suspected he was. I'm almost certain now that the Golden Legends is more than that, a legend".

"You think that the stories are what? True?" a bewildered Marie inquired.

"Some of them are", affirmed Tom, "you've just got to sort which ones are and which are not".

"So where does that leave us now then?" she responded with excitement in her voice.

"It means that the Santa Maria delle Grazie and anything contained within must be viewed with much more seriousness than before", said Tom as his eyes went back to his book, "considering it was designed by the same person who designed St. Peter's Basilica".

"How did you know that?"

"It's say's so right here", Tom responded tapping the book with his finger.

"Ok Einstein, what's our next move then?"

"Our next move Marie", said Tom as he gracefully sat back in his chair "is to visit the Santa Maria delle Grazie and see what that has to offer".

Tom and Marie, sat in the confines of the library confident that the Santa Maria delle Grazie would give them another clue in their progression of the truth, another step forward to isolating the reality from fiction and this time there was no Fossor, no one standing behind them in the shadows gloating over every mistake they made, this time it was there's for the taking and there's alone.

CHAPTER XLVI

The golden globe permeated the sky with a halo of gilded brilliance against the lazuline sky, as the leaves on the trees blew softly in the wind, the birds sang a chorus of triumphant tunes whilst the flowers raised their heads in approval. Mother nature herself was sensing that a change was approaching, a renewal in the faith of doing what was right, as opposed to what was thought to be right. A second renaissance was looming on the horizon, if and only if, the final pieces of the puzzle could be laid to rest on the board of truth. With all the pawns in the end game finally in their appropriate positions, it was time for the last piece to unveil the secrets it held, and tell the whole world the truth contained within it's time capsule canvas, all that remained was the door to be unlocked and the two protagonists to enter the kingdom which told of their forthcoming.

With interpretation and a sense of relief, Tom and Marie sat foot on the hallowed grounds of the dining hall in the Santa Maria delle Grazie, their footsteps echoing on the wooden paneled floor that lay beneath, as their voices resounded to the arched ceiling over their heads. Mystique filled the room with a sense of foreboding that was a precursor to the discovery that they were sure to unmask, the purity of the room cleansed all the apprehension from their bodies as calm waters encapsulated their souls.

Disappointment however would change their mood, as much to their surprise (and disgust) a long line of tourists wanting to view Leonardo's masterpiece stood between them and their hopeful discovery of their final missing piece of the jigsaw.

"Stinking, flipping, obnoxious, sneaker wearing tourists with their stupid fanny packs", snarled Tom in disbelief.

"Tom", said Marie in disgust, "remember, you're not in only the presence of the Master Artist, but a place of worship too".

"I'm sorry", he murmured hanging his head in shame, "I feel so close, yet so far away".

"That's okay, there's nothing else we can do as the Crucifixion painting is closed for repairs", Marie shrugged as she turned to face the exit.

"Hold on minute", Tom remarked grabbing Marie's hand preventing her from departing, "Where's your sense of adventure? Let's go see this other painting. There's got to a reason why it's here too".

"You've got a point", Marie conceded as she turned to face the cordoned off area in the room, "There has to be a reason why it's here. Let's go then Einstein".

Through the restricted area they moved, cautiously and as quietly as they could, stealthily moving forwards and onwards, between pots of cleaning fluids, scaffolding materials and an old lap top computer stacked on piles of dirty rags, until they discovered a painting no one took any notice of: *The Crucifixion by Giovanni Donato Montorfano*.

Fig. XI - CRUCIFIXION PAINTING BY GIOVANNI DONATO MONTORFANO C.1495

"You know", commented Marie to Tom as they both stood transfixed by the painting in their view, "I hate to admit it, I believe your right".

"About what?" a puzzled Tom queried, not entirely sure what he was right about, but was pleased he was right about something at least.

"That there has to be a reason why this painting is here, in the same room as Leonardo Da Vinci's painting of The Last Supper", Marie stated as she peered closer at the painting in question, her eyes trying to pierce the painted ozone with a Chlorofluorocarbon glare.

"You suspect this could be the painting we want and not *The Last Supper?*" Tom hypothesized a little taken aback that his flippant remark could be more profound that he originally intended.

"Yes I do", Marie confirmed taking a couple of paces back to be alongside Tom, "Let's put it into context with everything we've learnt on this quest shall we? Everything we've come across in one shape or form has been a clue, but a clue in plain sight and what better place to hide a secret message then in the presence of The Last Supper which everyone comes to visit and place it in a painting which no one hardly looks at ?".

"That would indeed make a lot of sense", Tom agreed as Marie's supposition got him viewing the art work with an all seeing eye of disbelief, "I mean why make the point of enlarging his name and the year of his work, when most artists try to hide them?"

A puzzled Marie looked closer at the painting, studying the bizarre nature of the point made by Tom about the artist's name and year of conception of the artwork. She was unsure of the reasoning behind the need to draw attention to the detail, but she was certain that it could be the breakthrough they were looking for. Marie was just about to concede defeat when she noticed something not quite right about the way the painter's surname was laid out, "Look", she exclaimed pointing to a particular part of the painting with an outstretched index finger, "There are extra letters in his name".

Fig. XII - GIOVANNI DONATO MONTORFANO's name on the Crucifixion Painting

Tom looked at the surname of the painter, and Marie was correct, there were extra letters in the name, but what was the purpose behind them? Surely it couldn't be a mistake, it had to have been put there for a specific purpose, but why? Why put them there? He took time to study the positioning of the letters and for a brief moment he thought they spelt a word, as the knowledge he held began to sink in, he also began to realize he was right too and what they spelt.

"ONORUS?" he shouted with a combination of excitement and skepticism.

"What?" Marie replied in total confusion.

"Look at the extra letters they spell the word ONORUS", Tom stated affirming his first remark with the hand of a teacher in front of his class.

Fig. XIII - GIOVANNI DONATO MONTORFANO name on the Crucifixion Painting containing the word ONORUS

"Jesus Christ", Marie swore as her eyes confirmed what Tom had seen and she had not.

"Not yet", Tom smiled in seriousness, "but I think we're on the right path".

The first shaft of light had shown down on them and they had what they believed was not only the correct painting with the hidden clue(s) contained within, but they were firm in their belief too that this finding of a word (and a word neither of them knew) was of great significant importance. They secretly prayed that this would in the end, give them all the information they sought including the meaning of this word, the word ONORUS.

CHAPTER XLVII

The transformation from darkness into light was progressively altered by different shades of grey, each one letting in more light until the final one completed the ambient transfer. For Tom and Marie their journey was the same. With each step they took, more of the historical bloodline's secrets became apparent, and the more obvious (to them at least) it became, that there was a cover up of massive proportions. Why and what for remained elusive, but the need to cover up this biblical secret in the manuscripts and artwork of artists was proof enough that a secret lay hidden. There remained one other question though left unanswered, why were the artists the ones trusted enough to not only be told the secret, but were given the commission (by their patrons) to leave hidden messages in their art ? Did the patrons know the secret too? If so, then that meant they were party to the knowledge imparted by others. If not then why would they let their family name be connected with those who had the secret information?

"There's still one thing I don't understand", Tom confessed to Marie as they sat resting on their laurels.

"What's that?" inquired Marie as she stood up again to look at the painting.

"How all the clues are hidden in the art work of great masters of their profession", Tom replied as he began to think openly more and more about those hiding the secrets.

"I think", she stated in earnest, "It's because either they were the ones chosen specifically by those with the knowledge of the bloodline, or it's because they wanted the ordinary man to seek the truth. Don't forget that in the time when these works of art were being produced, not many poor people could read or write, so it could be plausible that the secrets could be revealed even by the lowest of the low".

"Surely that would mean too, that those who employed the artists knew of the secrets also?" Tom said as he trudged slowly over to the laptop on a pile of rags that lay in the corner of the room.

"More likely they were the ones who told the artists what to paint, but then it depends on painter to painter. I mean would you tell Da Vinci what to paint? I know I wouldn't", Marie commented with a sense of foreboding that bewitched Tom with a sense of urgency "What are you doing anyhow?"

"I'm just seeing if this piece of junk works", Tom speculated looking for a power switch on the abused computer. He turned the computer around and around until he made himself dizzy trying to isolate the ON button, the fluid in his ear loops taking a while to settle themselves down.

"Here Einstein", Marie said walking over to Tom and flipping the power button into the correct position; "See if this helps".

The computer kicked into life, humming and whirling into action, as the disc contained within began to bring Frankenstein's creation to life. Tom looked at the computer, and then at Marie, before he shook his head in disbelief, "Thanks I think", he muttered under his breath.

"You're welcome", Marie laughed returning once more to her study of the painting.

Tom was pleasantly surprised to see that not only was the computer working, but there was a signal strong enough for him to receive a wireless connection to a localized internet receiver. His relief however was short lived, for upon entering the word they had found on the painting disappointment would tell him that no word existed matching to that entry.

Tom willfully relayed his findings to his counterpart, who began to suspect that there might be more than one clue on the painting.

"I wonder", suggested Marie searching for the key to unlock the door, "If 1495 is a clue in itself",

"I don't quite follow", Tom answered unsure of Marie's interpretation of the word *ONORUS* on the painting.

"I suspect that if we implement a basic code system, for example A=1 B=2 C=3 et cetera, we might get another longer message", Marie stated as she began to count the letters of the alphabet on her fingers, "Therefore 1=A, 4=D, 9=I and 5 =E and the message could read *ADIE ONORUS*. Can you see if there is an entry for that?"

Tom did as he was asked and entered the phrase into the computer, but much to his surprise yet again, there was still no entry for the term he entered, "Sorry there isn't", as he apologized scratching his head in hope that it would coerce a thought from his malnourished brain.

"Wait a minute", Marie exclaimed, noticing something about the painting, "The 1 looks like the letter *I,* therefore the message could read *I DIE ON ORUS.* What does that give us then Tom?"

Once more Tom went into the breach, suspecting that an entry would not materialize; however he was taken aback when much to his surprise an entry did appear on the screen in front of him, "*Orus*", he gleefully informed Marie, "is a village and commune in southwestern France. Isn't there a legend that suggests that Mary Magdalene went to France carrying the child of Jesus?"

"Yes there is", affirmed Marie, "However the legend states that she went to Marseilles along with her brother Lazarus and Maximinus (one of the Seventy Disciples expelled from the Holy Land during the persecution of Christians by the Romans)".

"I don't think that I *DIE ON ORUS* could be feasible then", sighed Tom as he began to think more about the 1495 at the top of the block where the painter's name sat. The more he thought about the number 1495, the more he began to realize that the number might not be a year as they originally thought, "I think I've got it, I think I've frigging got it", he shouted in excitement.

"Got what?" Marie queried as her excitement was triggered off by that of Tom's, "The flu?"

"No, no, no. 1495 it's not a year", he answered barely able to contain himself.

"It's not?" Marie shrilled, her excitement beginning to surface like a submarine from the depths of the oceans, "Then what the hell is it?"

"It's 1495 in Da Vinci's notebooks. 1495 is in frigging Da Vinci's notebooks", Tom burst out jumping up and down, before kissing Marie on the lips, embracing her delighted body with the touch of a long lost friend returning home for the first time in years.

Marie remained spellbound, held in the wonderment that was Tom, for she knew his assumption about the number 1495 was correct, neither one of them until now had even bothered to look at the master's notebooks. It was the notebooks that told Tom and Marie to '*Trust the Works*'. It was the notebooks that began their journey. It was the notebooks that they forgot about. Yet here they were, making their presence known, prompting them, urging them to seek the answers to the puzzle that lay before them.

Whatever 1495 was in Leonardo Da Vinci's own words would be the key to unlock not only one door, but several more doors that would follow, doors that would allow them to view the treasure that was the true bloodline of Jesus.

CHAPTER XLVIII

For the first time since Istanbul, Tom and Marie were no longer joined in psychological union, for their temporary divorce from one another was a necessary evil. The key they needed to unlock the 1495 puzzle was not in their possession, so Marie a willing volunteer, set off in search of a duplicate edition of Da Vinci's notebooks. Tom on the other hand was given the opportunity to fine tune his own take on the painting that stood guarding the secrets in front of him.

He took the task given to him with great seriousness, examining every inch of the painting with a fine tooth comb, but 1495 kept on calling him back, beckoning him, urging him to unravel the messages it contained. Occasional seasons of self doubt drained his tired psyche but he brushed them aside with the hand of a gentle giant.

Tom was about to retire gracefully from active duty, when something began to tickle his mind with the finger of inquisition. He took a look as his supposition again, before rubbing his eyes in disbelief; he couldn't be true in his assumption could he? Once more he viewed his own theory with suspicion before he confirmed what he originally believed to be correct. There was another secret message, a message he hoped that would make more sense than the previous one.

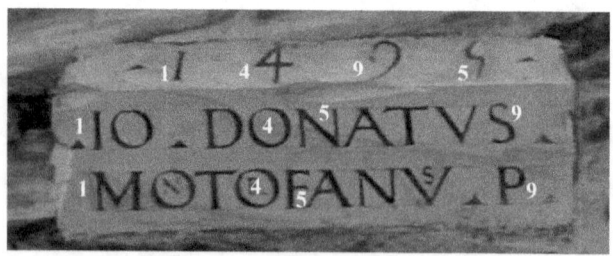

Fig .XIII - GIOVANNI DONATO MONTORFANO name on the
Crucifixion Painting containing secret message

One by one the letters on the painting began to reveal a secret message, "I, O, N and S. Then M, O, E and P, IONS MOEP. What the hell is IONS MOEP?" Tom thought to himself querying the letters he found, "Come on Tom, think. Think". Slowly he began to pace back and forth, not only on the wooden floor, but in his mind too. Tom could have sworn there was another message there, but what was it? The phrase *'IONS MOEP'* made no sense, no sense at all. Maybe there another explanation for the unpronounceable words he had discovered.

Time elapsed as did the reasoning in his head, explosions of hypothesis bouncing around inside his skull all falling to the cavity between his frontal lobe and his heart. Disappointment was beginning to slowly enter his soul, when silently a warrior was dispatched to remove it from his body, "Maybe the message is an anagram of something else", he thought as he stood pondering his next move. The words that he thought were unpronounceable began to unscramble, unveiling themselves into a more understandable message, a message he could finally comprehend.

"*SION POEM!!*", he screamed silently inwards to his subconscious, then he uttered it softly once more just to make sure he was correct, "SION POEM. Goddam it, the message is SION POEM".

His analytical mind began to process the information given to him, and it began to wonder if this was pertaining to the Priory of Sion, the alleged secret society associated with the French monarchy. If so then would that mean Giovanni Donato Montorfano as well as Leonardo Da Vinci was a member of the brotherhood? There was just one thing that did not make sense and that was the inclusion of the word POEM in the message. Perhaps there was no such thing as a SION POEM, but then again maybe there was, he wouldn't know unless he found definitive proof. The best cause of action, Tom decided, was to look for an entry on the computer attributed to both.

Tom's sweat ladened fingers began to type in the search query on the computer, pausing for a moment before pressing the final key and sending the computer on its way to find any and all records relating to a SION POEM. Maybe, just maybe this would provide the turning point. If so would this unlock yet another layer of the mystery they sought to resolve? There would only be one way of finding out, so without due need to delay the action any further, the final key was pressed, prompting the computer to locate the records needed. The delay was only a brief heartbeat away, before it came back with an answer that not only shocked but delighted Tom.

"SION POEM is the Priory of Sion poem, Le Serpent Rouge", Tom smiled in delight at his find, his delight however turned into confusion, for he was unsure of the interpretation of Le Serpent Rouge and what it meant relating to the painting. Quickly as he could, Tom entered the term *'Le Serpent Rouge'* onto the computer's keyboard and this time quickly pressing the final key that would send the computer into a rapturous delight that would signify its importance.

"Le Serpent Rouge (The Red Serpent), the archive of Rennes-le-Chateau written by Pierre Jarnac in the latter part of the 20th century", Tom quoted despairingly, "God frigging damnit, I thought I had a lead then".

"A lead to what?" echoed a friendly welcoming voice returning from the acquisition of resources.

"Marie", screamed Tom in delight as he ran to hug her with the absence of a long lost lover, "Oh boy how I missed you".

Marie laughed, "Yeah I kind of missed you too Einstein. So what you been up to then?"

"Nothing that won't wait", Tom answered as his frustration turned to that of pure relief upon his friend's return.

"Good", replied Marie, "I brought you some chocolate and something that might prove useful", she said handing Tom a chocolate bar that had been imported all the way from France, and both books of Leonardo Da Vinci's notebooks (translated into English with the original Italian beside it).

Finally they could solve the answer to the riddle that was contained in the painting. Was 1495 a significant number in the painting by Montorfano?

If so, then that not only meant Leonardo Da Vinci was a part of the conspiracy, but Montorfano too and that meant that this secretive painter, (which few knew very little about) was entrusted by the master with his secrets, secrets that may or may not prove what they already suspected, that there was a cover up by someone in the Church that kept the secret of the bloodline of Jesus, just that, a secret.

CHAPTER XLIX

The separation, albeit temporary, proved to one another how much they relied, not only their physical presence but their intellectual presence too, for as soon as Marie returned from her voyage to the outside, she was eager to find all about Tom's new discovery. Tom on the other hand was eager to find out about Marie's venture in the outside world, and so for a little while a stalemate occurred, both enraptured by the others aura, as they both sat silently eating the chocolate Marie brought with her.

As they sat eating the sweet bitter confectionary, Tom broke the silence and began to explain his latest discovery about how he counted the 1st, 4th, 9th and 5th on both the lines of the painters name, he then went on to explain how the letters he found (I,O,N,S,M,O,E and P) were an anagram of the phrase SION POEM, "So naturally I thought it was a Priory of Sion poem they were referring to", continued Tom, eager to demonstrate his analytical prowess.

"And?" queried Marie as she finished her last bite of chocolate.

"The only Priory of Sion poem I could find was, Le Serpent Rouge", sighed Tom disappointed at his lack of progression of the cryptogram designed by Da Vinci and executed by Montorfano.

"By Pierre Jarnac?" Marie responded, for the name of the poem she thought was similar to that of one in a journal she had the displeasure of reading some time ago.

"Yes it was. Why?" Tom pondered aloud as his eyes look down to the floor they were sat on.

"It was all a big massive hoax", Marie grumbled as the anger in her voice went to def com two, "Hell, they even had the audacity to imply that they used Tarot Cards as a secret system for transporting hidden messages".

"I take it you're not his biggest fan then?" Tom said trying to alleviate the anger in Marie's voice.

"No I'm not", she responded, "If you're going to make a big tissue of lies to cover up what really happened, then you're no better than those who cover up this lie of Jesus' true bloodline".

"God that reminds me", Tom exclaimed as the purpose for their being there re-materialized again in his head, "I better see what 1495 says in Da Vinci's notebooks".

"Damn", swore Marie in astonishment as she handed Tom the literary work, "I nearly forgot too".

Tom slowly began to turn pages in hesitation, praying that what he anticipated would be another step in the right direction. One by one he turned the pages, as one by one Da Vinci's secrets flashed in front of his dilated pupils, until 1495 appeared to him like a dove of peace carrying an olive branch, "1495", stated Tom, "*Of the error of those who practice without knowledge; -- [3] See first the 'Ars Poetica' of Horace [5]*".

"What do you think?" Marie asked Tom waiting for his input in the mystery.

"Hold on a minute", Tom stated peering at the bottom of the page, "It states that the number [3] and [5] of the title line of the text given, entire as No.19. We better see if we can find this Ars Poetica of Horace on the computer".

"Why? What are you thinking?"

"I think the numbers 19, 3, and 5 could be referring to the line number and word count in the piece of literary art Da Vinci is pointing us too", explained Tom as he stood up and went over to the laptop. He promptly entered the search query in question and before either of them knew, he had managed to bring up line 19 in Horace's Ars Poetica.

"God almighty", an astounded Marie stated in disbelief, "You didn't hang around did you? So what did you find?"

"Line 19 is in the part entitled *'Unity and Harmony'*", Tom quoted reading the text from the screen.

"Very apt", Marie commented joining Tom at his side to discover what he had found in the computer's records.

"It states *'Or the River Rhine, or the rainbow's being described'*".

"So what about the 3 and the 5 then?"

"I believe it means the words 3 to 5 inclusive", Tom replied as he began to count words on the screen in his head, "Which then gives us *'River Rhine or'*. That doesn't make a lot of sense"

Marie paused for a minute as an idea began to formulate in her head, "Tom can you re-read the clue from Da Vinci's notebook again?"

"Yes", Tom confirmed re-reading that article at Marie's bequest, "*Of the error of those who practice without knowledge; -- [3] See first the 'Ars Poetica' of Horace [5]*"

"It states *'Of the error of those who practice without knowledge'* agreed?" stated Marie as she slowly began to understand the clue left behind by Da Vinci.

"Agreed".

"So how do we get knowledge? We remove the error", explained Marie as she looked on the screen at words 3 to 5 inclusive. "We take the word *'error'* from *River Rhine or*".

Tom looked at the screen, then from his person he brought forward his notebook, "that leaves us *r, i, v, e, r, h, i, n*. I believe this possibly could be another anagram".

"Well you solved the last once", smiled Marie as she placed an arm around Tom, bracing herself for the moment when he would solve this new puzzle.

Tom thought Marie was challenging him to solve this new puzzle, and she was, but she had enough confidence and faith in his ability to crack the anagram and offer them a new view of the puzzle on the painting. Slowly one by one the letters in his head began to arrange themselves until they formed a new sentence.

"*Henri IV or VI*", stated Tom as he cracked the puzzle with glee. He sat in wonder, at the ease at which he solved puzzle, as he did something struck him, something that would finally give meaning to all the previous clues found, "*Henri Vision Poem*", he stated putting all the pieces of puzzle together.

"W.W.What?" a disbelieving Marie stuttered.

"*Henri Vision Poem*", confirmed Tom, "You put the two clues together, *Henri VI* from the new one and *SION POEM*, from the old one, which gives us".

"*Henri Vision Poem*", Marie confirmed with total and utter bewilderment, staring in the disbelief at the screen in front of them.

This was the biggest breakthrough to date, who or what was the *Henri Vision Poem*? Neither Tom nor Marie knew, but this now confirmed beyond any reasonable doubt that this painting was the one that contained a hidden message. They were the first ones on the entire planet to find it, and that made them feel alive, but above all eager, eager to find what other messages were contained, for in their hearts they were sure that more were to follow, and follow they would.

CHAPTER L

The temptations to taste the fruits of narrow mindedness were a powerful aphrodisiac for Tom and his master at arms Marie. They had concentrated (and rightly so) on the meaning of the 1495 cryptogram, but now was the time to diversify and spread their wings to different parts of the painting, hunting down whatever minuscule clues where left to find, for whatever was drawing their attention to the painting would also let them find other secretive messages that the painter had placed for those worthy enough to find.

Their decision to ignore the rest of the painting was starting to haunt their judgment, for although the 1495 clue was a very important find, it might pale to insignificance compared to other messages contained within, prompting Tom and Marie to peel back the layers of time, and begin the daunting task of scanning the horizon with their third eye.

"So what are we looking for?" Tom asked Marie as they stood in front of the painting, waiting for the preemptive strike that would open yet another door to the past.

"Anything that you think would help us with the mystery in our hands", Marie replied as she started to examine everything with a more receptive train of thought.

Tom with the absent mindedness of a patient suffering from amnesia, began his visual exploration in pursuit of the treasure that was captured in fresco, querying each particle created with the brush stroke of a master story teller, in hope that one small detail created by the purveyor of secrets would yet open another layer of the darkness that enveloped the mystery underneath.

He felt like a philanderer, as his eyes looked at pictures of women in medieval clothing, wondering if anyone of these people knew about the significance of the painting they found themselves in, querying the knowledge that they themselves were fully party to.

As Tom continued looking inwards and outwards at the painting his eyes began to focus on a figure dressed in the cloth of a religious figure. Nothing strange he thought at first, but then as he looked closer and closer at the figure it became apparent that it was not only a woman wearing a thorn crown, but the woman was with child too.

Fig. XV - Mysterious woman wearing the clothes of a friar on the Crucifixion Painting

"Hey Marie", Tom ushered, his eyes still locked on the fertile woman in question, "Come and take a look this, see what you make of it".

Marie ambled her way to where Tom was fixated with the mysterious person in his line of fire, "That's curious", she said as her eyes began to study the female in question, "This person wearing the cloth of the brotherhood of Friars, is not only female, but pregnant too".

"Have you seen what's on her head?" Tom asked moving his little finger to illustrate the thorn crown.

"If I didn't know any better, I'd swear that this person is related to Jesus and bearing his child too", Marie commented, fixated by the mysterious lady Tom had found, "and that usually means only one person"

"*MARY MAGDALENE*", stated Tom in excitement.

"Yes Mary Magdalene", confirmed Marie as she continued to stare at the vision of the alleged lover of Jesus.

"Does that mean that the legend of Mary Magdalene carrying Jesus' child is true then?" Tom asked curious about the implication of their find.

"I don't think it confirms it either way", stated Marie being as realistic as she could, "We need more proof to either deny or confirm the stories".

Tom was just about to ask another question, when his eyes began to stare closer and closer at the picture of the woman wearing the thorn crown. Marie sensing Tom was looking at something significant braced herself for Tom's forthcoming remark. "Look at this", Tom pointed as something new he had just witness came to life.

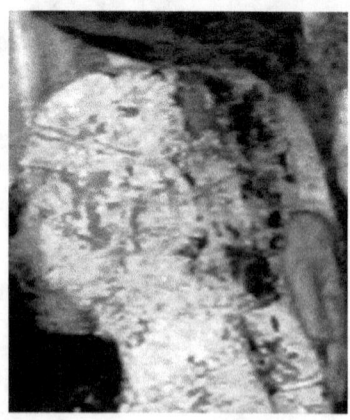

Fig. XVI - Mary Magdalene's left hand around the fresco of a woman on the Crucifixion Painting

"Isn't the hand of Mary Magdalene comforting this unusual portrayal of this figure?" Tom asked continuing his observation of the painting.

Marie peered in the vicinity of the figure's hand, and to her complete surprise Tom was absolutely correct in his perceptive detective work, "I believe your right", she confirmed as her eyes zoomed in closer to the artwork, "I think that these are paintings of Ludovico Sforza's family and are by Leonardo Da Vinci".

"So who has Mary Magdalene's hand on them?" Tom wondered as he continued his never ending staring contest with the painting.

"I seem to remember someone once telling me it was, his wife *Beatrice d'Este*", Marie said as she too joined the competition Tom was currently taking part in.

"Who?"

"*Beatrice d'Este*, who she was I've no idea, but she must be important to have Mary Magdalene's hand around her".

"Do you think that this means that Beatrice d'Este is related to Mary Magdalene?", Tom queried as his mind went off on different tangents, giving different answers to the same question.

"That could be one explanation", said Marie as she turned to look at Tom engaged in his own inner sanctuary, "but we can't confirm that one way or the other without further investigation, but if, and I repeat if, she is then we have just opened the gateway to a whole multitude of conspiracy theories".

As they both stood in awe of the painting, they also stood in awe of the cleverness behind the painter's deception, for if, as they suspected, Mary Magdalene was the pregnant woman in the picture, dressed head to foot in clothes of a Monk, then did that mean that not only hers, but Jesus' bloodline too was no longer a fable and was alive and well in the history of the brotherhood of the church?

But why and what for? And what was the connection between Mary Magdalene and Beatrice d'Este?

Only time and further investigation would explain the answer to both, for Tom and Marie the further possibilities of the lineage of one of the most, if not the most, important figures in history was starting to unravel as with each clue they solved, another layer of the mystery unmasked itself, and as the unmasking slowly revealed what history tried to hide, they were certain that whatever the reasons for hiding the truth, they were no longer in the hands of those who wanted the truth to remain hidden, the church.

CHAPTER LI

Just as the painting held the secrets of an Italian Master captive, the doors that led to the convent refectory locked firmly in place too, sentencing all those who were left behind to one night of captivity. Although try as they might, the doors to the outside world barricading their escape remained firmly closed. Tom and Marie looked at the door, then each other, before returning to the fight with the artist's unique coded message system. Within minutes of their arrival the lights in the corridor that gave entry to a world previously unknown, were slowly switched off, leaving only the light above the painting to guide them till the next day.

"I suppose we're here for the night" Marie sighed as the darkness began to lap like the sea at their feet.

"It appears so", Tom replied confirming Marie's suspicions as he went back to work, looking for more hidden clues on a less respected painting than Leonardo Da Vinci's Last Supper. Tom began to wonder if the world was ready for the truth about the bloodline of Jesus.

Maybe it wasn't that knowing the truth might do more harm than good, for those who believed in God needed Him. They felt something that was missing from their lives.

Who then purported the lie to increase their own wealth out of those less fortunate? The questions in his mind began to burden his soul, Marie began to burden hers with less trivial worries, for although she herself was concerned with revealing the truth, her main concern was that of Tom's psychological well being, for she knew that Tom's past was far from easy on him, so she took time to relieve the tension that sometimes he carried by lightening the mood.

"So what you going to do with your Nobel Prize when you win it then?" she asked joining Tom in his venture.

"I thought I'd use it as a book end", Tom said laughing at Marie's remark, "What about you?"

"I was prepared to use mine as a cat scratching post", she replied triggering off Tom's infectious laughter. As they stood for a little while laughing at the prospect of Marie's cat using a much sought after prize as a scratching post, they began to understand that they needed each other more than they knew.

Tom was Marie's knight in shining armor, protecting, taking care of her when danger threatened Marie was the nurse of Tom's soul, helping Tom when his self respect, his self belief, became perilously low on his list of priorities.

The awkward silence that soon followed the raucous outburst, gave both the time needed to think about all the time they had spent together, in situations no one on earth would place themselves in, the smile on their faces conveying the contentment that each situation they had been through, brought them closer together. Clasping hands together, Tom looked at Marie and said, "You know without you, I would be like a ship lost at sea".

"Without you I would be a chocolate bar better off", Marie reminded Tom, trying to lighten the somber mood, but then she realized when she looked at Tom, he was being deadly serious, "but then I too would be lost without you".

"Back to work?" Tom queried smiling at Marie.

"Back to work", Marie confirmed rubbing the back of Tom's hand.

Marie pondered for a moment, wondering what the significance of the left arm of Mary Magdalene around Beatrice d'Este.

"Perhaps", she thought to herself, "It could be a sign pertaining to something else". She had heard rumors through colleagues in the field, that it was thought that Mary Magdalene was the woman sat on the right of Jesus on The Last Supper, but there was no proof to either confirm it or deny it.

The Last Supper was purported to contain an image of Beatrice d'Este on it, "That could be the connection", she pondered, "If it was then that could be the meaning of Mary Magdalene's hand around Da Vinci's fresco painted woman on The Crucifixion painting".

Not entirely comfortable with the hypothesis she had given birth, she thought it wiser and more prudent to return to the painting and help Tom where ever she could.

Little by little the painting went under close scrutiny, examining each final detail, looking for the tiniest clue that would unleash another confined message from its prison cell.

Cell to cell they went, searching high and low until Marie realized that something was talking to her loudly in volumes, "I believe we could be looking at the Holy Trinity", she said walking a couple of steps backwards.

"What do you mean?" a slightly fatigued Tom asked.

"Look", said Marie pointing to the figure of a woman in blue, "I believe that this woman here is Mary the Mother of Jesus, Jesus is on the cross, and Mary Magdalene, is the pregnant woman dressed in the cloth of a monk".

"I still don't quite follow", Tom said handing her his notebook, "Draw it out for me in this would you please so I can understand?"

Marie sensing Tom was beginning to fall from grace, due to lack of sleep, suggested something more clearer than a drawn picture that tired Tom could understand, so gracefully she went to the computer and began to manipulate the pixels on the screen. Upon finishing her modern piece of art she beckoned Tom over so he could see the results of her foray into the electronic art world.

Fig. IX - CRUCIFIXION PAINTING BY GIOVANNI DONATO
MONTORFANO C.1495

"The crucifixion agreed?" Marie asked Tom as she flashed the picture of the painting they were stood beside.

"Agreed", confirmed Tom.

"Now this picture is of the Holy Trinity, The Father, The Son, and The Holy Spirit", Marie continued bringing up the next image in line for Tom's perusal.

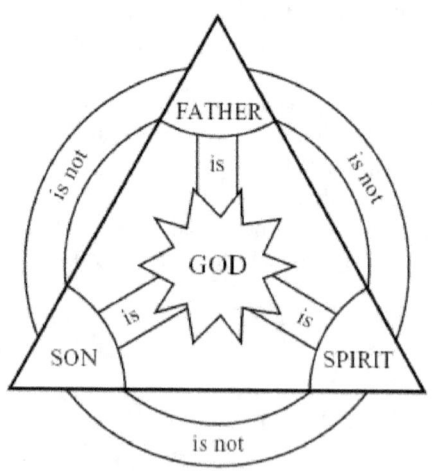

Fig.XVII - The Holy Trinity
(Father, Son & Holy Spirit)

"Yep I'm with you so far", Tom said to Marie as his eyes looked at the image on the screen.

As Marie pressed a few more keys on the computer she responded, "And this is the two together".

Fig. XVIII - Holy Trinity Superimposed on the
CRUCIFIXION PAINTING BY GIOVANNI DONATO MONTORFANO

"Holy crap", Tom exclaimed in disbelief, "You're absolutely correct. What's this place the word God is over?"

"I believe", Marie stated, pressing a few more keys to find the name of the building in the background, "It's the Temple of David in Jerusalem", as she spoke the last word, Marie looked at Tom, Tom looked at her as both knowing what the other was thinking.

"You do realize what this means?", an astonished Tom remarked taking in the gravity of the situation.

"It means Jesus was the son of David", Marie whispered in disbelief.

With one of the biggest secrets since the dawn of man in their possession, the pair of disbelieving truth seekers began to slowly understand what the painting was trying to tell those who sought the information it held, was that Jesus was the true son of King David.

No longer could the lies of the Immaculate Conception be true, for if as they suspected Jesus was the offspring of King David, then that meant the Virgin Mary could not be that when she gave birth, a virgin. This meant also, that the fable in the bible about the Virgin Mary giving birth to Jesus in a stable was untrue, but why perpetuate a lie about a woman of purity giving birth?

Whatever the reason, those who kept the lie a secret would not be pleased about the falsehood being revealed and that spelt danger, danger in the form of another man of Fossor's talents, an individual who would kill to keep the secret true to the version foretold in the Bible.

CHAPTER LII

The screams of the past had become the silence of the future, the voices that once proudly spoke were now reduced to secret whispers, incoherent to those but a select few. No longer were the tales of the brave few taught to those left behind, instead falsehoods created by men of mystery sought to replenish the truths unspoken with lies of the written word. The time was right for those predicted from the past to correct the wrong doings of the future, by unveiling the myths created and replacing them with the truth as it actually occurred. The damaged caused was insurmountable proof that greed above anything else was the reason behind the spread of maliciousness that drove those to keep the truth under lock and key.

The discussion between Tom and Marie, as to whether further knowledge was worth the price, was none existent, for they both understood the need to correct the mistakes of the past, mistakes that had been made by not questioning those whose power was defined by the lies they had created, the discussion was what path to follow to gain access to the hidden records.

"Do we continue on with looking for more clues in the painting or do we return back to the 1495 cryptogram and see if we can find what that Henri Vision Poem is?", Marie asked Tom as they stood both unsure of the next move in the chess game of hidden secrets.

"We could simply divide and conquer", Tom proposed standing silently in front of the puzzled painting.

"I'm not sure I'm up to the task", Marie replied uneasy about the prospect of solving a puzzle herself.

"Ok", Tom said breathing a sigh of relief, for he too was not totally confident in his ability, "I understand. What shall we tackle first?"

"I'm inclined to continue our search on the painting itself", Marie answered as her eyes began darting all over the painting before fixing themselves on the angels around the figure of Christ, "I'm sure there are several other puzzles in it before we return to the 1495 cryptogram, for instance the angels around the figure of the Jesus look a bit staged".

As soon as Marie uttered the words "a bit staged", Tom went off on one of his own inward journey's as he became one with the painting in unison with the energy it gave off, as the harmonics that bounced between the painting and his brain began to draw pictures in his mind, forming the outlines of letters as they went from blurred images to crystal clarity within seconds, "*JOHN*", he blurted out as the letters rearranged themselves in his mind.

"I.I.I beg your pardon?" Marie stammered in disbelief.

"The angels form the word *JOHN*", Tom answered drawing the outline of the letters with an index finger.

Fig. XIX - The word *JOHN* in the angels surrounding Christ being Crucified on the CRUCIFIXION PAINTING BY GIOVANNI DONATO MONTORFANO

As Marie stood in total amazement at the ease which Tom completed the puzzle, she began to realize too that he was correct in the name that projected itself from the past, it was "*JOHN*", but which John was it?

It could be John the Baptist, it could be John the Evangelist, or it could be another John entirely. What intrigued Marie the most was the location of the name around the figure of what they originally thought was Jesus. Did the appearance of the name John around the cross signify it wasn't Jesus who died on the cross, but was in reality John? If it was John who died on the cross, then did it mean also that it was John who was David's son?

The snake of 'ifs' and 'buts' coiled its head around Marie's intrigue until it made her head explode, so she decided to impart her question's on Tom, who in return collapsed to the floor in disbelief, for he did not expect the name John to hold so many queries, and so many unexplainable hypothesis. As he sat motionless on the floor barely able to articulate any thought, his vision was held captive by two little iconic books that lay on the ground that dominated the painting, "What are those two books in the painting?", he asked staggering to get to his feet.

"What two books?" Marie inquired still trying to get over the shock of Tom's original discovery.

"These two books", he replied gesturing with his hand the vicinity of the written compositions.

Fig. XX- Open book on the left   *Fig. XXI* - Closed book on the right

As soon as Marie saw the books Tom pointed out in the painting, she immediately recognized them as the red books of Florence artists, "Those are the Campagnia de Pittori, the red books of Florence artists. The closed book means it's the Master, the open book mean's it's the Apprentice".

A hesitant Marie stopped talking about the red books when she realized the significance behind them, "Oh my God", she swore in excitement.

"What? What is it?" Tom wondered slightly startled behind Marie's abortive remark.

"As we entered here what side was Da Vinci's painting on?" Marie asked Tom probing his intellectual reasoning.

"It was on the right, and", he too paused for a moment as he realized what Marie was grasping at, "You suspect Montorfano is Da Vinci's apprentice don't you?"

Marie nodded her in head in confirmation. As she began to start telling Tom that Montorfano must be a secret apprentice, for nothing is noted anywhere of his apprenticeship with Master Da Vinci, he in return then wondered if he was privy to all Da Vinci's secrets. Whilst Tom and Marie discussed the implications late into the night they began to realize that a secret apprentice, for now, must remain that, secret. Although they now knew who the secret apprentice was, they were uncertain about the reasons why he was kept secret.

Maybe they thought, pondering the question in hand, maybe he was kept secret for a reason, whatever the reason was, it was evident that keeping him secret was evidence enough that the mystery he held close to his heart would destroy those who sought to destroy him.

CHAPTER LIII

With the start of a fresh new day, came fresh new hope that the meaning of the word *ONORUS* would finally have meaning, for although they had a small town in south western France as a possibility, it made no sense to have such a place mentioned, for they now knew that nothing was as it first appeared. Shortly after the rising of the sun the temporary confinement that held its two convicts was slowly unlocked and the freedom that eluded them was finally theirs once more. They grasped the opportunity with both hands and made their way to the outside world, where the taste of fresh clean air reinvigorated their sleep deprived torsos.

The need for food, and some time away from the night's investigation drew Tom and Marie to a local cafe from which they ordered a breakfast of kings. As they sat in relative silence, Marie went to a table where a day old newspaper was sat. Picking it up she began to read the headlines on the front of paper, "*MAN FOUND DROWNED IN MILANESE CANAL*". Within seconds of her reading the major news story of the day, memories of the time they nearly died at the hand of Fossor came flooding back the coffee cup in her hand began to shake a little as Fossor's face broke her subconscious.

Tom witnessed the distress Marie was in and broke from his feast comforting his distressed friend with a protective arm, "Come sit Marie", he uttered guiding her back to their table, Marie still under Fossor's influence allowed herself to be seated by her knight.

"How...How long must I bear his face in my head?" Marie said placing the newspaper, headline up, back on the table.

"I don't know", Tom replied reaching for Marie's hand across the table, "but he's gone now".

"Still doesn't help in getting rid of his stinking, evil, smiling face", she stated slamming the table with every word she spoke.

"I know", Tom softly spoke, "I know, but at least you got me".

"That I do", Marie said placing her other hand on top of Tom's, "and I thank you for being my friend".

"Good", Tom replied as he and Marie shared a tender moment, "why don't you take your mind off Fossor and doing something frivolous like reading my horoscope, or reading the cartoons, or something else?"

Marie sensing Tom was trying to break Fossor's spirit from her head, lent forward and picked up the newspaper once more, opening the publication to the horoscope section. She began to read in earnest reading every letter, every character, as she did her eyes opened wider and wider staring in disbelief at the stupidity of her failure to identify the characters in the word ONORUS. Marie presented the newspaper to Tom pointing out her findings, who in return swore in disbelief.

Fig. XXII - Star sign of Leo
(23 July - 22rd August)

"You mean that the word we thought was ONORUS, is ORUS with the star sign Leo in the middle of it?" a bewildered Tom inquired, "so who the hell is ORUS?"

"I believe it is a shortened form of the Egyptian God Horus", Marie answered, "but I'm not entirely sure about it".

"Why Horus?" Tom asked Marie unsure of the connection between that and the painting in which it was found.

"It was always thought that Horus was what ......", but she never finished for she now understood what the significance behind that word Orus was.

Tom on tenterhooks waiting for Marie to finish her sentence gradually became frustrated and started urging Marie to finish what she was saying, "What?"

"It was always thought that Horus was what the legend of Jesus was based on", Marie finished staring off into space.

"So what you're saying, that this could be the symbol for what? Jesus?" Tom pondered scarcely believing the meaning of the word ONORUS.

"I believe so", confirmed Marie, "but as to the meaning of the star sign for Leo I'm at a lost end".

In a little cafe, in a little insignificant street in the city of Milan, two people sat astonished at the prospect of another suggestive idea pertaining to the genealogy of Jesus. They had solved part of the equation. But what was the connection between him and the star sign Leo? Nothing was starting to make sense as it first did, John, Jesus and Mary Magdalene all had hidden messages and hidden secrets in the painting, but what was the connection? What was the missing link that connected all these people together? Tom and Marie did not know, but they wanted to know all there was to find out, if the prospect of losing their sanity was their cross to bear, it was worth knowing what others had tried to hide.

CHAPTER LIV

Slowly from the flames the phoenix began to rise, the ashes of the past which lay dormant, began to slowly smolder creating a fire, a fire so intense that not even the holy water of a corrupt church would douse the burning truth that was being born to two proud parents. The aberration, that once seemed like an impossibility, was like Frankenstein's creation, slowly brought back to life.

Tom and Marie, whose child it was, were beginning to worry that they were no longer in control, they were starting to feel like they were trapped in a car with no brakes, running head long into a pedestrian filled shopping precinct, but they were not afraid for the casualties of war, who had already been mown down had given their lives up freely, had urged them to commit their lives in penance for those who sought to justify their own means by preying on the weak and infirm.

"Do you ever get that feeling of Déjà Vu?" Tom inquired as they revisited the Crucifixion painting in hope they would finally solve the riddles it contained.

"You mean that feeling of being here before?" Marie asked, "I sure do. I just hope that this time it will be the final occurrence".

"I hope so too", agreed Tom wearily as his spirit began to dwindle down just a little more.

"You want to check for a connection between Jesus and the star sign Leo", Marie asked Tom as she went to interrogate the painting further.

"Sure thing Batman", he replied playfully as he began to torture the computer with his typing.

"Ha, Ha, Batman I like that Einstein", Marie said laughing at her new nickname.

"I tell you what you're not going to like though", Tom said as he flickered over the electronic information in his sight.

"Let me guess", Marie said hesitantly, "Nothing".

"What are you? Psychic?" Tom wondered as he sat back trying to outplay the Grand Master at his game.

"Let's just call it intuition", Marie answered as she joined Tom's side, deciding that two heads were slightly better than one. The blankness that accompanied her suggested otherwise, for nothing, not one iota came to her, the light that once illuminated the path was now in dangerous peril of extinguishing itself. As try as they might nothing came to pass, ideas once fertile had now fallen on a barren wasteland, seeds of despair beginning to take their place.

"Could there possibly be another meaning for the star sign Leo?" juxtaposed Tom as his mind began to slowly pick up the pace of the race.

"Such as?" an inquisitive Marie pondered.

"I don't know", Tom answered as he began to slowly type more precariously on the keyboard of hope, "but I suspect we're not thinking outside the box enough".

"Okay", Marie said stretching her word out, "what does our little friend suggest?"

Tom paused for a moment trying to figure out what the computer's entry for the star sign Leo meant, "This doesn't make any sense at all", he sighed, hopelessly lost in the meaning that came to pass.

"What doesn't?" Marie inquired as she stopped what she was doing and listened intently to Tom's explanation.

"According to these records the astrological sign Leo is often associated with Jesus, just as Mary Magdalene is associated with the astrological sign Virgo. (In the Christian religion the Lion of Judah represents Jesus) ", he quoted reading the text off the screen.

Fig. XXII - Star sign of Virgo
(23 August - 22nd August)

"So what you're telling me is we've got Jesus in Jesus?"

"Apparently so", sighed Tom disappointed at what appeared to be another dead end, as his eyes went searching for something to corroborate his finding he noticed something else strange and unnerving, "It also states that Horus is often associated with the astrological symbol Leo too. None of this is making sense".

"Maybe", Marie commented, thoughts etched in her head that this was another puzzle, "We could interpret this as meaning Jesus in Leo, with perhaps Leo meaning something else".

"It states here that", Tom quoted reading more of the computer's records "Astrological signs are often associated with other things besides stars too like countries for instance".

"Really?" said a disbelieving Marie, "and what countries are connected with Leo?"

"_Zanzibar, Madagascar, Sicily, Romania, Macedonia, Italy_", quoted Tom stopping in his tracks before stating the final country, "and _France_".

"What _France_, _France_?", Marie asked Tom suddenly becoming aware of a situation fast approaching, Tom confirmed the answer to Marie's question, before he asked the reason for her line of question.

"I suspect", she implied "That this word ONORUS is trying to tell us that Jesus' bloodline is in France".

"You mean for real?" a hesitant Tom asked.

"For real", came Marie's response as she went back to look at the painting, "hence this pregnant woman in the cloth of a monk, could be carrying the child of Jesus"

"That makes a lot of sense, if indeed the word ORMUS relates to Mary Magdalene being in France, then this would confirm that Jesus is France also. So what's the connection between that and this Henri Vision Poem then?"

"I don't think we'll know until we solve that riddle. We've got to found out about this Vision Poem who inspired Da Vinci".

"I'm one step ahead of you on that", replied Tom with an air of relief in his voice, "As I was searching through records on the computer, I managed to find out that Da Vinci was inspired by the works of Dante degli Alighieri".

"That makes a lot of sense", Marie said alleviating her fears with a slight sigh of relief, "what about the name Henry though".

Tom in his infinite wisdom was already trying to locate the name in the computer's records, and for once he struck gold, for Dante was closely associated with *Henry VII, the Holy Roman Emperor*, (a man who he mentioned as the new Charlemagne), dedicating *Paradiso* to the said *Henry*.

"Dante saw Henry VII as the one person to restore the office of Holy Roman Emperor back to its former glory. He also had hoped the Henry would take back Florence from the Black Guelph (The Black Guelph were supporters of the Papacy, as opposed to The White Guelph were opposed to the influence of the Rome through Pope Boniface VIII). In fact Dante wrote several letters to Henry VII, asking for his help in removing the Pope's influence from his beloved Florence. There's a mystery contained within these letters too", Tom went on, "The key to riddle of 515 in Dante's Purgatory is supposed to be contained within the confines of the letters, but I can't locate that anywhere".

"Come on Tom", Marie said a little surprised her fellow companion had not leapt instantly to his feet with an instant solution, "perhaps Mr. Da Vinci's notebooks might help".

Tom witnessing Marie's breakthrough slapped himself on his forehead in disgust, skipping backwards through time and the pages of Da Vinci's notebook. Tom had only gone back a few pages when something surprising caught his attention, "*Notes on Pupils Section 1465 - I left Milan for Rome on the 24th day of September 1513, with Giovanni [2], Francesco di Melzi [3], Salai, Lorenzo and il Fanfoi*".

"1465? That's almost the same as 1495 with the 9 inverted", Marie noted as she listened to Tom quoting from Da Vinci's notebooks, "That then confirms our suspicion that Giovanni Donato Montorfano is indeed Da Vinci's secret apprentice".

"I believe it does", confirmed Tom as he began to turn the pages back to their original investigation, section 515 in Leonardo Da Vinci's notebook, "*The light for drawing from nature should come from the North in order that it may not vary. And if you have it in the South, keep the window screened with cloth, so that with the sun shining the whole day the light may not vary. The height of the light should be so arranged, as that every object shall cast a shadow on the ground of the same length as itself*".

He scratched his head, contemplating the possible meaning of the message it held, but for all tense and purposes the message was full of gobbledygook. The North and the South mentioned drawing a blank look from Tom's inwardly looking mind, whatever the message was, for now it remained hidden, hidden until there came a time when all would be revealed.

CHAPTER LV

Since the beginning of time, mankind has looked to the stars to provide answers to two major questions about his life: *[1] where are they coming from? And [2] where are they going to?*

Influenced by their own primitive desires to know more about the path that lay ahead, human beings have sought those individuals who claim to have the power of the second sight, where it be from reading messages that lay in the heavens above, or other sources available to them. Skeptics have and always will, follow these people hand in hand, as they seek to undermine their power and ridicule their beliefs, yet somehow they follow blindly in hope that one day, a true person (or persons) will come forth to reveal the future that has yet to materialize, for Tom and Marie they were neither skeptics nor believers, for they were people who sought their own path, not influenced by others, free thinking in their own ideological beliefs.

They too sought the stars for hidden messages, but not messages pertaining to the future, they sought messages from those who understood the meaning of star systems, whether they agreed with them or not.

"I tell you there is a reason for the triangles in the 1495 puzzle", argued Tom, as he and Marie stood together on opposite sides of the fence.

"What makes you think that?", she replied slightly annoyed at Tom's narrow minded attitude to her argument, that it made no sense to have the triangles arranged in a pattern to formulate yet another message.

"Everything we've found so far", he reminded her, "has been hidden, so why not hide a message in these triangles?"

"Let's suppose for an instance that you're correct in your assumption, what pattern do they join up to make?" Marie asked as her demeanor began to slowly calm down.

"I suppose it could be a number of things", Tom said looking at the items in question, "but the thing that immediately springs to mind, is it could be a star system".

Marie stood silently as she began to understand Tom's intellectual prowess, for as much as she hated it, she had to agree with his hypothesis. It could be the pattern of a star system. If it was as she now understood, a cluster of shapes in the form of a pattern of stars, then what was the meaning behind it? "Maybe", she argued in her own inner sanctum, "It's another message trying to elude us". As the thoughts entered her head of another secret message, she too began to wander about another possibility for the meaning of 515 in Dante's Purgatory.

"You know you could be right", she stated as her own mind went off on a parallel course, "That would make a lot of sense".

"I'm pleased you agree, but why do I suspect your concocting something else too?" Tom said with an air of expectation is his voice.

"I've been thinking about your number 515", Marie answered as she began to offer her take on the number puzzle.

"Ok", Tom replied, "I'm all ears".

"I know there's been several tries at breaking this 515 code for many years, all using complicated mathematical formulae, but I have my doubts at their answers for one very good reason", she stated as the thoughts from her head broke free, "and that is, those who the message was for, must have a damn good knowledge, not only of code breaking, but mathematics too, and to me that doesn't make a whole lot of sense".

"So you suspect something simpler?" Tom queried as he listened intently to Marie.

"I do. I'm beginning to suspect that there may be just something in Le Serpent Rouge, when they insinuated that they used Tarot Cards to hide secret messages. I also know that there is a set of tarot cards call the *Visconti-Sforza* tarot deck, although they didn't appear until the 15th century".

"Do you want me to look on the computer for you?"

"Thank you that would be great", praised Marie as they both sat on the floor, looking once more into the electronic oblivion. Soon they were both looking at the screen as Tom pulled up information regarding the *Visconti-Sforza Tarot Cards*. Line after line they read, searching, looking, and looking in hope that a small minute piece of lost information would assist them.

"I can't see anything", Tom replied as he drew a blank from the data presented to him, "What about the actual cards themselves? Maybe it could be cards *5 and 15* perhaps?"

"I'm not sure", Marie confessed slightly disappointed by the results they found, "but it wouldn't hurt to look".

Within seconds, Tom and Marie's slight disappointment turned to that of complete and utter bewilderment as they found the two cards in question.

Fig. XXIV - Tarot Card No.5
- The Hierophant

Fig. XXV - *Tarot Card No.15*
- *The Devil*

"Who is this Hierophant man?" Marie wondered in a voice of confusion. Tom understood what was being asked of him and began to look for any mention of the word Hierophant in the computer's records.

"Card Number 5 in the *Major Arcana* (*or Major Secrets*) is sometimes named the *Pope Card*", Tom stated as he read the meaning of the card on the computer's screen.

"The *Pope Card*?" asked Marie in disbelief, "You mean to tell me that the pope is what, *the devil?"*

"Not me", corrected Tom, "but it appears Dante is telling us so from beyond his grave".

Whether or not Tom and Marie chose to believe what they had found was true, was irrelevant. What was apparent though, was that the use of Tarot cards as a secret message system was a distinct possibility, not only that, but if they were correct in their assumption that the message contained alluded to the Pope being the Devil, then that meant they were dealing with a power whose influence ruled a large portion of the world's God fearing believers, and that could only mean one thing, trouble, and trouble on a scale much larger then they first thought. Now they were in a conundrum, whether to press on and release the information, or whether to keep quiet and try to help those who sought to reveal what they now knew, the fate of the world was now in their hands.

CHAPTER LVI

The damnation of Dante towards the church was obvious, two tarot cards hiding a message that few had seen had given up the secret to the code 515, and that was the Pope was the Devil. Yet what was the connection between that and this painting of the Crucifixion? Maybe, Tom theorized, the connection could be the use of Tarot cards to hide a message and that was the true meaning behind the numbers 1, 4, 9 and 5. They already knew what the number 5 card was, it was the Pope, but what about the other cards, 1, 4 and 9. Tom decided to play a hunch and went on a search for the other three cards.

Fig. XXVI - Tarot Card No.1
- The Magician

Fig. XXVII - Tarot Card No.4
- The Emperor

Fig. XXVIII -Tarot Card No.9
- The Hermit

Fig. XX IV-Tarot Card No.5
- The Hierophant

He found what he needed without much effort, but what was the message they contained? More research would have to be done before that could be read, so off he went into the annals of the computer's records.

"Basic meaning of the card number 1, the Magician Card, is the male power of creation. The Emperor Card number 4 naturally follows the pregnant Empress. Card number 9, the Hermit, is a card of introspection and virginity, and the meaning of the Pope card, number 5 is to bring the spiritual down to earth. So what we have is a male power of creation, Emperor following pregnant Empress, introspection and virginity, spirituality", Tom quoted as he read the meaning of each of the cards on the screen.

"I think I'm beginning to understand the message", Marie whispered as she bore witness to Tom's research, "I believe the meaning behind the cards is that the story of the virgin birth has been created by the Pope"

"If that's the case then, does that mean Jesus truly existed?" Tom asked in hope that all their time had not been wasted.

"I believe he did", Marie answered, "because there's too much hidden information to deny his existence, but the creation of the story of his immaculate conception was used to hide the fact he was an illegitimate child of Mary and King David".

"Ok then", responded Tom with an air of mystic, "Why would the Catholic Church, in the form of the Pope, create a story to hide Jesus' true birth?"

"I can only believe that it was done to hide the fact that he was the true son of David, and heir to the King of Israel, but why I don't know", Marie said only having enough information to best guess the reason behind the made up story of the virgin birth.

"None of this makes any sense", Tom said totally confused by the secrecy surrounding the myth of Jesus, "and I've still not found the star system created by the triangles either".

Fig. XXIX -
Pattern of Triangles in the Crucifixion Painting

"I believe I can answer that question my friend", a voice from behind them answered. Tom and Marie turned to face the person who offered sanctuary in their time of need, only to come face-to-face with a monk like figure covered head to foot in blue robes and wearing what appeared to be a mask in the shape of Horus on his face. They were not sure whether to trust this figure that hid in the shadows, for their previous encounters with another man dressed in the clothing of a religious bigot had almost cost them their lives.

"Who are you and want do you want?" snarled Tom protecting Marie by using himself as a shield

"I am a friend", replied the blue monk with a voice of reasoning, "I am here to help you finish what you started".

"Help us finished what we started?" Marie bravely asked coming from behind Tom's protection, "Does that mean you've been watching us all the time?"

"We've been watching you from the shadows, yes", answered the blue monk.

"Even when we were in danger?" snarled Tom staring into the expressionless face of his 'friend'.

"Yes", humbly answered the blue monk, "We had to see if you were worthy".

"WHY?" shouted an irate Tom at the top of his voice.

"You are the chosen ones", a solemn voice responded, "You are the ones prophecies foretold would bring the truth back from the darkness into the light. You are the ones ancient scribes predicted would transform the legend into reality. You are the ones to save mankind from falling into the clutches of the devil himself. So it shall be written. So it shall be done".

"Us? Why us", Marie pondered as the gravity of the situation began to sink in.

"Prophets foretold of a time when two individuals, a man and a woman, would be chosen to undertake the quest of enlightenment, and bring back the Holy Grail".

"The Holy Grail?" asked Tom in disbelief, "THE HOLY GRAIL?".

"In time yes", stated the monk, "but for now I am here to help you solve the final puzzle".

"You mean the pattern of triangles in the Crucifixion painting?" a bewildered Marie inquired.

"Yes", confirmed the monk, "and you are correct in your assumption Tom Raust. It is a star system. It's the star system Canis Major".

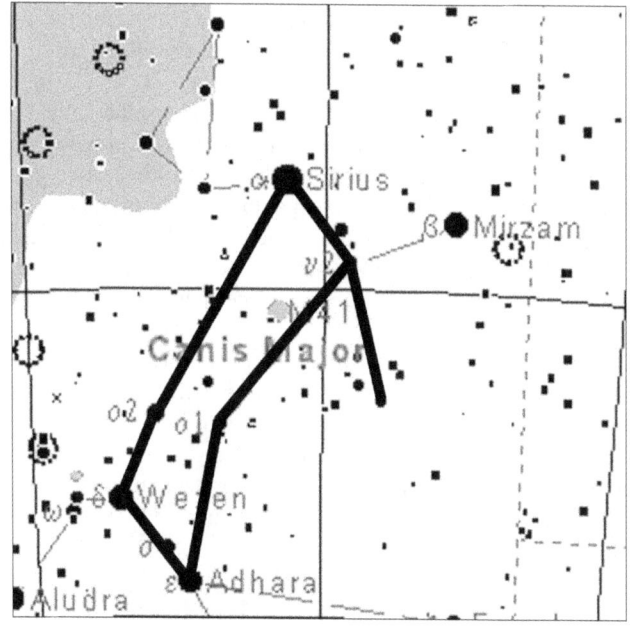

Fig. XXX -
Star System - Canis Major

"Why Canis Major?" asked Tom.

"Canis Major, The Great Dog", stated the monk, "Is the King of the North stated in Psalm 22:20 and Daniel 11:40".

"The King of the North? Goddam it", swore Tom, "That's the connection between 515 in Da Vinci's notebooks and Dante".

"So who is this King of the North?" Marie asked not having heard this member of royalty before.

"The first King of the North was a man called, Satan the King of Babylon and the King of Tyre. The final King of the North, is the leader of a Vatican influenced super state", answered the monk.

"You mean the Pope?" Tom inquired.

"The Pope or whoever is controlling the Pope", answered the monk, "Come, we have made preparations for your arrival".

Cautiously they followed the man dressed in blue holy cloth, into a secret part of the Santa Maria delle Grazie, a place where no one visited, darkness prevailing the arrival of the two chosen ones, as torches of a light flickering ambience transformed the aura into hopeful expectations. Through the retarded light they walked, marble columns leading the way to a throne that lay silently waiting for the king to be seated in the court of the silent few.

The blue monk stopped as they reached the throne and proceeded to seat himself down on the chair of authority, "My friends they have arrived", he stated to the shadows that lay in waiting as one by one a trinity of mysterious figures made themselves known to Tom and Marie. Encircling the two in an arch of protection the blue monk signaled to the others "It is time to reveal our true form".

Slowly and without hesitation, the mysterious figures began to unveil themselves to Tom and Marie, "Mister Edwards?", Tom said in disbelief as the first one made himself known, "Inspector Mancini, Miss Annunziata Montagna the curator, and Father Makom. What the hell is going on?", but they did not respond in words only issuing a pointing hand at the blue monk sat on the throne.

The blue monk arouse gracefully from the throne and began to unmask himself from the shackles of secrecy, "*MEDAD*", screamed both Tom and Marie as the mask of Horus fell silently to the floor. The surprise became too much for Tom as he became overcome with shock at seeing his allegedly dead friend, alive and well. As he awoke from his brief lapse into unconsciousness, Tom witnessed Medad's beaming presence smiling at him, "Hello my friend, long time no see".

"I don't understand", an astonished Tom remarked.

"Firstly, let me thank you for taking great care of my sister Marie", Medad said helping Tom gently to his feet.

"Your...your...Your sister?" Tom stammered in confusion.

"Yes my sister", Medad confirmed, "It appears she is overcome with joy too". He pointed to Marie who had fainted also with shock at seeing her long lost brother being attended to by the others of the group, "Let me explain a few things to you. We thought that allowing myself to be killed, it would bring those who sought to hide what we knew secret out of hiding and reveal themselves, and it did. My only regret was that it was not possible to let you in on the plan, for we wanted you to continue in searching for what you're now in possession of, the truth".

"We?"

"Yes Tom we .Who are we? We are The Cult of Horus".

"The C...C.Cult of Horus", stammered a shocked Tom, "So Emre was being truthful when he told me about The Cult of Horus?"

"Ah poor Emre", sighed Medad in disappointment shaking his head, "We always suspected Emre was in league with the devil and you coercing Emre's treachery out into the open confirmed our suspicions. The Cult of Horus is what the myths of Jesus were based on".

"I don't follow".

"Horus was born of a virgin, just like Jesus. Horus' birth was announced by angels, just like Jesus. Horus performed miracles just as Jesus was claimed to do".

"Isn't that wrong then?"

"Religion in its infancy, borrowed many things from many early beliefs. Did you know for instance that the wearing of a wedding ring is a paganistic symbol?"

"Another thing too Medad, What's it with all these number sevens?"

"That my friend", answered Medad, the echo in his voice trying to penetrate the silence in Tom's head, "Is because the number seven is half a pyramid turned upside down".

"But why me Medad? Why was I one of the chosen ones?" Tom asked as he began to slowly understand what was being told to him by his long lost friend.

"It's your name Tom", stated Medad.

"My name?" puzzled Tom, even more confused than before, "Why my name?"

"Your father was named Tom Raust, his father before him and so on, T. Raust or Traust is an Icelandic word meaning trust", explained Medad.

"Icelandic? Why Iceland?" Tom pondered scratching his head.

"That we don't know. All we know is that the first born son of your family has always carried the name".

"So what do we do now the truth has been revealed, about Jesus' bloodline being in France, The Pope being the devil, and everything else we discovered?"

"That my friend", comforted Medad placing an arm around Tom, "is something only you can decide for yourself. In time you will know what do with the knowledge you have gained, however I do want you to remember that people, not only this century, but others throughout history have given their lives in order to protect the legacy you are in possession of. I know it is a great burden to carry but I have faith in you, just as my sister has".

With the power now in their hands, Tom began to realize that this was a very serious gift they had been chosen to receive, not only did they have knowledge of the whereabouts of Jesus' heritage, but they had knowledge too that would unleash all hell on earth. Tom needed time to think and decide the best course of action to follow. Whatever it was, he would do so knowing that he did the best he could and that's all anyone could ask of him.

EPILOGUE

Tom sat with Marie by his side, staring at the water in the Naviglio Grande canal flow slowly towards the sea. The quest was over, the knowledge was theirs, but something was missing, a nagging doubt that a final puzzle dangled over their heads like a noose.

"I can't help but feel we've missed something", Tom commented as his eyes fixed on a leaf floating on the water's surface.

"I get that same feeling too", Marie responded as her hand probed its way into that of Tom's, "so why don't we do something about it?"

"Another library visit?" Tom asked as his brain began to reboot once more.

"Another library visit", confirmed Marie as they went off on another ramble into the past life of a man who held secrets within the confines of his works of art. Secretly she wasn't sure what they hoped to find would be worth knowing, but she did know that Tom was right in his assumption that another puzzle was taunting their mental capacity for lateral thinking.

"So what are you thinking then Einstein?" Marie asked Tom as they sat in yet another library.

"What I'm thinking is this", stated Tom, "1495 pointed us to the words SION and POEM in the painting agreed?"

"Agreed", confirmed Marie.

"What if it was the other way round?" Tom necessitated.

"You mean use the letters of a word to give us a number sequence?"

"Yes".

"What word?"

"I thinking ONORUS", stated Tom answering Marie's question.

"Ok", Marie responded, "can you remember what positions were the letters on ONORUS?"

"I think", began Tom, "they were at positions 2, 4 and 8. Hmmm I wonder".

"You wonder what?"

"I don't think it can be the basic code as that would give us B, D and H, which doesn't mean diddly squat. I wonder if it's connected to the word John we found in the shape of angels".

"The only thing I can think of would be its John 2 verses 4 to 8. Can you pass me the bible please?" Marie politely inquired.

"Sure thing", Tom responded passing Marie the bible on the desk. As he did, he sat waiting patiently for Marie to find something significant in the passage and it was not long before she answered with an astonishing find.

"Verse 6 reads 'Now there were six stone water pots set there for the Jewish custom of purification, containing twenty or thirty gallons each'", Marie quoted from the bible.

"I'm not sure I quite follow", Tom said unsure of the hidden meaning.

"Verse 6, six water pots, two multiplied by three, put them altogether and you get?"

"666", replied Tom in disbelief, "What does that have to do with John?"

"Don't you remember? It was John who wrote the book of Revelations?"

"I do. So where in the Book of Revelations is 666 mentioned?"

"In Revelations 13:18 it states 'This calls for wisdom. If anyone has insight, let him calculate the number of the beast, for it is man's number. His number is 666'"

"13:18 you say", Tom remarked picking up a loaned copy of Da Vinci's notebooks and running his hand over the pages to section 1318, "Section 1318 states *'All those things which in winter are under the snow, will be uncovered and laid bare in summer (for Falsehood, which cannot remain hidden)* '"

"You do realize what this means Tom?" Marie asked her trusted confidant.

"I think it's a message from Da Vinci himself to reveal the falsehoods for what they are", responded Tom answering Marie's question.

They sat together, side by side, in total agreement now what to do with the information they had, the truth had to be revealed not only for the interest of their own sanity, but at Da Vinci's bequest, however they did not have much time to sit and muster their plan of action, for from the streets a messenger was sent forth.

"Mr. Raust, Miss Dubois, I'm sorry for the interruption", said the messenger gasping for breath, "but your needed urgently".

"By who?" Tom inquired.

"He wouldn't give his name", replied the messenger, "All he said was *'All will be revealed soon* '".

THE END

LIST OF REFERENCE MATERIAL

The Notebooks of Leonardo Da Vinci - Vol.I
(Compiled and Edited From the Original Manuscripts
By Jean Paul Richter
ISBN: 0-486-22572-0)

The Notebooks of Leonardo Da Vinci - Vol.II
(Compiled and Edited From the Original Manuscripts
By Jean Paul Richter
ISBN: 0-486-22573-9)

From Cedar to Hyssop: A Study in Plant Folk Lore
(By Grace Mary Hood Crowfoot &
Mrs. Louise Baldensperger.)

Vatican Assassins:
"Wounded In the House of My Friends"
(By Eric Jon Phelps)

Purgatory
(By Durante degli Alighieri)

Ars Poetica' of Horace
(By Quintus Horatius Flaccus)

ALL SEEING EYES

FULL EXPLANATION OF THE
PYRAMID PUZZLE

Tom and Marie were correct in their assumption that the pyramid puzzle was an anagram.

The clue was: Heroes Fate Text in Bugs or Star.

Bugs or Star was correctly identified as Strasbourg, and Heroes Fate Text was indeed Street of the Axe.

Street of the Axe as Marie translated, became Rue de la Hache, however what they failed to realize was that the Rue de la Hache given in the puzzle was the key to unlock the word HORUS.

This can be explained by the following:

Using the basic code A=1, B=2, C=3 etc. transpose the word Horus into numbers

H = 8, O = 15, R = 18, U = 21, S = 19

Now we take this number 815182119 and put that into the form of an IP address thusly: 81.51.82.119

The IP address then points to a particular place in the world, that being Rue de la Hache, Strasbourg.

Whether this is coincidental or not, I'm not sure, but it does make you think more openly about conspiracy theories, considering the history behind Strasbourg Cathedral and its connection with Charlemagne and the Carolingian dynasty.

(As a side note if you do the word SATAN using the same method you get an IP address that points to the Ford Motor Company).

D. A. BROUGHTON

OTHER RECOMMENDED
READING MATERIAL

Holy Blood, Holy Grail
(By Michael Baigent, Richard Leigh
& Henry Lincoln
IBSN: 0-440-13648-2)

The Last Templar
(By Raymond Khoury
IBSN: 0-451-21995-3)

COPYRIGHT NOTICE

www.ingramcontent.com/pod-product-compliance
Lightning Source LLC
Chambersburg PA
CBHW072205030726
47501CB00015B/656